STORIES

ALSO BY SUSAN SONTAG

FICTION

The Benefactor
Death Kit
I, etcetera
The Way We Live Now
The Volcano Lover
In America

ESSAYS

Against Interpretation
Styles of Radical Will
On Photography
Illness as Metaphor
Under the Sign of Saturn
AIDS and Its Metaphors
Where the Stress Falls
Regarding the Pain of Others

FILM SCRIPTS

Duet for Cannibals
Brother Carl

PLAY

Alice in Bed

A Susan Sontag Reader
As Consciousness Is Harnessed to Flesh
At the Same Time

STORIES

COLLECTED STORIES

SUSAN SONTAG

EDITED BY BENJAMIN TAYLOR

HAMISH HAMILTON
an imprint of
PENGUIN BOOKS

HAMISH HAMILTON

UK | USA | Canada | Ireland | Australia
India | New Zealand | South Africa

Hamish Hamilton is part of the Penguin Random House group of companies
whose addresses can be found at global.penguinrandomhouse.com.

First published in the United States of America by Farrar, Straus and Giroux 2017
First published in Great Britain by Hamish Hamilton 2017

001

Grateful acknowledgement is made to the publications in which these stories first
appeared: 'Debriefing' and 'Old Complaints Revisited' appeared in *American Review*;
'Project for a Trip to China' in the *Atlantic Monthly*; 'The Dummy' in *Harper's
Bazaar*; 'Unguided Tour', 'Pilgrimage', 'The Letter Scene' and 'The Way We Live Now'
in the *New Yorker*; 'American Spirits' (originally entitled 'The Will and the Way')
and 'Doctor Jekyll' in *Partisan Review*; and 'Baby' in *Playboy*

Printed in Great Britain by Clays Ltd, St Ives plc

A CIP catalogue record for this book is available from the British Library

ISBN: 978–0–241–32741–8

CONTENTS

FOREWORD

Susan Sontag was an occasional rather than a habitual writer of short stories, turning to the form as certain expressive needs arose that couldn't otherwise be satisfied. Some pitched battle for wisdom is under way in each of the eleven works included here: A debriefing follows on some experiential blow. Such avowals did not come easily to Sontag. Reading them—particularly the most personal—one sees why. Anton Chekhov, the greatest of short-story writers, spoke of his "autobiographophobia," a condition Sontag strongly identified with. In masterworks like "Project for a Trip to China," "Debriefing," "Unguided Tour," and others, she outwits a native reticence. The weight of trouble such stories shift—the death of a father; the suicide of a friend; the threat of mortal illness—sets them at a distance from her much larger and more frequent production of essays. If the latter will always be more famous, the stories are where to go to know Sontag most intimately. She once told an interviewer that while the living room was fine for essays, short stories needed to be written in the bedroom. This distinction between outer and inner sancta seems a good way of approaching the contents of this volume. The stories are her innermost work.

A few critics have said that Sontag's stories might as well be called personal essays. This misses the point. Sontag regarded essays as arenas for coming to understand what she thought, for making up her mind. Her stories spring, by contrast, from a need to remain in suspense, to keep hold of contradictions, but also to make this perplexity bear fruit. "I would gladly consent to being silent," she writes in "Project for a Trip to China." "But then, alas, I'm unlikely to know anything. To renounce literature, I would have to be really sure that I could know. A certainty that would crassly prove my ignorance." Sometimes gnomic, as in "Baby" or "American Spirits," sometimes plangent, as in "Unguided Tour," "The Way We Live Now," and "Project," the voice is everywhere terse, bracing, distilled. "Sisyphus, I," she writes in "Debriefing." "I cling to my rock, you don't have to chain me. Stand back! I roll it up—up, up. And . . . down we go. I knew that would happen. See, I'm on my feet again. See, I'm starting to roll it up again. Don't try to talk me out of it. Nothing, nothing could tear me away from this rock." Craving more uncertainty than the essay allowed for, Sontag turned from time to time to a form in which one need only persevere, making up one's mind about nothing: the infinitely flexible, ever-amenable short story.

This book's contents originated in *Partisan Review*, *Harper's Bazaar*, *American Review*, *Playboy*, *The Atlantic Monthly*, and *The New Yorker* and are assembled here in their entirety for the first time. I suspect that a new generation of readers—less troubled about genre than their elders—will find these stories entirely contemporary. Sontag turns out, as usual, to have been ahead of the crowd.

BENJAMIN TAYLOR

PILGRIMAGE

Everything that surrounds my meeting with him has the color of shame.

December, 1947. I was fourteen, steeped in vehement admirations and impatience for the reality to which I would travel once released from that long prison sentence, my childhood.

End almost in sight. Already in my junior year, I'd finish high school while still fifteen. And then, and then . . . all would unfold. Meanwhile, I was waiting, I was doing time (still fourteen!), recently transferred from the desert of southern Arizona to the coastland of Southern California. Another new setting, with fresh possibilities of escape—I welcomed that. My peripatetic widowed mother's remarriage, in 1945, to a handsome, bemedaled and beshrapneled Army Air Forces ace who'd been sent to the healing desert to cap a year-long hospitalization (he'd been shot down five days after D-Day) appeared to have grounded *her.* The following year our newly assembled family—mother, stepfather, kid sister, dog, notionally salaried Irish nanny left over from the old days, plus the resident alien, myself—had vacated the stucco bungalow on a dirt road on the outskirts of Tucson (where we'd been joined by Captain Sontag) for a cozy shuttered cottage with rosebush hedges and three birch trees at the entrance of the San Fernando

Valley, where I was currently pretending to sit still for a facsimile of family life and the remainder of my unconvincing childhood. On weekends my now out-of-uniform but still military perky stepfather marshaled sirloins and butter-brushed corn tightly wrapped in tinfoil on the patio barbecue; I ate and ate—how could I not, as I watched my morose, bony mother fiddling with her food? His animation was as threatening as her apathy. They couldn't start playing family now—too late! I was off and running, even if I looked every inch the baby-faced, overgrown elder daughter effusively munching her fourth ear of corn; I was already gone. (In French one can announce, while lingering unconscionably, *Je suis moralemant partie*.) There was just this last bit of childhood to get past. For the duration (that wartime locution that gave me my first model of condescending to present time in favor of the better future), for the duration it was permissible to appear to enjoy their receptions, avoid conflict, gobble their food. The truth was, I dreaded conflict. And I was always hungry.

I felt I was slumming, in my own life. My task was to ward off the drivel (I felt I was drowning in drivel)—the jovial claptrap of classmates and teachers, the maddening bromide I heard at home. And the weekly comedy shows festooned with canned laughter, the treacly Hit Parade, the hysterical narratings of baseball games and prize fights—radio, whose racket filled the living room on weekday evenings and much of Saturday and Sunday, was an endless torment. I ground my teeth, I twirled my hair, I gnawed at my nails, I was polite. Though untempted by the new, tribal delights of suburban childhood that had quickly absorbed my sister, I didn't think of myself as a misfit, for I assumed my casing of affability was being accepted at face value. (Here the fact that I was a girl seeps through.) What other people thought of me remained a dim consideration, since other people seemed to me astonishingly unseeing as well as uncurious, while I longed to learn everything:

the exasperating difference between me and everyone I'd ever met—so far. I was certain there was a multitude like me, elsewhere. And it never occurred to me that I could be stopped.

If I didn't mope or sulk, it was not just because I thought complaining wouldn't do any good. It was because the flip side of my discontent—what, indeed, throughout my childhood had made me so discontented—was rapture. Rapture I couldn't share. And whose volume was increasing steadily: since this last move I was having near-nightly bouts of jubilation. For in the eight houses and apartments of my life before this one I had never had a bedroom to myself. Now I had it, and without asking. A door of my own. Now I could read for hours by flashlight after being sent to bed and told to turn off the light, not inside a tent of bedclothes but outside the covers.

I'd been a demon reader from earliest childhood (to read was to drive a knife into their lives), and therefore a promiscuous one: fairy tales and comics (my comics collection was vast), Compton's Encyclopedia, the Bobbsey Twins and other Stratemeyer series, books about astronomy, chemistry, China, biographies of scientists, all of Richard Halliburton's travel books, and a fair number of mostly Victorian-era classics. Then, drifting to the rear of a stationery and greeting-card store in the village that was downtown Tucson in the mid-1940s, I toppled into the deep well of the Modern Library. Here were standards, and here, at the back of each book, was my first list. I had only to acquire and read (ninety-five cents for the small ones, a dollar twenty-five for the Giants)—my sense of possibility unfolding, with each book, like a carpenter's rule. And within a month of arriving in Los Angeles I tracked down a real bookstore, the first of my bookstore-besotted life: the Pickwick, on Hollywood Boulevard, where I went every few days after school to read on my feet through some more of world literature—buying when I could, stealing when I dared. Each of my occasional thefts cost me weeks of self-revilement and dread of future humiliation, but what could I do, given my puny allowance? Odd that I never thought of going to a library. I had to acquire them, see them in rows along a wall of my tiny bedroom. My household deities. My spaceships.

Afternoons I went hunting for treasure: I'd always disliked going home directly from school. But in Tucson, visits to the stationery store excepted, the most cheering postponement I'd come up with was a walk out along the Old Spanish Trail toward the Tanque Verde foothills, where I could examine close up the fiercest saguaros and prickly pears, scrutinize the ground for arrowheads and snakes, pocket pretty rocks, imagine being lost or a sole survivor, wish I were an Indian. Or the Lone Ranger. Here in California there was a different space to roam and I had become a different Lone Ranger. Most days after school I boarded the trolley on Chandler Avenue to hasten into, not away from, town. Within a few blocks of the enchanted crossroads of Hollywood Boulevard and Highland Avenue lay my little agora of one- and two-story buildings: the Pickwick; a record store whose proprietors let me spend hours each week in the listening booths, gorging myself on their wares; an international newsstand where militant browsing yielded me *Partisan Review, Kenyon Review, Sewanee Review, Politics, Accent, Tiger's Eye, Horizons*; and a storefront through whose open door one afternoon I unself-consciously trailed two people who were beautiful in a way I'd never seen, thinking I was entering a gym, which turned out to be the rehearsal quarters of the dance company of Lester Horton and Bella Lewitzky. O golden age! It not only was, I knew it was. Soon I was sipping at a hundred straws. In my room I wrote imitation stories and kept real journals; made lists of words to fatten my vocabulary, made lists of all kinds; played conductor to my records; read myself sore-eyed each night.

And soon I had friends, too, and not very much older than

myself—to my surprise. Friends with whom I could speak of some of what absorbed and enraptured me. I didn't expect them to have read as much as I had; it was enough that they were willing to read the books I lent them. And in music, even better, I was the novice—what bliss! It was my desire to be taught, even more thwarted than my desire to share, that made me my first friends: two seniors at whom I flung myself soon after entering this new school as a sophomore, whose taste in music was far superior to mine. Not only were they each proficient on an instrument— Elaine played the flute, Mel the piano—but they had done all their growing up here, in Southern California, with its infusion of refugee virtuosi, employed in the full symphony orchestras maintained by the major film studios, who could be heard at night playing the canonical and the contemporary chamber repertory to small gatherings scattered across a hundred miles. Elaine and Mel were part of that audience, with tastes elevated and made eccentrically rigorous by the distinct bias of high musical culture in Los Angeles in the 1940s—there was chamber music, and then there was everything else. (Opera was so low on the scale of musical goodness it was not worth mentioning.)

Each friend was a best friend—I knew no other way. Besides my music mentors, who started at U.C.L.A. the following autumn, there was a fellow sophomore, my romantic comrade for the remaining two years of high school, who was to accompany me to the college I had already elected at thirteen as my destiny—the College of the University of Chicago. Peter, fatherless and a refugee (he was part Hungarian, part French), had had a life even more marked by displacements than my own. His father had been arrested by the Gestapo, and Peter and his mother escaped Paris to the South of France and from there, via Lisbon, to New York in 1941; after a spell in a Connecticut boarding school, he was now reunited here with the very single, tanned, red-haired Henya (whom I acknowledged to be as young-looking, if not as beautiful, as my own mother). Our friendship started in the school cafeteria with an exchange of boastful anecdotes about our glamorously dead fathers. Peter was the one with whom I argued about social-ism and Henry Wallace, and with whom I held hands and wept through *Open City, Symphonie Pastorale, The Children of Paradise, Mädchen in Uniform, The Baker's Wife, Brief Encounter,* and *Beauty and the Beast* at the Laurel, the theatre we'd discovered that showed foreign movies. We went bicycling in the canyons and in Griffith Park and rolled about, embracing, in the weeds—Peter's great loves, as I remember, were his mother, me, and his racing bicycle. He was dark-haired, skinny, nervous, tall. I, though always the youn-gest, was invariably the tallest girl in the class and taller than most of the boys and, for all my outlandish independence of judg-ment on matters Olympian, on the matter of height had the most abjectly conventional view. A boyfriend had to be not just a best friend but taller, and only Peter qualified.

The other best friend I made, also a sophomore, though at an-other high school, and also to enter the University of Chicago with me, was Merrill. Cool and chunky and blond, he had all the trap-pings of "cute," a "dish," a "dreamboat," but I, with my unerring eye for loners (under all disguises), had promptly seen that he was smart, too. Really smart. Therefore capable of separateness. He had a low sweet voice and a shy smile and eyes that smiled some-times without his mouth—Merrill was the only one of my friends I doted on. I loved to look at him. I wanted to merge with him or for him to merge with me, but I had to respect the insuperable barrier: he was several inches shorter than I was. The other barri-ers were harder to think about. He could be secretive, calculating (even literally so: numbers figured often in his conversation), and sometimes, to me, insufficiently moved by what I found moving. I was impressed by how practical he was, and how calm he remained when I got flustered. I couldn't tell what he really felt about the quite plausible family—mother, real father, younger brother (who was something of a math prodigy), even grandparents—with which he came equipped. Merrill didn't like to talk about feelings, while I was seething with the desire to express mine, preferably by focusing feeling away from myself onto something I admired or felt indignant about.

We loved in tandem. Music first—he'd had years of piano. (His brother played the violin, which made me equally envious, though it was for piano lessons that I'd implored my mother—rather, stopped imploring my mother—years before.) He introduced me to getting into concerts free by ushering (at the Hollywood Bowl in the summer), and I made him a regular at the Monday chamber-music series "Evenings on the Roof," to which I'd been brought by Elaine and Mel. We were building our nearly identical, ideal record collections (on 78s, happily unaware that this was the last year before L.P.s), and joined forces often in the cool, dark listening booths of the Highland Record Store. Sometimes he came to my house, even if my parents were there. Or I went to his house; the name of his frumpy, hospitable mother—I remember finding this embarrassing—was Honey.

Our privacy was in cars. Merrill had a real driver's license, while mine was the "junior" license one could hold from fourteen to sixteen in California then, entitling me to drive my parents' cars only. Since parents' cars were the only ones available to us, the difference was moot. In his parents' blue Chevy or my mother's green Pontiac we perched at night on the rim of Mulholland Drive, the great plain of twinkling lights below like an endless airport, oblivious of the mating couples in cars parked around us, pursuing our own pleasures. We pitched themes at each other in our inexact treble voices—"Okay, listen. Now, what's this?" We quizzed each other's memory of Köchel listings, knowing by heart long stretches

of the six hundred and twenty-six. We debated the merits of the
Busch and the Budapest Quartets (I'd become an intolerant partisan of the Budapest); discussed whether it would be immoral,
given what I'd heard from Elaine and Mel about Gieseking's Nazi
past, to buy his Debussy recordings; tried to convince ourselves
that we had liked the pieces played on the prepared piano by John
Cage at last Monday's "Evenings on the Roof" concert; and talked
about how many years to give Stravinsky.

This last was one of our recurrent problems. Toward John
Cage's squawks and thumps we were deferential—we knew we
were supposed to appreciate ugly music; and we listened devoutly
to the Toch, the Krenek, the Hindemith, the Webern, the Schoenberg, whatever (we had enormous appetites and strong stomachs).
But it was Stravinsky's music we sincerely loved. And since Stravinsky seemed grotesquely old (we had actually seen him on two
Mondays in the small auditorium of the Wilshire Ebell, when In-
golf Dahl was conducting something of his), our fears for his life
had given rise to a compelling fantasy à deux about dying for our
idol. The question, a question we discussed often, was: What were
the terms of the sacrifice we so relished contemplating? How many
more years of life for Stravinsky would justify our dying now, on
the spot?

Twenty years? Obviously. But that was easy and, we agreed, too
good to hope for. Twenty years granted to the ancient homely
person we saw Stravinsky to be—that was simply an unimagin-
ably large number of years to the fourteen-year-old I was and the
sixteen-year-old Merrill was in 1947. (How lovely that I.S. lived
even longer than this.) To insist on getting Stravinsky twenty more
years in exchange for our lives hardly seemed to show our fervor.

Fifteen more years? Of course.

Ten? You bet.

Five? We began to waver. But not to agree seemed like a failure of respect, of love. What was my life or Merrill's—not just our paltry California-high-school-students' lives but the useful, achievement-strewn lives we thought were awaiting us—compared to making it possible for the world to enjoy five years more of Stravinsky's creations? Five years, okay.

Four? I sighed. Merrill, let's get on.

Three? To die for only three additional years?

Usually we settled on four—a minimum of four. Yes, to give Stravinsky four more years either one of us was prepared right then and there to die.

Reading and listening to music: the triumphs of being not myself. That nearly everything I admired was produced by people who were dead (or very old) or from elsewhere, ideally Europe, seemed inevitable to me.

I accumulated gods. What Stravinsky was for music Thomas Mann became for literature. At my Aladdin's cave, at the Pickwick, on November 11, 1947—taking the book down from the shelf just now, I find the date written on the flyleaf in the italic script I was then practicing—I bought *The Magic Mountain*.

I began it that night, and for the first few nights had trouble breathing as I read. For this was not just another book I would love but a transforming book, a source of discoveries and recognitions. All of Europe fell into my head—though on condition that I start mourning for it. And tuberculosis, the faintly shameful disease (so my mother had intimated) of which my hard-to-imagine real father had died so long ago and exotically elsewhere, but which seemed, once we moved to Tucson, to be a commonplace misfortune—tuberculosis was revealed as the very epitome of pathetic and spiritual interest! The mountain-high community of invalids with afflicted lungs was a version—an exalted version—of that picturesque, climate-conscious resort town in the

desert with its thirty-odd hospitals and sanatoriums to which my
mother had been obliged to relocate because of an asthma-disabled
child: me. There on the mountain, characters were ideas and ideas
were passions, exactly as I'd always felt. But the ideas themselves
stretched me, enrolled me in turn: Settembrini's humanitarian
élan but also Naphta's gloom and scorn. And mild, good-natured,
chaste Hans Castorp, Mann's orphaned protagonist, was a hero
after my own unprotected heart, not least because he was an or-
phan and because of the chastity of my own imagination. I loved
the tenderness, however diluted by condescension, with which
Mann portrays him as a bit simple, overearnest, docile, mediocre
(what I considered myself to be, judged by real standards). Tenderness. What if Hans Castorp was a Goody Two-Shoes (appalling
accusation my mother had once let fly at me)? That was what made
him not like but unlike the others. I recognized his vocation for
piety; his portable solitude, lived politely among others; his life of
onerous routines (that guardians deem good for you) interspersed
with free, passionate conversations—a glorious transposition of
my own current agenda.

For a month the book was where I lived. I read it through almost at a run, my excitement winning out over my wish to go
slowly and savor. I did have to slow down for pages 334 to 343,
when Hans Castorp and Clavdia Chauchat finally speak of love, but
in French, which I'd never studied: unwilling to skip anything, I
bought a French-English dictionary and looked up their conversation word by word. After finishing the last page, I was so reluctant
to be separated from the book that I started back at the beginning
and, to hold myself to the pace the book merited, reread it aloud, a
chapter each night.

The next step was to lend it to a friend, to feel someone else's
pleasure in the book—to love it with someone else, and be able to
talk about it. In early December I lent *The Magic Mountain* to

Merrill. And Merrill, who would read immediately whatever I pressed on him, loved it, too. Good.

Then Merrill said, "Why don't we go see him?" And that's when my joy turned to shame.

Of course I knew he lived here. Southern California in the 1940s was electric with celebrity presences for all tastes, and my friends and I were aware not only of Stravinsky and Schoenberg but of Mann, of Brecht (I'd recently seen *Galileo*, with Charles Laughton, in a Beverly Hills theatre), and also of Isherwood and Huxley. But it was as inconceivable that I could be in contact with any of them as that I could strike up a conversation with Ingrid Bergman or Gary Cooper, who also lived in the vicinity. Actually, it was even less possible. The stars stepped out of their limos onto the klieg-lighted sidewalk of Hollywood Boulevard for the movie-palace première, braving the surge of besieging fans penned in by the police sawhorses; I saw newsreels of these apparitions. The gods of high culture had disembarked from Europe to dwell, almost incognito, among the lemon trees and beach boys and neo-Bauhaus architecture and fantasy hamburgers; they weren't, I was sure, supposed to have something like fans, who would seek to intrude on their privacy. Of course, Mann, unlike the other exiles, was also a public presence. To have been as officially honored in America as Thomas Mann was in the late 1930s and early 1940s was probably more improbable than to have been the most famous writer in the world. A guest at the White House, introduced by the vice president when he gave a speech at the Library of Congress, for years indefatigable on the lecture circuit, Mann had the stature of an oracle in Roosevelt's *bien-pensant* America, proclaiming the absolute evil of Hitler's Germany and the coming victory of the democracies. Emigration had not dampened his taste, or his talent, for being a representative figure. If there was such a thing as a good

Germany, it was now to be found in this country (proof of America's goodness), embodied in his person; if there was a Great Writer, not at all an American notion of what a writer is, it was he.

But when I was borne aloft by *The Magic Mountain*, I wasn't thinking that he was also, literally, "here." To say that at this time I lived in Southern California and Thomas Mann lived in Southern California—that was a different sense of "lived," of "in." Wherever he was, it was where-I-was-not. Europe. Or the world beyond childhood, the world of seriousness. No, not even that. For me, he was a book. Books, rather—I was now deep in *Stories of Three Decades*. When I was nine, which I did consider childhood, I'd lived for months of grief and suspense in *Les Misérables*. (It was the chapter in which Fantine was obliged to sell her hair that made a conscious socialist of me.) As far as I was concerned, Thomas Mann—being, simply, immortal—was as dead as Victor Hugo.

Why would I want to meet him? I had his books.

I didn't want to meet him. Merrill was at my house, it was Sunday, my parents were out, and we were in their bedroom sprawled on their white satin bedspread. Despite my pleas, he'd brought in a telephone book and was looking under "M."

"You see? He's in the telephone book."

"I don't want to see!"

"Look!" He made me look. Horrified, I saw: 1550 San Remo Drive, Pacific Palisades.

"This is ridiculous. Come on—stop it!" I clambered off the bed. I couldn't believe Merrill was doing this, but he was.

"I'm going to call." The phone was on the night table on my mother's side of the bed.

"Merrill, please!"

He picked up the receiver. I bolted through the house, out the always unlocked front door, across the lawn, beyond the curb to the far side of the Pontiac, parked with the key in the ignition (where else would you keep the car keys?), to stand in the middle of the street and press my hands to my ears, as if from there I could have heard Merrill making the mortifying, unthinkable telephone call.

What a coward I am, I thought, hardly for the first or the last time in my life; but I took a few moments, hyperventilating, trying to regain control of myself, before I uncovered my ears and retraced my steps. Slowly.

The front door opened right into the small living room, done up with the Early American "pieces," as my mother called them, that she was now collecting. Silence. I crossed the room into the dining area, then turned into the short hall that went past my own room and the door of my parents' bathroom into their bedroom.

The receiver was on the hook. Merrill was sitting on the bed's edge, grinning.

"Listen, that's not funny," I said. "I thought you were really going to do it."

He waved his hand. "I did."

"Did what?"

"I did it." He was still smiling.

"Called?"

"He's expecting us for tea next Sunday at four."

"You didn't actually call!"

"Why not?" he said. "It went fine."

"And you spoke to him?" I was close to tears. "How could you?"

"No," he said, "it was his wife who answered."

I extracted a mental picture of Katia Mann from the photographs I'd seen of Mann with his family. Did she, too, exist? Perhaps, as long as Merrill hadn't actually spoken to Thomas Mann, it wasn't so bad. "But what did you say?"

"I said we were two high-school students who had read Thomas Mann's books and would like to meet him."

No, this was even worse than I imagined—but what had I imagined? "That's so ... so dumb!"

"What's dumb about it? It sounded good."

"Oh, Merrill ..." I couldn't even protest any more. "What did she say?"

"She said, 'Just a minute, I'll get my daughter,'" Merrill continued proudly. "And then the daughter got on, and I repeated—"

"Go slower," I interrupted. "His wife left the phone. Then there was a pause. Then you heard another voice ..."

"Yeah, another woman's voice—they both had accents—saying, 'This is Miss Mann, what do you want?'"

"Is that what she said? It sounds as if she was angry."

"No, no, she didn't sound angry. Maybe she said, 'Miss Mann speaking.' I don't remember, but, honest, she didn't sound angry. Then she said, 'What do you want?' No, wait, it was 'What is it that you want?'"

"Then what?"

"And then I said ... you know, that we were two high-school students who had read Thomas Mann's books and wanted to meet him—"

"But I don't want to meet him!" I wailed.

"And she said," he pushed on stubbornly, "'Just a minute, I will ask my father.' Maybe it was 'Just a moment, I will ask my father.' She wasn't gone very long ... and then she came back to the phone and said—these were her words exactly—'My father is expecting you for tea next Sunday at four.'"

"And then?"

"She asked if I knew the address."

"And then?"

"That was all. Oh . . . and she said goodbye."

I contemplated this finality for a moment before saying, once more, "Oh, Merrill, how could you?"

"I told you I would," he said.

Getting through the week, awash in shame and dread. It seemed a vast impertinence that I should be forced to meet Thomas Mann. And grotesque that he should waste his time meeting me.

Of course I could refuse to go. But I was afraid this brash Caliban I'd mistaken for an Ariel would call on the magician without me. Whatever the usual deference I had from Merrill, it seemed he now considered himself my equal in Thomas Mann worship. I couldn't let Merrill inflict himself unmediated on my idol. At least, if I went along I might limit the damage, head off the more callow of Merrill's remarks. I had the impression (and this is the part of my recollection that is most touching to me) that Thomas Mann could be injured by Merrill's stupidity or mine . . . that stupidity was always injuring, and that as I revered Mann it was my duty to protect him from this injury.

Merrill and I met twice during the week after school. I had stopped reproving him. I was less angry; increasingly, I was just miserable. I was trapped. Since I would have to go, I needed to feel close to him, make common cause, so we would not disgrace ourselves.

Sunday came. It was Merrill who collected me in the Chevy, at one exactly, in front of my house at the curb (I hadn't told my mother or anyone else of this invitation to tea in Pacific Palisades), and by two o'clock we were on broad, empty San Remo Drive, with a view of the ocean and Catalina Island in the distance, parked some two hundred feet up from (and out of sight of) the house at 1550.

We had already agreed on how we would start. I would talk first, about *The Magic Mountain*, then Merrill would ask the question about what Thomas Mann was writing at present. The rest we were going to work out now, in the two hours we'd allotted to rehearse. But after a few minutes, unable to entertain any idea of how he might respond to what we were considering saying, we ran out of inspiration. What does a god say? Impossible to imagine.

So we compared two recordings of *Death and the Maiden* and then veered to a favorite notion of Merrill's about the way Schnabel played the *Hammerklavier*, a notion which I found wonderfully clever. Merrill seemed hardly to be anxious at all. He appeared to think that we had a perfect right to bother Thomas Mann. He thought that we were interesting—two precocious kids, minor-league prodigies (we knew neither of us was a real prodigy, which was someone like the young Menuhin; we were prodigies of appetite, of respect, not of accomplishment); that we could be interesting to Thomas Mann. I did not. I thought we were . . . pure potentiality. By real standards, I thought, we hardly existed.

The sun was strong and the street deserted. In two hours only a few cars passed. Then, at five minutes to four, Merrill released the brake and we coasted silently down the hill and re-parked in front of 1550. We got out, stretched, made encouraging mock-groaning sounds to each other, closed the car doors as softly as we could, went up the pathway, and rang the bell. Cute chimes. Oh.

A very old woman with white hair in a bun opened the door, didn't seem surprised to see us, invited us in, asked us to wait a minute in the dim entryway—there was a living room off to the right—and went down a long corridor and out of sight.

"Katia Mann," I whispered.

"I wonder if we'll see Erika," Merrill whispered back.

Absolute silence in the house. She was returning now. "Come with me, please. My husband will receive you in his study."

We followed, almost to the end of the narrow dark passageway, just before the staircase. There was a door on the left, which she opened. We followed her in, turning left once more before we were really inside. In Thomas Mann's study.

I saw the room—it seemed large and had a big window with a big view—before I realized it was he, sitting behind a massive, ornate, dark table. Katia Mann presented us. Here are the two students, she said to him, while referring to him as Dr. Thomas Mann; he nodded and said some words of welcome. He was wearing a bow tie and a beige suit, as in the frontispiece of *Essays of Three Decades*—and that was the first shock, that he so resembled the formally posed photograph. The resemblance seemed uncanny, a marvel. It wasn't, I think now, just because this was the first time I'd met someone whose appearance I had already formed a strong idea of through photographs. I'd never met anyone who didn't affect being relaxed. His resemblance to the photograph seemed like a feat, as if he were posing now. But the full-figure picture had not made me see the sparseness of the mustache, the whiteness of the skin, the mottled hands, the unpleasantly visible veins, the smallness and amber color of the eyes behind the glasses. He sat very erectly and seemed to be very, very old. He was in fact seventy-two.

I heard the door behind us close. Thomas Mann indicated that we were to sit in the two stiff-backed chairs in front of the table. He lit a cigarette and leaned back in his chair.

And we were on our way.

He talked without prompting. I remember his gravity, his accent, the slowness of his speech: I had never heard anyone speak so slowly.

I said how much I loved *The Magic Mountain*.

He said it was a very European book, that it portrayed the conflicts at the heart of European civilization.

I said I understood that.

What had he been writing, Merrill asked.

"I have recently completed a novel which is partly based on the life of Nietzsche," he said, with huge, disquieting pauses between each word. "My protagonist, however, is not a philosopher. He is a great composer."

"I know how important music is for you," I ventured, hoping to fuel the conversation for a good stretch.

"Both the heights and the depths of the German soul are reflected in its music," he said.

"Wagner," I said, worried that I was risking disaster, since I'd never heard an opera by Wagner, though I'd read Thomas Mann's essay on him.

"Yes," he said, picking up, hefting, closing (with his thumb marking the place), then laying down, open again, a book that was on his worktable. "As you see, at this very moment I am consulting Volume IV of Ernest Newman's excellent biography of Wagner." I craned my neck to let the words of the title and the author's name actually hit my eyeballs. I'd seen the Newman biography at the Pickwick.

"But the music of my composer is not like Wagner's music. It is related to the twelve-tone system, or row, of Schoenberg."

Merrill said we were both very interested in Schoenberg. He made no response to this. Intercepting a perplexed look on Merrill's face, I widened my eyes encouragingly.

"Will your novel appear soon?" Merrill asked.

"My faithful translator is at work on it now," he said.

"H. T. Lowe-Porter," I murmured—the first time I'd actually said this entrancing name, with its opaque initials and showy hyphen.

"For the translator this is, perhaps, my most difficult book," he said. "Never, I think, has Mrs. Lowe-Porter been confronted with such a challenging task."

"Oh," I said, having not imagined H. T. L.-P. to be anything in particular but surprised to learn that the name belonged to a woman.

"A deep knowledge of German is required, and much ingenuity, for some of my characters converse in dialect. And the Devil— for, yes, the Devil himself is a character in my book—speaks in the German of the sixteenth century," Thomas Mann said, slowly, slowly. A thin-lipped smile. "I'm afraid this will mean little to my American readers."

I longed to say something reassuring, but didn't dare.

Was he speaking so slowly, I wondered, because that was the way he talked? Or because he was talking in a foreign language? Or because he thought he had to speak slowly—assuming (because we were Americans? because we were children?) that otherwise we wouldn't understand what he was saying?

"I regard this as the most daring book I have written." He nodded at us. "My wildest book."

"We look forward very much to reading it," I said. I was still hoping he'd talk about *The Magic Mountain.*

"But it is as well the book of my old age," he went on. A long, long pause. "My *Parsifal,*" he said. "And, of course, my *Faust.*"

He seemed distracted for a moment, as if recalling something. He lit another cigarette and turned slightly in his chair. Then he laid the cigarette in an ashtray and rubbed his mustache with his index finger; I remember I thought his mustache (I didn't know anyone with a mustache) looked like a little hat over his mouth. I wondered if this meant the conversation was over.

But, no, he went on. I remember "the fate of Germany" . . . "the demonic" and "the abyss" . . . and "the Faustian bargain with the Devil." Hitler recurred several times. (Did he bring up the Wagner-Hitler problem? I think not.) We did our best to show him that his words were not wholly lost on us.

At first I had seen only him, awe at his physical presence blinding me to the room's contents. Now I was starting to see more. For instance, what was on the rather cluttered table: pens, inkstand, books, papers, and a nest of small photographs in silver frames, which I saw from the back. Of the many pictures on the walls, I recognized only a signed photograph of F.D.R. with someone else—I seem to remember a man in uniform—in the picture. And books, books, books in the floor-to-ceiling shelves that covered two of the walls. To be in the same room with Thomas Mann was thrilling, enormous, amazing. But I was also hearing the siren call of the first private library I had ever seen.

While Merrill carried the ball, showing that he was not entirely ignorant of the Faust legend, I was trying, without making the divagations of my glance too obvious, to case the library. As I expected, almost all of the books were German, many in sets, leather-bound; the puzzle was that I could not decipher most of the titles (I didn't know of the existence of *Fraktur*). The few American books, all recent-looking, were easy to identify in their bright, waxy jackets.

Now he was talking about Goethe . . .

As if we had indeed rehearsed what we would say, Merrill and I had found a nice, unstrained rhythm of putting questions whenever Thomas Mann's glacial flow of words seemed to be drying up, and of showing our respectful appreciation of whatever he was saying. Merrill was being the Merrill I was so fond of: calm, charming, not stupid at all. I felt ashamed that I'd assumed he would disgrace himself, and therefore me, in front of Thomas Mann. Merrill was doing fine. I was, I thought, doing so-so. The surprise was Thomas Mann, that he wasn't harder to understand.

I wouldn't have minded if he had talked like a book. I wanted him to talk like a book. What I was obscurely starting to mind was that (as I couldn't have put it then) he talked like a book review.

Now he was talking about the artist and society, and he was using phrases I remembered from interviews with him I had read in *The Saturday Review of Literature*, a magazine I felt I'd outgrown since discovering the fancy prose and convoluted arguments of *Partisan Review*, which I had just started buying at the newsstand on Hollywood Boulevard. But, I reasoned, if I found what he said now a little familiar it was because I had read his books. He couldn't know he had in me such a fervent reader. Why should he say anything he hadn't already said? I refused to be disappointed.

I considered telling him that I loved *The Magic Mountain* so much that I had read it twice, but that seemed silly. I also feared he might ask me about some book of his which I had not read, though so far he hadn't asked a single question. "*The Magic Mountain* has meant so much to me," I finally ventured, feeling that it was now or never.

"It sometimes happens," he said, "that I am asked which I consider to be my greatest novel."

"Oh," I said.

"Yes," said Merrill.

"I would say, and have so replied recently in interviews . . ." He paused. I held my breath. "*The Magic Mountain.*" I exhaled.

The door opened. Relief had come: the German wife, slow-gaited, bearing a tray with cookies, small cakes, and tea, which she bent over to set down on a low table in front of the sofa against one wall. Thomas Mann stood up, came around the table, and waved us toward the sofa; I saw he was very thin. I longed to sit down again, and did, next to Merrill, where we'd been told to sit, as soon as

Thomas Mann occupied a wing chair nearby. Katia Mann was pouring tea from a heavy silver service into three delicate cups. As Thomas Mann put his saucer on his knee and raised the cup to his mouth (we followed, in unison), she said a few words in German to him in a low voice. He shook his head. His reply was in English—something like "It doesn't matter" or "Not now." She sighed audibly, and left the room.

Ah, he said, now we will eat. Unsmiling, he motioned to us to help ourselves to the cakes.

At one end of the low table that held the tray was a small Egyptian statuette, which sits in my memory as a funerary votive figure. It reminded me that Thomas Mann had written a book called *Joseph in Egypt*, which in the course of a cursory browsing at the Pickwick I'd not found enticing. I resolved to give it another try.

No one spoke. I was aware of the intense, dedicated quiet of the house, a quiet I had never experienced anywhere indoors; and of the slowness and self-consciousness of each of my gestures. I sipped my tea, tried to control the crumbs from the cake, and exchanged a furtive glance with Merrill. Maybe it was over now.

Putting down his cup and saucer, then touching the corner of his mouth with the edge of his thick white napkin, Thomas Mann said that he was always pleased to meet American young people, who showed the vigor and health and fundamentally optimistic temper of this great country. My spirits sank. What I had dreaded— he was turning the conversation to us.

He asked us about our studies. Our studies? That was a further embarrassment. I was sure he hadn't the faintest idea what a high school in Southern California was like. Did he know about Drivers' Education (compulsory)? Typing courses? Wouldn't he be surprised by the wrinkled condoms you spotted as you were darting across the lawn for the first period (the campus was a favorite nighttime trysting spot)—my own surprise having revealed, the very first week I entered, my being two years younger than my classmates, because I'd witlessly asked someone why there were these little balloons under the trees? And by the "tea" being sold by a pair of pachukes (as the Chicano kids were called) stationed along the left wall of the assembly building every morning recess? Could he imagine George, who, some of us knew, had a gun and got money from gas-station attendants? Ella and Nella, the dwarf sisters, who led the Bible Club boycott that resulted in the withdrawal of our biology textbook? Did he know Latin was gone, and Shakespeare, too, and that for months of tenth-grade English the visibly befuddled teacher handed out copies of the *Reader's Digest* at the beginning of each period—we were to select one article and write a summary of it—then sat out the hour in silence at her desk, nodding and knitting? Could he imagine what a world away from the Gymnasium in his native Lübeck, where fourteen-year-old Tonio Kröger wooed Hans Hansen by trying to get him to read Schiller's *Don Carlos*, was North Hollywood High School, alma mater of Farley Granger and Alan Ladd? He couldn't, and I hoped he would never find out. He had enough to be sad about—Hitler, the destruction of Germany, exile. It was better that he not know how really far he was from Europe.

He was talking about "the value of literature" and "the necessity of protecting civilization against the forces of barbarity," and I said, yes, yes . . . my conviction that it was absurd for us to be there—what, all week, I'd expected to feel—at last taking over. Earlier, we could only say something stupid. Actually having tea, the social ritual that gave a name to the whole proceeding, created new opportunities for disgrace. My worry that I would do something clumsy was driving out of my head whatever I might have ventured to say.

I remember beginning to wonder when it would not be

awkward to leave. I guessed that Merrill, for all the impression he gave of being at ease, would be glad to go, too.

And Thomas Mann continued to talk, slowly, about literature. I remember my dismay better than what he said. I was trying to keep myself from eating too many cookies, but in a moment of absent-mindedness I did reach over and take one more than I had meant to. He nodded. Have another, he said. It was horrible. How I wished I could just be left alone in his study to look at his books.

He asked us who our favorite authors were, and when I hesitated (I had so many, and knew I should mention only a few) he went on—and this I remember exactly: "I presume you like Hemingway. He is, such is my impression, the most representative American author."

Merrill mumbled that he had never read Hemingway. Neither had I; but I was too taken aback even to reply. How puzzling that Thomas Mann should be interested in Hemingway, who, in my vague idea of him, was a very popular author of novels that had been made into romantic movies (I loved Ingrid Bergman, I loved Humphrey Bogart) and wrote about fishing and boxing (I hated sports). He'd never sounded to me like a writer I ought to read. Or one my Thomas Mann would take seriously. But then I understood it wasn't that Thomas Mann liked Hemingway but that we were supposed to like him.

Well, Thomas Mann said, what authors do you like?

Merrill said he liked Romain Rolland, meaning *Jean-Christophe*. And Joyce, meaning *Portrait of an Artist*. I said I liked Kafka, meaning *Metamorphosis* and *In the Penal Colony*, and Tolstoy, meaning the late religious writings as much as the novels; and, thinking I must cite an American because he seemed to expect that, I threw in Jack London (meaning *Martin Eden*).

He said we must be very serious young people. More embarrassment. What I remember best is how embarrassing it was.

I was still worrying about Hemingway. Should I read Hemingway?

He seemed to find it perfectly normal that two local high-school students should know who Nietzsche and Schoenberg were . . . and up to now I'd simply rejoiced in this first foretaste of the world where such familiarity was properly taken for granted. But now, it seemed, he also wanted us to be two young Americans (as he imagined them); to be, as he was (as, I had no idea why, he thought Hemingway was), representative. I knew that was absurd. The whole point was that we didn't represent anything at all. We didn't even represent ourselves—certainly not very well.

Here I was in the very throne room of the world in which I aspired to live, even as the humblest citizen. (The thought of saying that I wanted to be a writer would no more have occurred to me than to tell him I breathed. I was there, if I had to be there, as admirer, not as aspirant to his caste.) The man I met had only sententious formulas to deliver, though he was the man who wrote Thomas Mann's books. And I uttered nothing but tongue-tied simplicities, though I was full of complex feeling. We neither of us were at our best.

Strange that I don't recall how it ended. Did Katia Mann appear to tell us that our time was up? Did Thomas Mann say he must return to his work, receive our thanks for granting this audience, and take us to the study door? I don't remember the goodbyes—how we were released. Our sitting on the sofa having tea and cakes cross-fades in my memory to the scene in which we are out on San Remo Drive again, getting into the car. After the dark study, the waning sun seemed bright: it was just past five-thirty.

Merrill started the car. Like two teenage boys driving away after their first visit to a brothel, we evaluated our performance. Merrill thought it was a triumph. I was ashamed, depressed, though I agreed that we hadn't made total fools of ourselves.

"Damn, we should have brought the book," Merrill said as we neared my neighborhood, breaking a long silence. "For him to sign."

I gritted my teeth and said nothing.

"That was great," said Merrill as I got out of the car in front of my house.

I doubt we spoke of it again.

Ten months later, within days of the appearance of the much-heralded *Doctor Faustus* (Book-of-the-Month Club selection, first printing over a hundred thousand copies), Merrill and I were at the Pickwick, giddily eyeing the piles of identical books stacked on a metal table in the front of the store. I bought mine and Merrill his; we read it together.

Acclaimed as it was, his book didn't do as well as Thomas Mann expected. The reviewers expressed respectful reservations, his American presence began to deflate slightly. The Roosevelt era was really over and the Cold War had started. He began to think of returning to Europe.

I was now within a few months of my big move, the beginning of real life. After January graduation, I started a term at the University of California at Berkeley, luckless George started doing his one-to-five at San Quentin, and in the fall of 1949 I left Cal and entered the University of Chicago, accompanied by Merrill and by Peter (both of whom had graduated in June), and studied philosophy, and then, and then . . . I went on to my life, which did turn out to be, mostly, just what the child of fourteen had imagined with such certitude.

And Thomas Mann, who had been doing time here, made his move. He and his Katia (who had become American citizens in 1944) were to leave Southern California, returning to the somewhat leveled magic mountain of Europe, for good, in 1952. There had been fifteen years in America. He had lived here. But he didn't really live here.

Years later, when I had become a writer, when I knew many other writers, I would learn to be more tolerant of the gap between the person and the work. Yet even now the encounter still feels illicit, improper. In my experience deep memory is, more often than not, the memory of embarrassment.

I still feel the exhilaration, the gratitude for having been liberated from childhood's asphyxiations. Admirations set me free. And embarrassment, which is the price of acutely experienced admiration. Then I felt like an adult, forced to live in the body of a child. Since, I feel like a child, privileged to live in the body of an adult. The zealot of seriousness in me, because it was already full-grown in the child, continues to think of reality as yet-to-be. Still sees a big space ahead, a far horizon. Is this the real world? I still ask myself that, forty years later . . . as small children ask repeatedly, in the course of a long, tiring journey, "Are we there yet?" Childhood's sense of plenitude was denied me. In compensation, there remains, always, the horizon of plenitude, to which I am borne forward by the delights of admiration.

I never told anyone of the meeting. Over the years I have kept it a secret, as if it were something shameful. As if it happened between two other people, two phantoms, two provisional beings on their way elsewhere: an embarrassed, fervid, literature-intoxicated child and a god in exile who lived in a house in Pacific Palisades.

PROJECT FOR A TRIP TO CHINA

I

I am going to China.

I will walk across the Luhu Bridge spanning the Sham Chun River between Hong Kong and China.

After having been in China for a while, I will walk across the Luhu Bridge spanning the Sham Chun River between China and Hong Kong.

Five variables:
> Luhu Bridge
> Sham Chun River
> Hong Kong
> China
> peaked cloth caps

Consider other possible permutations.

I have never been to China.

I have always wanted to go to China. Always.

II

Will this trip appease a longing?

> *Q.* [stalling for time] The longing to go to China, you mean?
>
> *A.* Any longing.

Yes.

Archaeology of longings.

But it's my whole life!

Don't panic. "Confession is nothing, knowledge is everything." That's a quote but I'm not going to tell who said it.

Hints:

> —a writer
> —somebody wise
> —an Austrian (i.e., a Viennese Jew)
> —a refugee
> —he died in America in 1951

Confession is me, knowledge is everybody.

Archaeology of conceptions.

Am I permitted a pun?

III

The conception of this trip is very old.

First conceived when? As far back as I can remember.
      —Investigate possibility that I was conceived in China
      though born in New York and brought up elsewhere
      (America).
          —write M.
             —telephone?

Prenatal relation to China: certain foods, perhaps. But I don't remember M. saying she actually *liked* Chinese food.
      —Didn't she say that at the general's banquet she spit the
      whole of the hundred-year-old egg into her napkin?

Something filtering through the bloody membranes, anyway.

Myrna Loy China, *Turandot* China. Beautiful, millionaire Soong
sisters from Wellesley and Wesleyan & their husbands. A landscape of jade, teak, bamboo, fried dog.

Missionaries, foreign military advisers. Fur traders in the Gobi
Desert, among them my young father.

Chinese forms placed about the first living room I remember (we
moved away when I was six): plump ivory and rose-quartz elephants on parade, narrow rice-paper scrolls of black calligraphy in
gilded wood frames, Buddha the Glutton immobilized under an
ample lampshade of taut pink silk. Compassionate Buddha, slim,
in white porcelain.

—Historians of Chinese art distinguish between porcelain and proto-porcelain.

Colonialists collect.

Trophies brought back, left behind in homage to the other living room, in the real Chinese house, the one I never saw. Unrepresentative, opaque objects. In dubious taste (but I only know that now). Confusing solicitations. The birthday gift of a bracelet made of five small tubular lengths of green jade, each tiny end capped in gold, which I never wore.

> —Colors of jade:
>> green, all sorts, notably emerald green and bluish
>>> green
>> white
>> gray
>> yellow
>> brownish
>> reddish
>> other colors

One certainty: China inspired the first lie I remember telling. Entering the first grade, I told my classmates that I was born in China. I think they were impressed.

I know that I wasn't born in China.

The four causes of my wanting to go to China:
> material
> formal

efficient

final

The oldest country in the world: it requires years of arduous study to learn its language. The country of science fiction, where everyone speaks with the same voice. Maotsetungized.

Whose voice is the voice of the person who wants to go to China? A child's voice. Less than six years old.

Is going to China like going to the moon? I'll tell you when I get back.

Is going to China like being born again?

Forget that I was conceived in China.

IV

Not only my father and mother but Richard and Pat Nixon have been to China before me. Not to mention Marco Polo, Matteo Ricci, the Lumière brothers (or at least one of them), Teilhard de Chardin, Pearl Buck, Paul Claudel, and Norman Bethune. Henry Luce was born there. Everyone dreams of returning.

　　—Did M. move from California to Hawaii three years ago
　　to be closer to China?

After she came back for good in 1939, M. used to say, "In China, children don't talk." But her telling me that, in China, burping at the table is a polite way of showing appreciation for the meal didn't mean I could burp.

Outside the house, it seemed plausible that I'd made China up. I knew I was lying when I said at school that I was born there; but being only a small portion of a lie so much bigger and more inclusive, mine was quite forgivable. Told in the service of the bigger lie, my lie became a kind of truth. The important thing was to convince my classmates that China actually did exist.

Was the first time I told my lie after or before I announced in school that I was a half-orphan?
          —That was true.

I have always thought: China is as far as anyone can go.
          —Still true.

When I was ten, I dug a hole in the back yard. I stopped when it got to be six feet by six feet by six feet. "What are you trying to do?" said the maid. "Dig all the way to China?"

No. I just wanted a place to sit in. I laid eight-foot-long planks over the hole: the desert sun scorches. The house we lived in then was a four-room stucco bungalow on a dirt road at the edge of town. The ivory and quartz elephants had been auctioned.
          —my refuge
          —my cell
          —my study
          —my grave

Yes. I wanted to dig all the way to China. And come bursting out the other end, standing on my head or walking on my hands.

The landlord came by in his jeep one day and told M. the hole had to be filled in within twenty-four hours because it was dangerous. Anyone crossing the yard at night might fall in. I showed him how it was entirely covered by boards, solid boards, except for the small square entrance on the north side where, with difficulty, I myself could just fit through.

      —Anyway, who was going to cross the yard at night? A coyote? A lost Indian? A tubercular or asthmatic neighbor? An angry landlord?

Inside the hole, I scraped out a niche in the east wall, where I set a candle. I sat on the floor. Dirt fell through the cracks between the planks into my mouth. It was too dark to read.

      —About to jump down, I never worried that I might land on a snake or a Gila monster curled up on the floor of the hole.

I filled in the hole. The maid helped me.

Three months later I dug it again. It was easier this time, because the earth was loose. Remembering Tom Sawyer with the fence that had to be whitewashed, I got three of the five Fuller kids across the road to help me. I promised them they could sit in the hole whenever I wasn't using it.

Southwest. Southwest. My desert childhood, off-balance, dry, hot.

I have been thinking about the following Chinese equivalences:

EAST	SOUTH	CENTER	WEST	NORTH
wood	fire	earth	metal	water
blue-green	red	yellow	white	black
spring	summer	end of summer / beginning of autumn	autumn	winter
green	red		white	black
dragon	bird		tiger	tortoise
anger	joy	sympathy	grief	fear

I would like to be in the center.

The center is earth, yellow; it lasts from the end of summer through the beginning of autumn. It has no bird, no animal.

Sympathy.

V

Invited by the Chinese government, I am going to China.

Why does everybody like China? Everybody.

Chinese things:
>   Chinese food
>   Chinese laundries
>   Chinese torture

China is certainly too big for a foreigner to understand. But so are most places.

For the moment I am not inquiring about "revolution" (Chinese revolution) but trying to grasp the meaning of patience.

And cruelty. And the endless presumption of the Occident. The bemedaled officers who led the Anglo-French occupation of Peking in 1860 probably sailed back to Europe with trunks of *chinoiserie* and respectful dreams of returning to China someday as civilians and connoisseurs.

    —The Summer Palace, "the cathedral of Asia" (Victor
    Hugo), pillaged and burned
    —Chinese Gordon

Chinese patience. Who assimilates whom?

My father was sixteen when he first went to China. M. was, I think, twenty-four.

I still weep in any movie with a scene in which a father returns home after a long desperate absence, at the moment when he hugs his child. Or children.

The first Chinese object I acquired on my own was in Hanoi in May 1968. A pair of green and white canvas sneakers with "Made in China" in ridged letters on the rubber soles.

Riding around Phnom Penh in a rickshaw in April 1968, I thought of the photograph I have of my father in a rickshaw in Tientsin taken in 1931. He looks pleased, boyish, shy, absent. He is gazing into the camera.

A trip into the history of my family. I've been told that the Chinese are pleased when they learn that a visitor from Europe or America has some link with prewar China. Objection: My parents were on the wrong side. Amiable, sophisticated Chinese reply: But all foreigners who lived in China at that time were on the wrong side.

La Condition Humaine is called *Man's Fate* in English. Not convincing.

I've always liked hundred-year-old eggs. (They're duck eggs, approximately two years old, the time it takes to become an exquisite green and translucent-black cheese.

    —I've always wished they *were* a hundred years old.

    Imagine what they might have mutated into by then.)

In restaurants in New York and San Francisco I often order a portion. The waiters inquire in their scanty English if I know what I'm ordering. I affirm that I do. The waiters go away. When the order comes, I tell my eating companions how delicious they are, but I always end up having all the slices to myself; everyone I know finds the sight of them disgusting.

    Q. Didn't David try the eggs? More than once?

    A. Yes. To please me.

Pilgrimage.

I'm not returning to my birthplace, but to the place where I was conceived.

When I was four, my father's partner, Mr. Chen, taught me how to eat with chopsticks. During his first and only trip to America. He said I looked Chinese.

Chinese food
Chinese torture
Chinese politeness

M. watched, approvingly. They all went back on the boat together.

China was objects. And absence. M. had a mustard-gold liquescent silk robe that belonged to a lady-in-waiting at the court of the Dowager Empress, she said.

And discipline. And taciturnity.

What was everybody doing in China all that time? My father and mother playing Great Gatsby and Daisy inside the British Concession, Mao Tse-tung thousands of miles inland marching, marching, marching, marching, marching, marching. In the cities, millions of lean coolies smoking opium, pulling rickshaws, peeing on the sidewalks, letting themselves be pushed around by foreigners and pestered by flies.

Unlocatable "White Russians," albinos nodding over samovars as I imagined them when I was five years old.

I imagined boxers raising their heavy leather gloves to deflect the hurtling lead of Krupp cannons. No wonder they were defeated.

I am looking in an encyclopedia at a photograph whose caption reads: "Souvenir photograph of a group of Westerners with the corpses of tortured Boxers. Honghong. 1899." In the foreground, a row of decapitated Chinese bodies whose heads have rolled some distance away; it is not always clear which body each head belongs to. Seven white men standing behind them, posing for the camera. Two are wearing their safari hats; a third holds his at his right side. In the shallow-looking water behind them, several sampans. The beginning of a village on the left. Mountains in the background, lightly touched with snow.

    —The men are smiling.

    —Undoubtedly it is an eighth Westerner, their friend, who is taking the picture.

Shanghai smelling of incense and gunpowder and dung. A United States Senator (from Missouri) at the turn of the century: "With God's help, we shall raise Shanghai up and up and up until it reaches the level of Kansas City." Buffalo in the late 1930s, disemboweled by the bayonets of invading Japanese soldiers, groaning in the streets of Tientsin.

Outside the pestilential cities, here and there a sage crouches at the breast of a green mountain. A great deal of elegant geography separates each sage from his nearest counterpart. All sages are old but not all are hirsute enough to grow white beards.

Warlords, landlords; mandarins, concubines. Old China Hands. Flying Tigers.

Words that are pictures. Shadow theatre. Storm Over Asia.

VI

I am interested in wisdom. I am interested in walls. China famous for both.

From the entry on China in the *Encyclopaedia Universalis* (Vol. 4, Paris, 1968, p. 306): "Dans les conversations, on aime toujours les successions de courtes phrases dont chacune est induite de la précédente, selon la méthode chinoise traditionelle de raisonnement."

Life lived by quotations. In China, the art of quotation has reached its apogee. Guidance in all tasks.

There is a woman in China, twenty-nine years old, whose right foot is on her left leg. Her name is Tsui Wen Shi. The train accident that cost her her right leg and her left foot occurred in January 1972. The operation that grafted her right foot onto her left leg took place in Peking and was performed, according to the *People's Daily*, "under the guidance of the proletarian line of Chairman Mao on matters of health, but also thanks to advanced surgical techniques."
>—The newspaper article explains why the surgeons didn't graft her left foot back on her left leg: the bones of her left foot were smashed, the right foot was intact.
>—The reader is not asked to take anything on faith. This is not a surgical miracle.

I am looking at the photograph of Tsui Wen Shi, sitting erect on a table covered with a white cloth, smiling, her hands clasping her bent left knee.

Her right foot is very large.

The flies are all gone, killed twenty years ago in the Great Fly-Killing Campaign. Intellectuals who, after criticizing themselves, were sent to the countryside to be reeducated by sharing the lot of peasants are returning to jobs in Shanghai and Peking and Canton.

Wisdom has gotten simpler, more practicable. More horizontal. The sages' bones whiten in mountain caves and the cities are clean. People are eager to tell their truth, together.

Feet long since unbound, women hold meetings to "speak bitterness" about men. Children recite anti-imperialist fairy tales. Soldiers elect and dismiss their officers. Ethnic minorities have a limited permission to be folkloric. Chou En-lai remains lean and handsome as Tyrone Power, but Mao Tse-tung now resembles the fat Buddha under the lampshade. Everyone is very calm.

VII

Three things I've been promising myself for twenty years that I would do before I die:
 —climb the Matterhorn
 —learn to play the harpsichord
 —study Chinese

Perhaps it's not too late to climb the Matterhorn. (As Mao Tse-tung swam, didactically old, eleven miles down the Yangtze?) My fussed-over lungs are sturdier today than when I was in my teens.

Richard Mallory vanished forever, behind a huge cloud, just as he was sighted nearing the top of the peak. My father, tubercular, never came back from China.

I never doubted I would go to China someday. Even when it became hard to go, impossible even, for an American.

—Being so confident, I never considered making that one of my three projects.

David wears my father's ring. The ring, a white silk scarf with my father's initials embroidered in black silk thread, and a pigskin wallet with his name stamped in small gold letters on the inside are all I possess that belonged to him. I don't know what his handwriting was like, not even his signature. The flat signet of the ring bears his initials, too.

—Surprising that it should just fit David's finger.

Eight variables:
    rickshaw
    my son
    my father
    my father's ring
    death
    China
    optimism
    blue cloth jackets

The number of permutations here are impressive: epic, pathetic. Tonic.

I have some photos too, all taken before I was born. In rickshaws, on camels and boat decks, before the wall of the Forbidden City. Alone. With his mistress. With M. With his two partners, Mr. Chen and the White Russian.

It is oppressive to have an invisible father.

Q. Doesn't David also have an invisible father?
A. Yes, but David's father is not a dead boy.

My father keeps getting younger. (I don't know where he's buried. M. says she's forgotten.)

An unfinished pain that might, just might, get lost in the endless Chinese smile.

VIII

The most exotic place of all.

China is not a place that I—at least—can go to, just because I decide to go.

My parents decided against bringing me to China. I had to wait for the government to invite me.
        —Another government.

For meanwhile, while I was waiting, upon their China, the China of pigtails and Chiang Kai-shek and more people than can be counted, had been grafted the China of optimism, the bright future, more people than can be counted, blue cloth jackets and peaked caps.

Conception, pre-conception.

What conception of this trip can I have in advance?

A trip in search of political understanding?
        —"Notes Toward a Definition of Cultural Revolution"?

Yes. But grounded in guesswork, vivified by misconceptions. Since I don't understand the language. Already six years older than my father when he died, I haven't climbed the Matterhorn or learned to play the harpsichord or studied Chinese.

A trip that might ease a private grief?

If so, the grief will be eased in a willful way: because I want to stop grieving. Death is unremittable, unnegotiable. Not unassimilable. But who assimilates whom? "All men must die, but death can vary in its significance. The ancient Chinese writer Szuma Chien said, 'Though death befalls all men alike, it may be heavier than Mount Tai or lighter than a feather.'"

    —This is not the whole of the brief quote given in
    Quotations from Chairman Mao Tse-tung, but it's all I
    need now.
    —Note that even in this abridged quote from Mao Tse-
    tung there is a quote within a quote.
    —The omitted final sentence of the quote makes clear that
    the heavy death is desirable, not the light one.

He died so far away. By visiting my father's death, I make him heavier. I will bury him myself.

I will visit a place entirely other than myself. Whether it is the future or the past need not be decided in advance.

What makes the Chinese different is that they live both in the past and in the future.

Hypothesis. Individuals who seem truly remarkable give the impression of belonging to another epoch. (Either some epoch in the past or, simply, the future.) No one extraordinary appears to be entirely contemporary. People who are contemporary don't appear at all:

they are invisible.

Moralism is the legacy of the past, moralism rules the domain of the future. We hesitate. Wary, ironic, disillusioned. What a difficult bridge this present has become! How many, many trips we have to undertake so as not to be empty and invisible.

IX

From *The Great Gatsby*, p. 2: "When I came back from the East last autumn I felt that I wanted the world to be in uniform and at a sort of moral attention forever; I wanted no more riotous excursions with privileged glimpses into the human heart."

—Another "East," but no matter. The quote fits.

—Fitzgerald meant New York, not China.

—(Much to be said about the "discovery of the modern function of the quotation," attributed by Hannah Arendt to Walter Benjamin in her essay "Walter Benjamin."

—Facts:

a writer

someone brilliant

a German [i.e., a Berlin Jew]

a refugee

he died at the French-Spanish border in 1940

—To Benjamin, add Mao Tse-tung and Godard.)

"When I came back from the East last autumn I felt that I wanted the world . . ." Why shouldn't the world stand at moral attention? Poor, bruised world.

First half of second quotation from unnamed Austrian-Jewish refugee sage who died in America: "Man as such is the problem of our time; the problems of individuals are fading away and are even forbidden, morally forbidden."

It's not that I'm afraid of getting simple, by going to China. The truth *is* simple.

I will be taken to see factories, schools, collective farms, hospitals, museums, dams. There will be banquets and ballets. I will never be alone. I will smile often (though I don't understand Chinese).

Second half of unidentified quote: "The personal problem of the individual has become a subject of laughter for the Gods, and they are right in their lack of pity."

"Fight individualism," says Chairman Mao. Master moralist.

Once China meant ultimate refinements: in pottery, cruelty, astrology, manners, food, eroticism, landscape painting, the relation of thought to written sign. Now China means ultimate simplifying.

What doesn't put me off, imagining it on the eve of my departure for China, is all that talk about goodness. I don't share the anxiety I detect in everyone I know about being *too* good.
> —As if goodness brings with it a loss of energy, individuality;
>> —in men, a loss of virility.

"Nice guys finish last." American saying.

"It's not hard for one to do a bit of good. What is hard is to do good all one's life and never do anything bad. . . ." (*Quotations from Chairman Mao Tse-tung*, Bantam paperback edition, p. 141.)

A teeming world of oppressed coolies and concubines. Of cruel landlords. Of arrogant mandarins, arms crossed, long fingernails sheathed inside the wide sleeves of their robes. All mutating, peaceably, into Heavenly Girl & Boy Scouts as the Red Star mounts over China.

Why *not* want to be good?

But to be good one must be simpler. Simpler, as in a return to origins. Simpler, as in a great forgetting.

X

Once, leaving China to return to the United States to visit their child (or children), my father and M. took the train. On the Trans-Siberian Railroad, ten days without a dining car, they cooked in their compartment on a Sterno stove. Since just one breathful of cigarette smoke was enough to send my father into an asthmatic attack, M., who smokes, probably spent a lot of time in the corridor.

> —I am imagining this. M. never told me this, as she did tell me the following anecdote.

After crossing Stalin's Russia, M. wanted to get out when the train stopped in Bialystok, where her mother, who had died in

Los Angeles when M. was fourteen, had been born; but in the 1930s the doors of the coaches reserved for foreigners were sealed.

>—The train stayed for several hours in the station.
>—Old women rapped on the icy windowpane, hoping to sell them tepid kvass and oranges.
>—M. wept.
>—She wanted to feel the ground of her mother's faraway birthplace under her feet. Just once.
>—She wasn't allowed to. (She would be arrested, she was warned, if she asked once more to step off the train for a minute.)
>—She wept.
>>—She didn't tell me that she wept, but I know she did.
>>I see her.

Sympathy. Legacy of loss. Women gather to speak bitterness. I have been bitter.

Why *not* want to be good? A change of heart. (The heart, the most exotic place of all.)

If I pardon M., I free myself. She has still not, after all these years, forgiven her mother for dying. I shall forgive my father. For dying.

>—Shall David forgive his? (Not for dying.) For him to decide.

"The problems of individuals are fading away . . ."

XI

Somewhere, some place inside myself, I am detached. I have always been detached (in part). Always.

—Oriental detachment?

—pride?

—fear of pain?

With respect to pain, I have been ingenious.

After M. returned to the United States from China in early 1939, it took several months for her to tell me my father wasn't coming back. I was nearly through the first grade, where my classmates believed I had been born in China. I knew, when she asked me to come into the living room, that it was a solemn occasion.

—Wherever I turned, squirming on the brocaded sofa, there were Buddhas to distract me.

—She was brief.

—I didn't cry long. I was already imagining how I would announce this new fact to my friends.

—I was sent out to play.

—I didn't really believe my father was dead.

Dearest M. I cannot telephone. I am six years old. My grief falls like snowflakes on the warm soil of your indifference. You are inhaling your own pain.

Grief ripened. My lungs wavered. My will got stronger. We went to the desert.

From *Le Potomak* by Cocteau (1919 edition, p. 66): "Il était, dans la ville de Tien-Sin, un papillon."

Somehow, my father had gotten left behind in Tientsin. It became even more important to have been conceived in China.

It seems even more important to go there now. History now compounds my personal, individual reasons. Bleaches them, displaces them, annihilates them. Thanks to the labors of the greatest world-historical figure since Napoleon.

Don't languish. Pain is not inevitable. Apply the gay science of Mao: "Be united, alert, earnest, and lively" (same edition, p. 81).

What does it mean, "be alert"? Each person alertly within himself, avoiding the collective drone?

    —All very well, except for the risk of accumulating too many truths.

    —Think of the damage to "be united."

Degree of alertness equals the degree to which one is not lazy, avoids habits. Be vigilant.

The truth is simple, very simple. Centered. But people crave other nourishment besides the truth. Its privileged distortions, in philosophy and literature. For example.

I honor my cravings, and I lose patience with them.

"Literature is only impatience on the part of knowledge." (Third and last quote from unnamed Austrian-Jewish sage who died, a refugee, in America.)

Already in possession of my visa, I am impatient to leave for China. To know. Will I be stopped by a conflict with literature?

A nonexistent conflict, according to Mao Tse-tung in his Yenan lectures and elsewhere, if literature serves the people.

But we are ruled by words. (Literature tells us what is happening to words.) More to the point, we are ruled by quotations. Not only in China, but everywhere else as well. So much for the transmissibility of the past! Disunite sentences, fracture memories.

    —When my memories become slogans, I no longer need them. No longer believe them.

        —Another lie?

        —An inadvertent truth?

Death doesn't die. And the problems of literature are not fading away . . .

XII

After walking across the Luhu Bridge spanning the Sham Chun River between Hong Kong and China, I will board a train for Canton.

From then on, I am in the hands of a committee. My hosts. My gracious bureaucratic Virgil. They control my itinerary. They know what they want me to see, what they deem proper for me to see; and I shall not argue with them. But when invited to make additional suggestions, what I shall tell them is: the farther north the better. I shall come closer.

I hate the cold. My desert childhood left me an intractable lover of heat, of tropics and deserts; but for this trip I'm willing to support as much cold as is necessary.

    —China has cold deserts, like the Gobi Desert.

Mythical voyage.

Before injustice and responsibility became too clear, and strident, mythical voyages were to places outside of history. Hell, for instance. The land of the dead.

Now such voyages are entirely circumscribed by history. Mythical voyages to places consecrated by the history of real peoples, and by one's own personal history.

The result is, inevitably, literature. More than it is knowledge.

Travel as accumulation. The colonialism of the soul, any soul, however well intentioned.
        —However chaste, however bent on being good.

At the border between literature and knowledge, the soul's orchestra breaks into a loud fugue. The traveler falters, trembles. Stutters.

Don't panic. But to continue the trip, neither colonialist nor native, requires ingenuity. Travel as decipherment. Travel as disburdenment. I am taking one small suitcase, and neither typewriter nor camera nor tape recorder. Hoping to resist the temptation to bring back any Chinese objects, however shapely, or any souvenirs, however evocative. When I already have so many in my head.

How impatient I am to leave for China! Yet even before leaving, part of me has already made the long trip that brings me to its border, traveled about the country, and come out again.

After walking across the Luhu Bridge spanning the Sham Chun River between China and Hong Kong, I will board a plane for Honolulu.

—Where I have never been, either.

—A stop of a few days. After three years I am exhausted by the nonexistent literature of unwritten letters and unmade telephone calls that passes between me and M.

After which I take another plane. To where I can be alone: at least, sheltered from the collective drone. And even from the tears of things, as bestowed—be it with relief or indifference—by the interminably self-pitying individual heart.

XIII

I shall cross the Sham Chun bridge both ways.

And after that? No one is surprised. Then comes literature.

—The impatience of knowing

—Self-mastery

—Impatience in self-mastery

I would gladly consent to being silent. But then, alas, I'm unlikely to know anything. To renounce literature, I would have to be really sure that I could know. A certainty that would crassly prove my ignorance.

Literature, then. Literature before and after, if need be. Which does not release me from the demands of tact and humility required for this overdetermined trip. I am afraid of betraying so many contradictory claims.

The only solution: both to know and not to know. Literature and not literature, using the same verbal gestures.

Among the so-called romantics of the last century, a trip almost always resulted in the production of a book. One traveled to Rome, Athens, Jerusalem—and beyond—in order to write about it.

Perhaps I will write the book about my trip to China before I go.

AMERICAN SPIRITS

The story begins in a crowded place, something like a Greyhound bus station, only more refined. The main character is an intrepid young woman of irreproachable white Protestant ancestry and even, regular construction. Her only visible fault was mirrored in her name, Miss Flatface.

Buffeted by mechanical stares, Miss Flatface decided to enter upon a career of venery. The spirits of Ben Franklin and Tom Paine whispered hoarsely in her ears, beckoning and forbidding.

Miss Flatface lifted up her skirts. A gasp was heard from one and all. "No sex, no sex," the crowd chanted. "Who could inspire desire with that face?"

"Try me," she murmured bravely, backing against a white tile wall. They continued to taunt her, without moving.

Then Mr. Obscenity bounded into the room, wearing white knickers, a plaid shirt, and a monocle. "The trouble with you fellows," he said, leering at Miss Flatface, then ripping open her nylon blouse without bothering to undo the buttons, "is that you've got principles. Too aesthetic by far, that's what's wrong with you." He gave Miss Flatface a shove for emphasis; she stared, surprised, her eyelids fluttering. "Mild as any sucking dove," he added, seizing her left breast and aiming it at the enrapt spectators.

"Hey, I'm her husband, you know," said a sturdy young fellow—Jim was his name—who separated himself from the crowd. "Miss Flatface is only her maiden name. Back home she's plain Mrs. Jim Johnson, proud wife and mother of three, Den Mother, Vice President of the PTA at the Green Grove School—that's where our kids go—and Recording Secretary of the local League of Women Voters. She has 9 and ¾ books of King Korn trading stamps and a 1962 Oldsmobile. Her mother—that's my mother-in-law—would be mad as hell if I let you get away with this." He paused. "If I let you get away with this, Mr. Obscenity, sir."

"That's better," said Mr. Obscenity.

"Jim," Miss Flatface called out crossly. "It's no use, Jim. I've changed. I'm not coming home."

Something like a chariot, drawn by a team of roan horses, pulled up before the frosted-glass doors. Mr. Obscenity vaulted into his seat and, with a gesture that admitted of no refusal, summoned Miss Flatface to hers. Above the clatter of hoofs, as they sped away, moans and giggles could be heard.

Back home, Miss Flatface—formerly Mrs. Johnson—had been renowned for having the cleanest garbage on the block. But in the place to which Mr. Obscenity had spirited her, nothing seemed amenable to the laws of sanitation as she had known them. Overripe peaches were languidly let fall, half eaten, onto the whitewashed wood floors. Sheets of sky-blue legal-size paper were scrawled with drawings of the male and female genitals, crumpled, then hurled into a corner of the room. Wine stains flourished on the damask tablecloths, which were never changed. A faded lipstick-smeared magazine photo of Marlon Brando was pinned to the inside of the closet door; the windowsills remained undusted;

there was barely time for Miss Flatface to brush her teeth once a day; and the condition of the bed—particularly that of the pillow, bristling with tiny feathers—was not to be believed.

From her window Miss Flatface could see the ocean, and a carrousel and a roller coaster called The Hurricane, and small figures—grouped in twos and in families—sauntering along the boardwalk. It was summertime, and several greasy fans about the room roiled the air without vanquishing the heat. Miss Flatface longed to bathe in the ocean, though she would not have dreamed of washing off the pungent body smells that Mr. Obscenity relished. Her craving for cotton candy was more easily satisfied. Practically no sooner had she voiced a wish for some than there it lay, wrapped in newspaper, at her door. But when she was only half through, merrily pulling off wads of the pink fuzz with her unnecessary teeth, Mr. Obscenity leaped on the bed and took her. Amid the twanging of bedsprings the cardboard cone swathed with the sticky mess fell unnoticed to the floor.

Sometimes people dropped in for dinner. While Mr. Obscenity presided at one end of the oak trestle table, various swarthy figures bandied talk of Communism, free love, race mixing. Some of the women wore long gold earrings. Some of the men had pointed shoes. Miss Flatface had a notion of foreigners from movies. What she hadn't known about was their dreadful table manners, such as the way they tore off chunks of bread with their fingers. And the rich garlicky stews and foamy custards did not always agree with her. After dinner there was usually a good deal of solemn belching. Miss Flatface happily joined in.

Though sometimes unnerved, as much by the pulpy confusion of foods as by the tenor and momentum of the conversation, Miss Flatface had by now a good deal of confidence in Mr. Obscenity. He, whatever the state of his guests, was always immaculate and neatly buttoned. Her confidence was further increased by the mimeographed pages in the clipboard that Mr. Obscenity often carried and frequently consulted, even at the dinner table. This augurs well, thought Miss Flatface. There is some system here.

Hearty and ready for fun at the drop of a hat—that was how Miss Flatface tried to think of the guests. When lewd plaster statuettes were passed around the table, her neighbor might nudge her in the groin to express enthusiasm. Occasionally a pair of guests would sink beneath the table, which would shudder for a while until the flushed and disheveled couple reemerged.

Observing that Mr. Obscenity seemed to wish to show her off to his friends, Miss Flatface resolved to be as friendly as possible. One day, she hoped, there would be nothing that he might ask of her that she could not do.

"Nice little woman you got there," observed one of his black chums, a man everyone called Honest Abe. He flicked his cigar ash into a gold-plated diaphragm that served as an ashtray, and tilted back in his chair.

"Take her," said Mr. Obscenity with a genial wave of his hand. Then he jotted something on the clipboard.

"Well I dunno," said Honest Abe. He rubbed the fringe beard that decorated his chin, musing.

Miss Flatface wondered. Was this big black Honest Abe afraid of slim Mr. Obscenity? Or did he find her undesirable?

"Ain't much of a face . . ."

That settled it! Tears got ready behind Miss Flatface's eyes.

"And white women ain't good for my blood. That's what the Prophet says."

"Abe!" said Mr. Obscenity, menacingly.

"Yes, Mr. Obscenity. I mean yeah, boss. I mean yes, sir."

Honest Abe hoisted his great bulk wearily from the table, dropping his napkin, scattering breadcrumbs from his lap to the floor.

"Well, little woman, let's see what you and me can do. Can't do you no more harm than it does me." He chuckled.

Miss Flatface rose eagerly. She felt the faint tingling in her stomach. The spirits of James Fenimore Cooper and Betsy Ross whispered in her ears, beckoning and forbidding. "It's my duty, isn't it?" she asked Mr. Obscenity, wishing to quell the last flecks of doubt that soiled her perfect resolution. "The national will, I mean. The national purpose. And the national presence."

"You must do what you have to do," said Mr. Obscenity coldly. "This, after all, is the American dilemma." He made a notation on his clipboard and turned back to his guests.

Honest Abe carefully removed his maroon velvet jacket and hung it on the back of his chair, then unstrapped the transistor radio that nestled in his armpit.

So that's where the music was coming from, thought Miss Flatface.

Their union took place in a bathtub whose hard white enamel surface had been draped with gaily colored bath towels, blue and purple and brown and yellow, like the tent of a sheik. Over the faucets someone had considerately, perhaps even reverently, laid the Stars and Stripes. They do smell different, Miss Flatface had the presence of mind to observe. But it's a nice strong smell. I wonder why I was so afraid of them when I went into that candy store late one night to buy a pack of Luckies, or in the movie-theatre balcony (I was just a kid then) when that big one sat down beside me. Seeing them in the newsreels rioting and throwing bricks in their own dingy streets, it makes you afraid. There seem to be so many of them. But one at a time they're not so frightening once you get really close. They deserve all the rights they can get, she concluded.

As day followed night, which was followed by day, all spent in riotous pleasures, Miss Flatface sometimes wondered if she still deserved her name. But Mr. Obscenity proved a stern taskmaster. He
would not allow her near a mirror. He refused to answer any questions about her appearance, her talents, or her destiny.

Never once did she think of her mother, the widow of a railroad
engineer and now living in St. Louis, not even to the extent of
wishing to send her a postcard. Occasionally, very occasionally, she
thought of Jim and the three children. Had he sold the Oldsmobile, she wondered; he wouldn't need two cars. But there was no
turning back.

"You have some power," she said to Mr. Obscenity one day.
"But why are people afraid of you?" The spirits of Henry Adams
and Stephen Crane whispered hoarsely in her ears, beckoning and
forbidding. Surely it wasn't forbidden to ask questions? Not in a
free country.

"I mean, how did you get Jim to let me go so easy?"

Mr. Obscenity, plunged deep in Miss Flatface, did not reply. He
merely placed a pillow over her animated visage.

She flung off the pillow. "And Honest Abe?" she said, looking
up into his calm faraway eyes. "Why was *he* afraid of you?" Still
no answer. "He's bigger—I mean taller—than you."

Mr. Obscenity continued to leaf, as it were, through her body. A
gale, premonitory of something, had just come up. Somewhere
a shutter was banging against a wall.

Miss Flatface's attention began to wander. She watched a fly
sipping at a puddle of cold coffee on the night table. Next, the label
on Mr. Obscenity's new tan jodhpurs, bunched on the floor, caught
her eye. Then she wondered if Mr. Obscenity had any trouble getting listed in the telephone book.

"Pay attention," he barked, withdrawing from Miss Flatface,
turning on his side and lightly dusting her torso with sugar.

"I am."

"Don't contradict me. You aren't."

"Well, what if I do think of other things? Who says I have to think about it all the time? Doesn't thinking spoil it anyway?"

"Look," he said, "this isn't a eurhythmic exercise."

"Well, I don't know what that means," she said self-righteously, "but I know it isn't supposed to be hard labor either."

"Don't play innocent with me! I don't have all these people parked here for nothing."

Above the buzzing of flies about her breasts, Miss Flatface tuned in on a chorus of raspy breathing. In the hallway just beyond the open door, four Air Force lieutenants appeared to be playing bridge.

"I didn't see them," she protested.

Mr. Obscenity grunted.

"Honest I didn't."

"I bet you were a fussy eater when you were a kid," muttered Mr. Obscenity.

"No, really—"

Mr. Obscenity replaced the pillow. Miss Flatface resigned herself to pleasure. She would ask her questions another time.

———

"How do you like this life?" Mr. Obscenity deigned to inquire one afternoon in a muffled voice while nuzzling between Miss Flatface's legs.

"Gosh," she exclaimed, "I never imagined life could be like this!"

"Want to continue to live like this?" he asked.

"Sure!" Since childhood, Miss Flatface had always said "Sure!" when she wasn't. "Who'd want to live different? I can hardly imagine it," she went on, with a tremor of anxiety at this untimely chain of consecutive words.

"Ah my dear," sighed Mr. Obscenity, sitting upright amid the damp, rumpled sheets and patting Miss Flatface on the thigh. "I'm afraid you've had it. One must never think that no other life than this is possible. All other lives are imaginable, possible, even probable."

"What have I done?" she cried, dismayed to see that he had inserted his monocle in the socket of his left eye. Mr. Obscenity never removed his monocle except when engaged in the most profound carnal inquiry.

"Unless you wish to risk your life in one of the most picturesque exploits known to man—an orgy with no holds barred—I'm going to send you on your way. With references, of course. And some cash to see you through your first week."

An orgy with no holds barred? Drugs? Instruments of torture? Perversions? Artificial phalluses three feet long? She bowed her head in thought. The spirits of William James and Fatty Arbuckle whispered hoarsely in her ears, beckoning and forbidding. Mr. Obscenity drummed an indecipherable tune on her belly with his fingertips, waiting for her to come to a decision.

She was a brave girl, but not that brave. One sought an education in order to use it. She had not left Jim to die but to live. For Miss Flatface there was a limit, even to voluptuousness. Innocent as she might be, despite all she'd experienced, she had some sense of her own worth.

"Want to flip a coin?" said Mr. Obscenity, languidly sketching with a soft orange lipstick the outline of her pudenda in the vicinity of Miss Flatface's navel.

"Don't bother. I'll go," she said.

Someone put a dime in the jukebox. "Anyone Who Had a Heart," thought Miss Flatface, "Would Love Me." Mr. Obscenity whisked a mirror from his pocket and began preening himself. First he inspected the insides of his nostrils, then punched his midriff for signs of flabbiness. Miss Flatface had never felt so let down in all her life. Suddenly she felt terribly, terribly alone.

———

Yet Miss Flatface knew she was not alone in this place. There were other young American women here, in the charge of other educators like Mr. Obscenity. Just possibly they might be all in the charge of Mr. Obscenity himself. Miss Flatface preferred not to think about that.

All houses by the ocean are damp, and it was getting on to winter now. Workmen came trooping through her room; buckets of paint, stiff abandoned brushes, rollers, cans of turpentine, and huge rough paint-encrusted ladders lay about, adding to the confusion. The premises were being renovated. Miss Flatface gave way to a profound gloom.

Days went by without a glimpse of Mr. Obscenity. Miss Flatface tried to recall everything she owed him. At first she supposed that her tantrum was desire. It wasn't that. Not being of a grateful disposition, what Miss Flatface craved was revenge. She even had a plan. She would persuade some of the other boarders to leave with her. Then Mr. Obscenity would regret the whim that had prompted him to decree her expulsion.

Whom would she take? Only women, she decided. Dragging men along would make it too complicated. Miss Flatface had never thought of herself as a feminist before—certainly not when she had been Jim's wife and the mother of three. But now she felt the tug of sex loyalty. The spirits of Edith Wharton and Ethel Rosenberg whispered hoarsely in her ears, beckoning and forbidding.

Or was it that?

That very night, looking a bit slovenly in her blue flowered wrap-around housecoat, she crept about the drafty corridors, listening and, whenever she could, watching at keyholes. Scenes of aching delight assaulted her senses. Was this the Eden she was losing? Then no one else should have it either.

In the hall she accosted a dark-haired hoyden wearing nothing but a beige trench coat.

"You look like you can be trusted," said Miss Flatface cheerfully. "And I'm clearing out of here—I mean, I've had enough. How about coming with me? Wouldn't you like to bathe in the ocean, or ride The Hurricane? You know, do whatever you want and not have to be taking down your bloomers all the time?"

Quick as a flash, the girl reached under her coat and pulled out a dark metal object. A gun? Miss Flatface drew back in terror. No, a camera. The girl laid the cold instrument to her eye and rapidly snapped nine close-ups of her astonished companion.

"These can be developed by morning," said the girl. "I'll send you copies, if you want 'em."

"But what for?" cried Miss Flatface, realizing that her conspiracy was not even getting off the ground.

"They're for my album." Noting Miss Flatface's uncomprehending stare, she added, "My collection."

"Your collection?"

"For Soc. 1046y, Marriage & the Family," replied the girl. "A research project for my junior year. Four credits."

Although mystified, Miss Flatface now grasped enough to confirm her suspicion that this place was not the haven of spontaneous misrule it might appear. How else explain this girl, a crisp secretarial type, who probably took dictation at some phenomenal speed? Miss Flatface felt like a frump.

The girl bared her large white teeth in a smile, then glided down the corridor.

"Wait," called Miss Flatface. "I *would* like a picture. I mean, so I can see what I look like in it."

"Why not," said the girl. "Tomorrow morning. And I won't use your name. Everyone is anonymous, you know. It makes the project more scientific."

Scientific! There's an idea! Why hadn't she thought of that before? Every large institution requires great machines, and this one couldn't be different. All she had to do was to get control of the machinery. That's what a revolution is. Not simply using force, but seizing the tools of power. Miss Flatface hastened to the boiler room. The floor had recently been under water, piles of moldy soaked books were precariously balanced on top of orange crates, and the stench of urine was distracting. But the only machinery she found was a row of television screens, each carrying a different image, topped by a single screen which repeated one or another image from the row. Below the screens was a large prickly table studded with switches and buttons and dials and levers; and before that table, operating the panel and sporting a set of earphones, sat a bulky figure wearing a white plastic hood.

"Mr. Obscenity," she whispered, fearing the worst and preferring immediate censure to suspense.

Instead of turning, the figure convulsively manipulated some dials. The image on the master screen changed from a roller derby to a woman, legs agape, in the last stages of childbirth. Demoted, the roller derby continued as one of the images on the row beneath.

"Please tell me who you are. I know I shouldn't be here."

Competing with all these images, Miss Flatface feared she would never get an answer. The figure in the white hood threw a switch. A bald, toothy state governor addressing a Shriners' convention was promoted from the row to the master screen, and the anguished mother-to-be seemed much calmer alongside the roller derby. The political speech lasted a few moments. It was erased by the image Miss Flatface had had her eye on from the beginning— a delightful erotic scene between two women and a Nisei youth with an enormous erection.

Making an effort, Miss Flatface wrenched her glance from the master screen.

"Mr. Obscenity, I love you." This was a feckless lie.

A commercial for a new roll-on deodorant blanked out the erotic scene. The impassive figure turned, its attention for the moment released. Miss Flatface, tremblingly, undid her blue flowered housecoat, yearning to seduce. So far so good: now she had the attention of the eyes (which were all of the hooded face she could see) quite to herself. A hand reached toward her clammy thighs, a hand that seemed more slender than Mr. Obscenity's.

"Yes, yes," she cried, leaning toward the hand.

But at that very moment the commercial ended, and the Nisei youth and the two women resumed their sport. The hooded technician's delicate hand hovered in midair, suspended between Miss Flatface and the instrument panel. Seconds that seemed like hours passed. Then the machine won: the hand lunged toward a dial. Humiliated, Miss Flatface wrapped the housecoat around her shivering loins and found her way back to her room.

———

Next morning Miss Flatface, her eyes reddened by her first good cry since she left Jim, was scooped from sleep by a loud knocking.

"Laura," said the man at the door, who wore a gray chesterfield coat and a gray porkpie hat. "Laura?" he said again.

No one had ever called Miss Flatface by her first name in this place before.

"Miss Laura Flatface?"

Miss Flatface was daunted but intrigued.

"Let me innerduce myself." The man handed Miss Flatface an embossed card. *Inspector Jug, Detective*, it read. *By appointment only.*

"Now let's get this straight, Laura," said the man, all ceremony seemingly concluded. He had sat down but hadn't removed his hat.

"Who said you could call me by my first name?" wailed Miss Flatface, indignant.

"Now lookee here, Laura," said the man soothingly. "I don't mean to frighten yer"—he said yer instead of you—"but I've gotten wind of what yer up to and it won't wash. No ma'am, it just won't wash. Them girls stay here, and the TV sets too, and you gotta go. That's what the boss called me in to tell yer."

Provoked by her rejection the night before, Miss Flatface decided to see if Inspector Jug was proof against her charms.

"Music, Inspector? And perhaps a little wine?"

"Don't mind if I do, ma'am."

"You can call me Laura."

Ignoring the spirits of Eddie Duchin and John Philip Sousa which whispered hoarsely in her ears, beckoning and forbidding, she put on a pop ballad rapidly climbing to the top of the Top 40. The voices of an androgyne quaternity and the quakings of their electric guitars resounded in a heavenly echo chamber. Miss Flatface, ever attuned to the new, was entranced. But Inspector Jug was clearly of the older generation. "Turn off that record," he howled, pulling at his tie. "How can you stand all that bawlin'?"

"I like it," said Miss Flatface sweetly, lowering herself into his lap.

"Hey, whatcha—"

Just then, another knock on the door.

"God damn!" muttered Miss Flatface.

It was the dark-haired girl, good as her word, who silently proffered a small manila envelope.

Miss Flatface tore it open and gazed with delight upon her own features. Thank God, things had not gone too far: they were not indecently protruding. Perhaps they didn't protrude even in an average way. But that a definite change had taken place—a distinctly forward, assertive movement of her face—there could not be the slightest doubt. In her glee, she threw her arms around the dark-haired girl and kissed her.

"Who's there?" called out the Inspector, who, although he'd been backing off from Miss Flatface's attentions, was now beginning to feel ignored. It seemed that this day he would not have his mind solely on his professional duties. "Why doncha invite yer friend in?" he said, feigning casualness. Perhaps, he thought quickly, Mr. Obscenity could use a report on this one, too.

"Okay," said the girl. "For my collection," she explained to Miss Flatface, who didn't know whether she wished to share Inspector Jug with anyone else.

"Well, well, well," said the Inspector. "What a pretty pair of ladies we have here. One a little older"—he pointed to Miss Flatface, who was gratified to be mentioned first. "One a little younger," he said, pointing to the student of Marriage & the Family. "One blond"—Miss Flatface again. "And one brunette"— the girl. "One with dimpled knees"—it was Miss Flatface's knees that were being fondled; "one with knees like a tennis player"— the Inspector stroked the back of the girl's leg. "One with a mole on her—"

"Inspector Jug!"

Alas, here Inspector Jug's anatomical inventory was rudely interrupted. At the fireplace stood Mr. Obscenity, black-robed and arms extended like a great winged bat. His monocle glinted with the reflected rays of the sun, making one eye obsidian and relentless. His teeth seemed longer, and his face was a thing of terrible wrath. There was not a trace of mockery or compassion on it. Inspector Jug blanched, but held his ground; he did not move his hands, which rested on the buttocks of both women.

"You can't talk to me like that, Mr. Obscenity."

The girl broke away from Inspector Jug's grasp and pulled down her skirt.

"You were my most trusted assistant, Jug," said Mr. Obscenity sternly. "And you have betrayed that trust. You know my motto: every man to his business. I know my business. And you should have known yours."

Inspector Jug had, visibly, begun to quail. Miss Flatface, feeling the hand that had grasped her buttocks so avidly now loosening its grip, becoming more tentative in its lust, moved away. She had a faintly unpleasant sensation of coolness in the place where Inspector Jug had held her.

Mr. Obscenity advanced, hands like claws.

"But Mr. Obscenity—sir—"

At these halting deferential words Miss Flatface knew the game was up. Inspector Jug couldn't brave Mr. Obscenity any more than the others could. The king of the jungle, she concluded, will ever be king.

"You!" called Mr. Obscenity to Miss Flatface, imperiously. "Stay where you are. I want a word with you, as soon as I've lopped a piece off this sniveling rogue."

"Don't go, Laura," pleaded Inspector Jug. "Tell him how businesslike I was when I first came in the door. I wasn't doin' nothin' wrong. You can tell him that, Laura. Tell him! Please!"

Mr. Obscenity sank his fangs, through winter coat and all, into Inspector Jug's shoulder.

"Is there a way out of here?" Miss Flatface asked, addressing herself to the dark-haired girl cowering by the door. The girl pointed, mutely. Miss Flatface heard the sound of prancing hoofs. "Consider this an escape," she announced to the two men.

"I'll get you," shouted Mr. Obscenity. "No one escapes from here. You must be expelled." Saliva streamed from the corners of his mouth.

"Me too, Laura!" shouted Inspector Jug, pressing a handkerchief to his bleeding shoulder. "I'll get yer for gettin' me in dutch with my boss. Hellion! Bitch!"

"I'm staying," said the dark-haired girl, dropping her skirt to her ankles and lifting her sweater over her head. The two men ignored her—their first act in unison. All their hot desire, tardy as the hottest desire ever is when it is not premature, was flung at the proud departing figure of Miss Flatface.

She never regretted her departure. Her apprenticeship was over. Strictly speaking, her chosen career of venery could only be practiced on the outside, in the world proper. It all worked out handsomely. Because the life of a woman not drawn to this profession either by breeding (remember her impeccable white Protestant descent) or by background (Jim, the three children, the League of Women Voters, the trading stamps) is a hard and lonely one, she might have faltered. As it was, she had reason to court solitude. She knew those two would not give up easily.

Pursued by Mr. Obscenity and Inspector Jug, Miss Flatface traversed the length and breadth of the United States, carrying her warm treasure between her legs. Wherever she went, she spied replicas of her former self—pale, greedy, self-denying women fortified by pop-up toasters with infrared rays and boxed sets of stainless-steel steak knives made in West Germany. Miss Flatface, penitent for her former life, traveled light. Of course, she sold herself for money. The spirits of William Jennings Bryan and Leland Stanford chided her when she didn't get a good price.

Her mentor, Mr. Obscenity, first caught up with her in a lumber camp in the Northwest, somewhere near the Canadian border. He was not wearing his monocle or his knickers. His plaid shirt was carelessly stuffed into a pair of faded blue-jeans. Miss Flatface, plying her trade in front of the town's only movie theatre, did not at first recognize him. His recent exertions seemed to have aged him. He had grown a little fat and was less well groomed.

What rang a bell was the low mocking bow he made as she ambled seductively past him.

"Come near me and I'll scream," Miss Flatface retorted with surprising aplomb.

"Don't panic. I'm not going to force you. Did I ever force you to do anything?"

Miss Flatface remembered. The answer was no.

"Just come back," he said. "We'll forget everything that's happened."

"You sound like Jim," she said.

A sulky, coquettish expression passed across Mr. Obscenity's features. He had decided to ignore her last remark. "I'm not as spry as I used to be," he mused aloud. "I don't know why, but I'm tired."

"I'm not," she said. "At least not yet."

"Well just tell me one thing. Has that rat Jug found you yet?"

Miss Flatface slowly began to appreciate this new, unearned power she had over Mr. Obscenity.

"Because if he does," he snarled, "and you listen to him, I'll kill you both. Listen to me! Don't you realize he's the undoing of all that you and I have done?"

Miss Flatface considered that this was possibly so, but she wouldn't give Mr. Obscenity the satisfaction of letting him know she agreed with him.

"Well," he said, "let's get it over with. On the house, of course."

"Certainly not," said Miss Flatface with great severity. "I'm not a charitable institution."

"I was," said Mr. Obscenity.

His irony, intended to arouse sympathy, backfired. Miss Flatface laughed. Mr. Obscenity's lips became foamy, and he parted them in a sinister smile that disclosed a set of razor-sharp teeth. He advanced gruesomely, inexorably.

Miss Flatface made the sign of the cross. It didn't work. But, opportunely, a tree toppled and grazed him on the skull, leaving Miss Flatface plenty of time to slip down an alley and make her escape.

Her suppliant, Inspector Jug, first accosted her some months later while the roof of her mouth was burning from an impetuously gobbled slice of pizza-with-pepperoni. They were squeezed side by side in an all-night eatery in Times Square.

"Gee, Laura," he sighed, wheezing. "It's been a long time catchin' up with yer."

"I've nothing to say to you," she said, wiping her mouth with a paper napkin.

"You don't hafta say nothin' to me. Just clear me with my boss. That guy's awful mad at me."

"How's your shoulder?" asked Miss Flatface with routine sympathy.

"Poorly, Laura."

"Well, I can't help you. I've got to think of myself first. Anyway, stop passing the buck. Be a man! What do you care what he thinks? Don't you know this is a free country? You're free. So am I. And I intend to make use of the liberty granted me by God and the Constitution."

Inspector Jug looked distinctly crestfallen at this militant declaration.

"Are you on the level?" inquired Miss Flatface. "I mean, is this the real reason, the only reason you've been following me around? I did get that smutty wire in New Orleans, you know. I just didn't see any reason to answer it." She ordered another slice of pizza.

"Well, little lady—I reckon not. I really like yer. For yerself. You've got spunk. I sorta thought we might team up, Laura, maybe start a little agency with yer as a full partner. Lots of divorce cases, stuff like that. A lady investigator does even better than a man. How about it?"

"You mean you've been following me all over the country to make me a business proposition?" The spirits of John Brown and Dashiell Hammett whispered hoarsely in her ears, beckoning and forbidding.

"Well, maybe it isn't just that I'm attracted to yer, I admit it. Why don't we go to my hotel now and—"

"Look," said Miss Flatface. "I meant it when I said this was a free country. It took me a long time to find my freedom and I'm not giving it up. At least not until it's my idea, not somebody else's." And after these forceful words, she abandoned her uneaten second slice of pizza and marched out into the turbulent street. Looking back, she saw that Inspector Jug did not follow her.

Miss Flatface's brave words to Mr. Obscenity and Inspector Jug were sincere. She did love her freedom. But that did not mean she was not occasionally lonely.

To stave off loneliness, Miss Flatface indulged a newfound taste for disasters. Not political disasters (in Times Square she rarely looked up at the streaming news); the private, domestic ones. Between tricks, for which she used a convenient hotel on Tenth Avenue, she would buy and pore over all the weekly scandal papers, finding the headlines irresistible. "My Milk Killed My Nine Babies." "For My Husband's Sake I Was Blind For Forty-Two Years." "I Looked Like This Until I Had Plastic Surgery." "Cooked

Alive!" "I'm A Member Of The Fourth Sex." "My In-Laws Drove Four Nails Into My Skull." "I'm Not Ugly, I'm Just Funny-Looking." "They Left Me Outside For Seventeen Years." The stories were often less vivid than the headlines, but no matter. From the headlines alone Miss Flatface received sufficient and vicarious pleasure. For she had decided that she herself was perfectly normal-looking. Never did she meet the slightest reluctance from clients because of her flat face.

But although men generally found her attractive, she had to admit that she was not drawn to every man. A total sensual thrill was not always forthcoming. Yet her ardor might flare up simply at the sight of someone whom she thought at first was Mr. Obscenity or even the insipid Inspector Jug.

Miss Flatface tried to humor her occasional discontents by keeping on the move. That way she got to know this country extremely well—its unlimited human resources, its majestic natural setting. From time to time she would take a vacation, travel just for the sake of traveling (this also helped to throw her mentor and her suppliant off the track), saving a little money and hitch-hiking or taking a bus to the Grand Canyon or Yosemite National Park or Carlsbad Caverns. Once, she spent two whole weeks in a little cabin in the Ozarks, catching up on back issues of *The Saturday Evening Post*, sleeping twelve hours a day, and occasionally yielding to the advances of George, the proprietor of the nearby Friendly Ed Motel.

She knew some other work would be less strenuous than hustling. A telephone operator or a clerk at J. C. Penney's or a waitress had it easier than she. It was not just the risk of disease but the standing, and even worse, the walking; her feet swelled and it was hard to find attractive heels that didn't pinch her corns. But really she wouldn't have changed her life for any other. It had brought her a peace of mind and a vitality she'd never known before. She who had often flagged in her daily tasks as a fully mechanized suburban housewife with only three children, two of them school age, now found herself always on the go, full of pep. Truly the power of sex, even when discovered late in life, is a magical one.

So great was her energy that when she first encountered both Mr. Obscenity and Inspector Jug at the same time—it was a deserted street lined with warehouses, on the near north side of Chicago—she had the mother wit to call the police and have them arrested for molesting her. Actually, they hadn't gotten around to that yet. Mr. Obscenity, monocled, clad in a parka, corduroy pants, and high rubber snowboots, was leading Inspector Jug by some sort of harness. That's what I call a sick relationship, she thought.

The Chicago police are not noted for their courage or their incorruptibility, but they did not seem in the least fazed by the odd-looking pair that Miss Flatface consigned to their care.

"I bet that's not the last of them," Miss Flatface reflected aloud as she left the station after the disreputable twosome had been booked. Mingled with anxiety there was a wistful note in her voice.

———

Mr. Obscenity and Inspector Jug, usually singly, rarely in tandem, accosted Miss Flatface no less than one hundred seventy-four times within the next five years, by telephone, telegram, and personal appearance. Often the interruption was embarrassing, and Miss Flatface lost her composure. Gradually, however, her strongest emotion toward the pair became condescension, touched with alarm. Would they never give up? Didn't they know the meaning of rejection? Had they no pride?

———

While eating in a diner outside of Tulsa, Oklahoma, Miss Flatface finally fell in love for the first time in her life. He was a sailor named Arthur; seated next to her at the counter, his feet twined around the bar stool, he was bulldozing his way through three hamburgers doused with ketchup and relish. Miss Flatface longed to reach out and touch his smooth, healthy cheek. The spirits of Warren G. Harding and John F. Kennedy whispered hoarsely in her ears, beckoning and forbidding. For Arthur looked a little like Jim. Something in the eyes, in the shape of the head, the way the hair curled at the nape of his neck. Watch out! the spirits cried. But he's not Jim, said Miss Flatface to herself. Nor am I I.

He's a man, that's the resemblance, Miss Flatface observed after a few nights in Arthur's tireless arms. Like Jim, he isn't very interested in sexual variety. But who needs that, she said to herself, sternly repressing all memories of the unpredictable Mr. Obscenity. The main thing is that he loves me. And he won't sit on me—a figure of speech—as Jim did, because now I know my own mind.

She went with Arthur to San Diego, where a wedding ceremony was performed. They rented a room at the Magnolia Arms with cooking privileges, but Miss Flatface no longer liked to cook. When Arthur was away—he regularly shipped out for weeks at a time—she lived on canned ravioli, which she ate cold, and sardines, and spiced ham. In the morning, after going down to get the mail, she would wander over to the local Bowl; in the afternoon there was bingo. Needless to say, she was faithful to Arthur—sealing her fidelity by wearing loafers and white socks, an ungainly fashion from her high-school days. And Arthur, when he returned home, was as affectionate as ever.

"Laurababy," he would shout as he burst in the door, his tanned face beaming. "Boy did I miss my baby! Boyoboyoboy." Miss Flatface loved the boy in Arthur even more than the lover. When she undressed him upon his return from a voyage, it was first to see if he had new tattoos. That was a game between them. Arthur's fore-arms and biceps were already printed with colorful designs; now he made sure to get them in less likely places. He would fall on the bed squealing—he was ticklish too, another one of his charms—as Miss Flatface examined his armpits, his navel, the folds of his groin, and other secret zones. "Just wait till I get hold of you," he would mutter with mock fierceness, between his giggles. Miss Flatface would insist on continuing to look carefully for the tat-toos. This game was a lovely part of their joy. In her happiness with Arthur Miss Flatface began to forget her former lives.

She had a reminder, though, after one evening while he was in port and out with some of his seamen buddies. On such evenings Miss Flatface knew better than to ask to come along, but she al-lowed herself to question Arthur afterward. "Aw, you know," he said this particular evening. "A lot of booze. And chasing after girls—not that I'm interested in any other girl when I got my baby here at home waiting for me. And talking to a couple of funny fellows at the Blue Star."

"What fellows?"

"Oh, just some guys." He laughed and slapped his chest. "The weirdest dudes you ever laid eyes on, honey. One had a monocle and some kind of crazy outfit, like he was English or something. Like one of them polo players. Real stuck up. But the other guy, he was real friendly. Got me to talking about myself. I told them all about you, what a great little wife I got." He smacked his lips appreciatively, then planted them on her neck.

"Arthur," Miss Flatface cried shrilly. "You just stay away from those two men. Don't ask me to explain. Just stay away from them. Promise me! You hear?"

"Okay, okay, okay." Arthur's spirits drooped, for he was not ac-customed to being berated by his wife. A mean thought, one of the few ever to cross his mind, came without ado to his lips. "I guess I understand. I know you got a pretty wild past—"

"Arthur!"

"Aw I'm sorry." Kiss. "Let's forget about it. Come on, let's watch some TV and get to bed, huh?"

Throughout the night Miss Flatface could not rid herself of the suspicion that Mr. Obscenity and Inspector Jug, at separate windows, were watching her and Arthur making love. She longed to get up and look. But she was unwilling to alarm Arthur. She doubted—since he was groggy with beer—that his potency could have survived such an interruption.

At dawn, with Arthur curled up on one side of the bed, Miss Flatface made her way outdoors. It was as she'd suspected. Her two pursuers were nonchalantly sitting on the curb, near the bus stop.

"I thought you two hated each other," she said irritably.

"We've made up," said Inspector Jug. "Joined forces."

"Pay no attention to him," said the familiar imperious voice of Mr. Obscenity, tinged with silver mockery. "You know your place, my dear. And it's not at the side of that—boy." He spat the word out with something less than contempt. "Was it for this childish purple, red, and green Arthur that I rescued you from Jim, taught you all you know? Good God, woman, do you realize how much older you are than he? Does *he* realize it?"

"We've never talked about it," said Miss Flatface tearfully. "He loves me."

"But does he *know* you?" persisted Mr. Obscenity. "Does he know you as I do?"

"Mr. Obscenity—sir," interjected the ever apologetic Inspector Jug.

"Quiet, you moron!"

"But shouldn't we tell her the dope I've got on him? I got this whole dossier."

"What dossier?" she cried.

"Well, Laura," began Inspector Jug in a confidential tone, "yer Arthur wasn't always a sailor. Before that he was a—"

"You shit!" screamed Mr. Obscenity, losing altogether for the first time in Miss Flatface's knowledge his splendid self-control. "Don't you see that's no way to get her back!"

"It doesn't matter," said Miss Flatface, growing firmer in the face of Mr. Obscenity's disarray. "You can't spoil Arthur for me. I need him. And I won't give him up."

"And when he's thirty? Do you realize what an old bag you'll be?"

"Doesn't matter," said Miss Flatface. "Let me be, both of you. I've done my duty, I had my pleasures. Now I want to be."

Suddenly Mr. Obscenity's knickers looked wrinkled and absurd in the bright sunshine. His monocle seemed grotesquely affected. And no one, but no one, wears a hat in Southern California, least of all on a sunny early morning. Miss Flatface began to laugh.

———

After only a few more months of second marriage, Miss Flatface, still in the flower of her womanhood, became mortally ill. It began as ptomaine poisoning, contracted just over the border, in Tijuana. As she had approached the aged vendor's cart, and even while she was chewing the tacos, a food she had never particularly liked, the spirits of Margaret Fuller and Errol Flynn screamed warnings in her ears. But she hadn't heard them. Ever responsive to the American spirit in its broader manifestations, she had never been particularly attuned to its more direct signals. Arthur, who never heard voices, had settled for a Pepsi.

Two weeks after she took to their Castro Convertible, sustained by the best medical care the seamen's union could provide, she became delirious. Eyeing the grieving man slumped nearby in a chair, she cried, "Jim, I didn't know that you were here!" Then, with just the slightest touch of insincerity: "It was grand of you to come!"

But it was not Jim. It was still Arthur, who faithfully nursed her through the endless hours of bedpans and cups of consommé and damp washcloths laid on her still far from prominent features. And although he was the one romance in her life, Miss Flatface barely acknowledged Arthur's care. In a lucid interval between deliriums she called for a lawyer and dictated her will. Even here, Arthur wasn't mentioned. Miss Flatface did not take the present at all into account. Her mind as she approached death was unexpectedly preempted by effusions of a patriotic nature and by thoughts of her former husband and children. In the end we all return to our beginnings.

Miss Flatface's Last Will and Testament.

"To America—I salute you, especially those parts of you which are not beautiful: your new banks; your candy bars; your parking lots. I have tried always to see the best in you and your people who while friendly and full of fun on the outside are often rather mean on the inside. But no matter. My life has been spent in the discovery of you—that is, of myself. I am what I am because I am a citizen of this country and a votary of its way of life. Therefore, let my body be cremated and my remains scattered among the cigarette ashes next to the potatoes which lie uneaten (because you are dieting) on your dinner plates.

"To the National Association of Mental Health, to Radio Free Europe (sending beams of hope behind the Iron Curtain), to the League of Women Voters, to the NAACP (for helping speed the integration of our two great races), to the National Convention of Christians and Jews, to the Girl Scouts of America, to the Bahá'í Temple in Chicago, to the University of Vermont (the college of my choice)—I haven't forgotten the TVA or the Book-of-the-Month Club, except that they don't need my help—to all the bodies which contribute to the way of life distinctly American, I would give generously, if I could I would leave ten thousand dollars to each;

"To my children, who must be grown by now and have certainly forgotten their wayward mother—Jim Jr., Mary, and little Willums, the baby—I leave a mother's blessing and my aquarium, which my own mother has faithfully kept for me (or so she promised) since I left home to marry your father, if the fish have not all died;

"To my former husband Jim, in the hopes that he has long since forgiven me, all my policies, fully paid up, with the Equitable Life Insurance Company;

"To Inspector Jug, my contempt, this not being intended to reflect on the honor of policemen and detectives generally;

"To Mr. Obscenity, the ingratitude he richly deserves.

"(Signed) Laura Flatface Johnson Anderson."

———

Anderson was Arthur's last name.

At the Easy Come Easy Go Funeral Home on Las Madrinas Boulevard a crowd of mourners gathered. Arthur, flustered by the unexpected turnout, sped off unnoticed by a side door, later returning with a large carton of sugar cones and four gallons of vanilla ice cream. He loaded the cones with ice cream, three at a time, and distributed them among the guests. A photographer was circulating about. Several mourners concealed their cones when they saw their picture being taken.

Among the mourners were to be seen a monocled figure, some-what downcast in mien, attended by a burly man in a squashed porkpie hat. "What a waste," the man with the monocle kept mutter-ing. "What a damned waste." When Arthur came around with a cone for the monocled man, he waved it aside haughtily, then stalked from the room. Snatching the now dripping cone from Arthur's hand, the man in the porkpie hat raced after him. "Rude bastards, aren't they?" whispered some of the mourners, relatives of Arthur's, who had never approved of his marriage but had has-tened to the funeral.

In the back of the funeral parlor, a sturdy man—graying at the temples—sat alone, weeping into a large yellow handkerchief.

Just as the cremation was about to start, the weeping man lurched to the guardrail and grabbed Arthur by the collar.

"I'm Jim Johnson, you know. Her first husband." Then he broke down utterly. "It's hers," he said, his words broken by sobs and muffled by the handkerchief that covered his face and to which he referred. "Did you ever know that she loved yellow?"

"No," said Arthur sadly. Perhaps Arthur would have been a little less sad if he had known that this fondness for yellow was an item about Miss Flatface that not even Mr. Obscenity, urbane and sensually observant as he was, had guessed.

With a manly gesture of tenderness, Arthur threw his arm around Jim. Together they knelt in silence as the body was con-sumed. Up in heaven, Miss Flatface watched approvingly. May she be pardoned if she gloated a little. It may be that none of us is ever wholly known. But who among us has been loved so well?

THE LETTER SCENE

Take a deep breath. Don't attempt anything just yet, you're not ready. When will you be ready? Never never never.

That means I must start now.

Don't start, don't even think of it, it's too difficult. No, it's too easy.

Let me start, it's already started, and I have to catch up.

Not like that, you oaf. Perched on the chair's edge, that's no way to start. Sit all the way back.

Don't cool me down, can't you see I'm already off and running? Taking a deep breath, floated by feeling . . . the proper implements at hand. Pen, pencil, typewriter, computer?

You know you'll wreck everything, don't you. These things take time. Ground has to be prepared. The others alerted to your coming.

My intrusion, you mean. My demands, entreaties.

You have a right, I admit that. Take a deep breath.

My right to breathe? Thanks. How about my right to have a hemorrhage? I won't be stopped, stanched, bandaged. Let me try. Just don't pay attention while I try.

———

Act I, Scene 2. Brow furrowed, palms moist, Tatyana sits down at the escritoire in her bedroom to write Eugene a letter. After the salutation, she stalls. How to proceed, when, after all, they have met only once, a few evenings ago, downstairs, and from her shy vantage point at the windowsill in the conservatory, though she followed him everywhere with her gaze, she could hardly lift her eyes from the gleaming buttons on his jacket? That rush of warmth: she wants to declare something. She gets up and asks her nurse to prepare some tea. Nanny brings fudge cakes, too. Tatyana frowns and sets to work again. She pictures him against a background of air, and he becomes slimmer, denser, more remote. It's a declaration of love she wants to declare. She begins to sing.

The wind is rattling the shutters, and Eugene's scratchy quill pen moves swiftly over the paper like a small fish waving its tiny fin. "Dearest Father, there are many things I have long waited to tell you but never dared to utter to your face. Perhaps I shall find the courage in this letter. In a letter, perhaps, I can be brave." By starting thus Eugene would delay as long as he can what he means to say. This will be, is trying to be, a letter of denunciation. It will be very long. He throws some wood on the fire.

———

The night before Dumane's execution by hanging: after the special meal, and to the accompaniment of the hymns and freedom songs his comrades in neighboring cells will sing throughout the night to comfort him. Dumane is sitting on the cement floor of his cell, nine by twelve, knees drawn close to his chest, paper on his knees, stump of pencil clenched between three lacerated fingers of his left hand—they have broken his right hand—slowly, laboriously printing out his last written words. "When you read this

I will be dead. You must be brave. I am calm. Mbangeli and I die confident that our sacrifice will not be in vain. Do not grieve too long for me. I want you to remarry. Comfort Granny. Kiss the children." There was more to it than that, eked out in tottering capitals, but these were the salient points. The letter ends, "P.S. My darling daughter, remember always that your father loves you and wants you to grow up to be just like your mother. Dearest son, please take care of your mother, who will need you, and do your best at school until you are ready to take your place in our just struggle."

———

Think of it, all those artless letters dashed off between bouts of tormentingly slow composition of the intricate, severe novels and essays that had made her quickly famous, and now a two-volume collection of her letters has come out, which, they say, may be the finest writing she ever did. It's not only her spirited sentences that enchant; everybody is moved by the portrait of the idyllic loving family from which she sprang. Is it possible such united families still exist? Even now? Nobody knows about the embittered letters to her sister that the widower burned in the barbecue. The world is tired of disillusionment, of unseemly revelations, the world is famished for models of probity. Our world. No one would ever know her as he did, would ever know how valiant she was during the last months of her terrible illness, when the brain tumor gnawed at her language, and he took to writing letters for her, from her, the letters she would have written if she still could. As the guardian of her reputation, now he can be inside the skin of her work in a way she had never let him be while she was alive. He will be exigent, as she was. Somebody, but this professor isn't distinguished enough, has embarked on a biography: he hasn't decided whether or not to cooperate. A newspaper correspondent in the Far East writes him a maudlin letter about "the irreparable loss to literature." He replies, a correspondence ensues. Could this be an old lover of hers? From Hong Kong arrives a packet of her letters, sixty-eight of them, done up in red string. These he reads with astonishment. Posthumous shock: this is *not* the woman he knew.

———

Act I, Scene 2. Tatyana gulps down the fresh glass of tea which Nanny brings. Slipping her left hand inside her blouse, she rubs her thumb against her downy shoulder. She has barely begun the letter. The rush of ecstasy in declaring something should be its own reward, but no, there is already the need for an answer. "You didn't look at me," Tatyana has written on the first page. And in the middle of the second page, "I am writing you now to ask if you ever think of me." Then she weeps, and (not in the poem or the opera—no, in real life) begins the letter again. In the opera there is a gush of feeling that floats her through to the end.

———

Here I am, with my irrevocable feelings, at least they feel irrevocable, and it is clear that all this could well *not* have happened. We did not have to meet.

We met because there had been a fire, nothing serious, in the six-story tenement where I have the great fortune to have found a rent-stabilized apartment. A drowsy pot-smoker on the fifth floor ignited his horsehair sofa. Smoke, black acrid smoke; nothing serious. I was shivering on the street, coatless, and you were feeding nickels into a vending machine for the *Times*. Seeing me staring at you, you inquired about the fire. Nothing serious. We went past the fire engines to have coffee across the street. That was last January, now I am perishing from seriousness. Why did you leave me? Don't you mind how coldly he treats you? What is this white paper outspread on my desk? I have sat down to write you a letter, do you think you could love me again, but perhaps I won't.

———

The letter that was never sent, ghost of.

The letter that never arrived, two more sorts of ghosts. The letter that is lost (in the mail). The letter that was not written, but she said she wrote one and that it must have gotten lost (in the mail). You can never trust the mail. You can never trust the mailer.

———

To write at all is to say . . . all. An act of ardor. That is why she hesitates, while she goes on writing letters in her head. But a letter in the head is a letter, too. It is told that Artur Schnabel used to practice in his head.

———

Act I, Scene 2. "I write to you," Tatyana has begun, begun again— she's found the cadence. "No more confession is needed, nothing's left to tell. I know it's now in your discretion with scorn to make my world a hell."

The taper on the escritoire is flickering. Or is the moon, the quivering moon, becoming brighter?

Go to sleep, my darling, murmurs the old nurse.

"Oh, Nanny. Oh oh oh . . ." But she will not seek consolation on her dear, kind Nanny's breast.

There, there, my darling . . .

"Nanny, I'm stifling, open the window." The musty old crone moves to obey. "Nanny, I'm chilled, bring me a coverlet." She pauses at the window, perplexed. "Oh oh oh . . ."

Let me sing to you, my darling.

"No, Nanny, it is I who must sing. In my girlish treble. Leave me, Nanny, my darling old Nanny, I must sing . . ."

———

This is a letter that breaks the bad news. I don't know how to begin. It didn't seem as bad when it first started. We were quite hopeful. The situation got worse only toward the end. I hope you will accept this as best you can. I hate to be the bearer of, etc.

———

Why people don't write letters any more. (Much to be said about this, without ever mentioning the telephone.) People just don't want to take the time, what proves to be a great deal of time, because they lack confidence. Pen poised over the sheet of blank paper, they hesitate. The initial moment of exuberance refuses to translate fluently, rapidly into a voice that meets the standards of . . . what standards? More hesitations. They make a draft.

And then letters seem so—well, one-sided. Or lacking in velocity. One is too impatient for the answer.

———

The bad news is worse now. This is real bad news, the kind that invites ceremoniousness. He wrote to console me in a florid formal diction that I found heartrending.

Unlike lovers, unlike best friends, children and parents cannot revel in or despair at the thought that they did not have to have met. And don't necessarily have to part, except when they do. Eugene is getting closer to what he wants to say. "You have been generous, Father, and clearly think of yourself as having the best intentions toward me. Do not think me ungrateful for the monthly stipend you have provided since I graduated from Cadet School. But as you have acted according to your own principles, I must henceforth act in accord with mine." A frigid letter—the tone he is seeking is a kind of opaque sincerity—that will turn into a passionate, violent one.

The Hong Kong Letters, as the widower dubbed them, disclosed a relationship lasting nearly a decade whose inventive lechery he would never have dreamed his wife capable of. Their sexual transports are graphically recalled, as is her facility at giving herself full pleasure when they are apart at any moment, even fully clothed, in public (chatting at a cocktail party, giving a reading), if she had something to press herself against discreetly, with the merest thought of the rough pleasure they gave each other. And "he"—always "he," strewn respectfully throughout the letters: "he" and his endearingly limited needs, his protective asexual presence, outside whose lull she feared she could not write. Christ! Was that what his uxorious ardor was, for her? The conjugal drone? He would show his fangs now—it is never too late for a crime of passion. He purchases a plane ticket for Hong Kong.

And the forty-three-year-old salaryman from Osaka on the crippled jumbo jet now circling wildly as it loses altitude, plunging toward the mountain, who is able to master the white-hot blast of animal terror and pull a sheet of paper from the pad inside his briefcase, he too, like Dumane, is writing a farewell letter to his wife and children. But he will have three minutes only. Other passengers are screaming or moaning; some have dropped to their knees to pray as the overhead bins rain parcels and luggage and pillows and coats on their heads. His legs braced against the seat in front of him to keep from being pitched into the aisle, with his left arm, cradling, clutching the briefcase on which he writes, rapidly but legibly, he enjoins his children to be obedient to their mother. To his wife he declares that he regrets nothing—"we've had a full life," he writes—and requests that she accept his death. He is signing as the plane turns upside down, he is stuffing the letter in his jacket pocket when he is hurled past his seatmate against the window, head first, and smashed into the mercy of unconsciousness. When his broken body is recovered on the cedared slopes among the more than five hundred others, the letter is found, delivered by a red-eyed J.A.L. official to his wife, published on the first page of the newspapers. As one, all of Japan dissolves in tears.

Her letters were so cozily aligned with loneliness. Separation became a value, the occasion and justification for writing letters.

This, from one of her letters to me:

"Soon after that I stayed a month on a lavender-scented island off the Dalmatian coast. I found a room to rent in a fisherman's house and fellow-tourists I liked, with whom I spent much of my time: scuba diving from a boat with a four-horsepower outboard engine we hired, picnicking on broiled silver mackerel and freshly baked flat loaves of bread called *lepinja* on the pine-shaded rocks of a peninsula, recounting the lives we led elsewhere during long evenings in the café at the port. It was I who left first, before they scattered to Houston, London, Munich; and as the steamer pulled away from the jetty I waved more energetically. 'Write!' I shouted. 'Write!'

"The first one I met again was the lawyer from Texas, whom I saw the following spring in Geneva; we had exchanged many letters. 'You shouted "write,"' he teased me, 'as though you thought we were abandoning you. But it was you who decided to leave us, to move on.' My pride was stung. I have not written him since."

Again to me (a fragment): ". . . not to be taken as lack of trust or withdrawal. Or as rejection. One lives so badly when one is afraid to live alone."

To another, not me, she permits herself the lyrical tremolo.

With his four dromedaries Don Pedro d'Alfaroubeira traversed the world and admired it. He did what I would like to do. If I had three dromedaries! Or two! I am writing this astride the steed at hand. I am seeing the world, the marvels therein. It is what I've always wanted to do, in my one and only life. But, meanwhile, I want to keep in touch. Do want to keep. In touch.

With you. And you.

———

"You will be glad to hear, Father," Eugene adds, "that I have paid off my gambling debts." He means to be sarcastic, but perhaps he is trying to placate the old man. What does he care, what does he care, is he still seeking his father's approval? This part, where the failed poet indicates how he has not misspent his life, should be treated *presto*, in the manner of a note challenging someone to a duel.

———

Actually, one other passenger is writing as the plane falls— a fourteen-year-old girl who, returning to Tokyo after being treated by her aunt in Osaka to a joyous weekend of Takarazuka perfor- mances and about to start the thank-you note to her aunt when the pilot makes his first hoarse announcement, lifts her pen, shudders, then plunges it down to the paper to write instead: I'm scared. I'm scared. Help. Help. Help.

The characters are illegible. Her letter is never found.

———

Here's a cache of old letters. Old leaves . . . I have been having a go at rereading them. They are from my ex-husband. We had been married for seven years, and since we were going to be married forever we had granted me a sabbatical, I'd won a fellowship to Oxford, we had separated for the academic year, and we wrote each other blue aerograms every day. One didn't use the trans- atlantic telephone in those days, so long ago. We were poor, he was stingy. I was drifting away, discovering life was actually possible without him. But I did write, each evening. During the day I'd be composing my letter to him in my head, I was always talking to him in my head. I was, you see, so *used* to him. I felt safe. I didn't feel like a separate person. Whatever I saw when I was apart from him for an hour made me think first of how I would describe it to him; and we never separated for more than a few hours, just the time he taught his classes and I took mine—we were insatiable. My bladder might be aching, but I didn't want to interrupt myself or him; talking, he would follow me into the bathroom. Returning at midnight from what academics in that staid era were pleased to call parties, more than once we sat in the car until dawn lightened the street, forgetting to go into our own apartment, so absorbed were we in our dissections of his exasperating colleagues. So many years of that, the delirious amity of nonstop talking—now more than three times those years ago! I wonder if he kept my letters. Or did he, the better to unite with his second wife, pitch them into the fireplace? For a year after the divorce I awoke most mornings with a foolish smile on my face, from the surprise, the relief, of no longer being married to him. I've never felt so safe with anyone since. It's not right to feel so safe. I don't, I can't reread his letters. But I need to think of them there, in the shoebox, in the bottom of my closet. They are part of my life, my dead life.

———

Act I, Scene 2. "Why did you visit us, but why? Lost in our backwoods habitation, I would not have known you. Therefore I would have been spared this laceration. In time—who knows?—the agitation of inexperience would have passed. I would have found a friend, another, and calmly grown into my part, of virtuous mother and faithful wife." Tatyana has her indisputable feeling. But how does a feeling in one breast ignite a feeling in another? What are the laws of combustion? She can speak only of her own feeling— indisputably hers, after migrating from the lachrymose epistolary novels about love she loves to read. Of uniqueness. "Another! Now there can be no thought of another. Never could another rule my heart. My feeling for you is decreed forever, by Heaven's will. For you I'm set apart. And my whole life, whether you will or not, is pledged to you."

Pledges, promises—doesn't the fervor with which we make them testify to the strength of the opposing force, that of forget-fulness? An indomitable power of forgetfulness is necessary to close the doors and windows of consciousness, to make room for something new. Tatyana leans back in her chair, quivering, perspiring, and passes a hand over her brow. Nothing in her fragrant childhood spent among the silver birches has prepared her for this dire contraction. She tries vainly to conjure up her dear sister, her plump, kindly parents. The whole world has shrunk to the image of Eugene's grim, restless face. Then away with the past, let it be dissolved by the pale moon, evaporate like the treble notes of a perfume. Without forgetfulness there could be no happiness, no cheerfulness, no hope, no pride, no *present*. Without forgetfulness there could be no despair, no anxiety, no abjection, no longing, no *future*.

———

Other pleas for love, other styles of diffidence.

The first time I saw you, you had a white scarf knotted at the throat, the sun lay in your hair, your blouse was striped, you were wearing linen pants and espadrilles. From the table on the café terrace overlooking the Piazza del Popolo, I saw you approaching. I didn't think you were beautiful. Talking gaily of having spent the night in jail for seizing the ticket for speeding the policeman had just written out and tearing it up, you sat down and ordered a lemon sherbet. I saw you and thought, If I cannot say I love you I am lost. But I didn't. Instead I am going to write a letter. The weakest move.

Now that I see how beautiful you are, your face gets in the way.

As on a lenticular screen, the eyes follow me. I do not want to tell you you are beautiful. I must think of something else. Custom and my unfair heart demand that I flatter you. To coax a feeling from you. I want to pronounce those blessed words: love, love, love.

I received a letter from a close friend. I did not open it for a week. It lay smoldering on my night table. The envelope bearing the name of a mere acquaintance I tore open eagerly as I came up the stairs, confident that the letter inside would contain nothing that could disturb me or hurt me.

I have to tell you that I write in a very tiny script, so tiny it could be thought impossible to decipher; except that it is not. This script might seem to express my unwillingness to be known, my retreat from human contact; except that I want you to know me, which is why I am writing you, my dear.

My love, this morning I received your wonderful letter (typed) and hasten to answer. Please write more.

More effort than you can imagine—that's what it means. In my lair, under a dirty-paned window that lets in the sour light, I sit at the kitchen table pondering what I might say to you. This causes me to brush the frame of my typewriter with the flat of my hand, twiddle my hair, finger my chin, pass a hand over my eyes, rub my nose, push the lock back from my forehead, as if my task lay in that, and not in the sheet of paper which lies folded into the type-writer. Perhaps I will fail in my effort to write you, and yet not to try means to fail in the same way.

A black-bordered envelope arrives from Germany, the printed an-nouncement of a dear acquaintance's death, which I had learned about by telephone a week earlier. I would find it easier to open my mail if all the major messages were color-coded. Black for death. (Christoph died at forty-nine of his second heart attack.) Red for love. Blue for longing. Yellow for rage. And an envelope with a border the color once known as ashes of roses—could that announce kindness? For I'm prone to forget this kind of letter exists, too: the expression of sheer kindness.

Hello, hello, how are you, how are you, I'm well, I'm well, how are, how is . . .

And you, my dear?

———

Act I, Scene 2. Sighing, trembling, Tatyana continues writing her letter, riddled with mistakes in French. (She's feverish, as I've suggested.) She hears herself, her words. And the nightingale's cadence. (Have I mentioned there was a nightingale in the garden?) Dawn is close to breaking, but she still needs the taper's flickering light. She sings her love. Or, rather, it is the opera singer singing Tatyana. Though Tatyana is very young, the role is often sung by a mature diva whose voice can no longer perform as it should. It should float. But when there is a tendency to labored phrasing, the vocal line rarely floats or springs; it seems held back or driven forward. Happily, this is a good performance. The line soars. Tatyana writes. And sings.

———

I cannot bear not getting a letter from you, and no longer go out. Can it be that I was once carefree and giddy? Now I drag a long shadow behind me that withers the greenery as I pass.

I stay indoors, waiting for your reply. My self-imposed house arrest is turning out to be a longer sentence than I ever envisaged. Sometimes I go back to bed in the late morning or early afternoon, after the mail has been delivered: the daytime sleep that inmates of prisons call fast time. Your letter *will* come.

———

I write your name. Two syllables. Two vowels. Your name inflates you, is bigger than you. You repose in a corner, sleeping; your name awakes you. I write it. You could not be named otherwise. Your name is your juice, your taste, your savor. Called by another name, you vanish. I write it. Your name.

———

"Dear Friend! Dear Friend! You are all that remains, my only hope, my one friend. Only you can save me. I want to come where you are, be near you, next to you. I won't bother you, I won't come visiting, I won't interrupt your work, I only need to know you are there, that beyond the wall of my room there is a living human presence. You. I need your warmth. They have crushed me! I am beaten! I am worn out! After the nightmare of this year I must come to you—under your wing! Could you find me a room? Anything will do, all I need is a table, and a view, that is, a window to look out from, where I see something, not a wall, but if it does look out onto a wall, then it doesn't matter, as long as I am close to you. You will save me, you will show me what I must do, how I must live. And could you lend me the money for a ticket? I need nothing, I will ask nothing from you. I will not bother you once I am there, you have my solemn promise. Who understands better than I your need for privacy? How I admire your independence, your strength! And your generous heart. With you as my guiding star, I will be as independent as you. I will cook my own meals if I have to, I'm used to taking care of myself, but if you could find someone in the village who can look after my few simple needs, that would make it easier for me to just stay in my room, looking out the window, serenely thinking of you, never daring to bother you. You are the only one I can turn to, but you are the only one I need. Do you remember our first meeting, and how the filaments of the copper lamps glowed above our heads? You understood then. You have always understood me. Please work a miracle. Arrange it! Hide me! Find me a room!"

And I found him a room, a room in the house next to mine, on a hill above the dunes. And I wrote him that from the windows he would see trees and open spaces, and children flying kites by the sea. And that we would fly them, too.

"It's the handwriting of a lunatic," said a friend to whom I showed the letter, with its oversized script, after his death. No, not of a lunatic but of a child: they were the same large letters a child makes, writing not with the hand alone but with the arm, from the shoulder. Dear Mommy, I LOVE YOU WITH ALL MY HEART. I WILL ALWAYS LOVE YOU.

I found him a room. And he never came.

———

In actual size above, fig. 1 (illustration to come), and enlarged below, fig. 2 (ditto), is an example of a writing used by Richard Anton in the 1920s, apparently as a means of protecting his manuscripts from unwelcome scrutiny. Prof. Joachim Greichen has established that most such texts are decipherable as scribbled drafts of prose texts which Anton completed and later published. Although by 1931 he had returned to his normal hand, shown opposite, fig. 3 (ditto), he was still wont to vary the size of his writing. For in-

stance, in his most personal correspondence he often wrote in very
large printed capitals.

I NEED, I WANT. I NEED, I WANT.

I love a tender climate. I loll by the swimming pool. My letters are
my diary. I deposit my life with another. With you. A summer
thunderstorm is on its way. Shall I describe the weather (or landscape), using weather (or landscape) to portray the vexations of
self? If I write, I feel safe. I am humming something. I am bristling with sexual trepidation.

Desire is rapid as the postal system is slow. These delays in the
mail make my letters obsolete at their creation, make whatever I
write wrong. For even as I write, taking up each of the points in
your last letter, there already exists a subsequent letter from you,
written in response to the last one received from me, saying something else. As I write, there is already a letter from you *which I
have not read.* The Letter God is sporting with us. Our letters
cross, but our limbs do not.

Mused the diva:

"I adore having visitors, I detest going to see people. I adore
receiving letters, even reading them. But I detest writing letters.
I adore giving advice but I detest being its recipient, and I never
follow at once any wise advice that is given me."

Sometimes the letters contain a photograph, which the diva is pleased to sign. Yours, she writes. My best wishes. Your friend. Warmly. Love. Yes, on photographs to perfect strangers, but they are fans—exactly, that's what I said, perfect strangers—she signs Love.

———

Letters are sometimes a way of keeping someone at a distance. But for this purpose one must write a great many letters—at least one, sometimes two, a day. If I write you, I don't have to see you. Touch you. Put my tongue on your skin.

———

At first he writes mainly about his astonishing and now legendary discovery, that of a "six-class" marriage system on nearby Mortimer Island. He is happy. She can feel that. And she is happy for him, and tells him that. And he feels it, feels her wanting him to be happy, to give himself over entirely to his work, to be indivisible from his work, not to think of her, worry about her. And he seems to fall deeper in love through writing; he longs to be with his correspondent, though not back in England (but neither could she come out and join him); then the writing stops. Trevor's last letter arrived more than a month after Elizabeth had heard by telegram that he was dead, carried off at the age of twenty-four by blackwater fever. She recounts the moment sparely, with almost no comment, leaving us—as she was left for a half century—with the wound, the silence and the possibility, open. Would they have lived happily ever after?

———

I couldn't tell him I wanted a divorce, not by letter. My letters had to be loving. I had to wait till I returned. He met me at the airport, breaking out of the waiting area onto the tarmac as I stepped off the plane. We embraced, collected my suitcase, reached the parking lot. Once in our car, before he put his key in the ignition, I told him. We sat in the car, talking; we wept.

Of course, it should be easier to say no—or never, or no longer—in a letter. Easier, far, than face to misery-darkened face. And to say yes? Yes.

Act I, Scene 2. Tatyana rereads the three pages she has written, and signed. Words are crossed out, tears stain the paper—but no matter, this is not a school exercise. It will stand as written, sealed.

Sunrise. She pulls the bell rope to summon her befuddled Nanny, who supposes her high-strung darling has simply risen earlier than usual, and instructs the old woman to give the letter to her grandson, who must carry it quickly, quickly to their new neighbor. Who? Who? Tatyana points mutely to the beloved name on the envelope.

And Eugene? Tatyana's Eugene. The pale, slim scowler in the expensive foreign boots, who had barely talked to anyone the other night when he had come, everyone hoped, to visit. The lover always sees the beloved as solitary. But Eugene (Eugene's Eugene) is, actually, as solitary and miserable as Tatyana imagines him.

So is this Eugene (my Eugene), who has finished a haughty letter of six pages breaking off all relations with his father. He will allow no claims on his heart; from now on he will be dead, he vows, to all claims of affection.

But then he learns that his father has died (did he, before dying, receive Eugene's letter?) and—here my story rejoins theirs—returns to Petersburg for the funeral and to settle the estate, is about to go abroad, hears that his father's elder brother is dying (how mortal are these fierce old men!), arrives dutifully at his uncle's high-ceilinged manor in the remote countryside to find his uncle in the yard, already laid out in a coffin, and decides to stay for as long as it pleases him (could rustic life revive his poetic gift?), stays much alone, but after a month of seclusion most disapproved of by the neighboring gentry allows himself reluctantly to be brought to a gathering in the house of a local family with two daughters, a simple family night, really, with a few neighbors. And he does notice the pretty gravity of the figure in the window seat, and thinks, If I could fall in love, it might be with a girl like that. He finds her air of melancholy . . . well-bred.

And when he receives Tatyana's letter, he is moved, but more from pity at her artless innocence, for love has been banished from his imagination. He rereads her letter, sighs; he does not wish to hurt her. At the end of the day, the longest day of Tatyana's life, he will ride over to her house—he will find her in the garden—to explain with as much gallantry as he can muster that he is not meant for marriage and might feel for her no more than the sentiments of a brother. No letter for Tatyana. She does not obsess him. He will do it face to face.

———

In the same way that you find the courage to write me, I find the courage to read your letter. Do not imagine that I mull over every line, but I think I've understood why it is hard for you to write me. (See, you *have* allowed me to know you.) It's because with each letter it is as if you were writing me for the first time.

Eugene does not know that, after their conversation in the garden, Tatyana falls ill, that she almost dies. Of shame, of grief. But he does hear two years later, from an old classmate at the Cadet School, that she has married, married well—indeed, her husband, a general and a decent man, is a friend of Eugene's family—and now lives in Petersburg.

Has he forgotten when, some two years after that, he is invited to a reception at the Gremin mansion in Petersburg? Presented by General Gremin to his young wife, at first Eugene doesn't recognize in the stately, tiaraed, even more beautiful woman the vulnerable, dark-browed girl he dismissed in her parents' garden. Her eyes see but they don't look. They don't ask anything.

Torchères, chandeliers.

He finds himself returning often to the Gremin mansion, contriving to meet her at the opera, at other parties, but he and Tatyana never exchange anything more than calm civilities. Sometimes he manages to be the one who sets her fur cape on her shoulders. She nods gravely—meaning what? Sometimes she seems to be hiding her dear face in her muff. Bewildered, he slowly acknowledges that he loves her, loves her beyond saying. That it is a love decreed by Heaven. He knows this because he wants to write her. Could this be the solution to the riddle of his arid heart? Now he's ridiculous—no matter. One night he stays up until dawn writing a four-page epistolary howl of love. He writes another letter the next day. A third.

And he waits and waits. For a reply.

What did he do with the letter she sent him four years earlier? He did not even accord it the dignity of burning; it was simply tossed away. If only he could have it now, secreted in his wallet, to fold and unfold, to wet with his tears.

Please write me, just one letter, he asks humbly, at their last meeting. He has discovered her weeping: Tatyana has no more secrets. Irrevocably married, she has never ceased to love him. He kneels at her feet.

There will be no letter.

She forgets nothing.

There is no future.

———

Now I take a deeper breath. Readying myself, ready, faltering. My longing is pithed. It lies at hand, in words.

Turn up the halogen lamp. There's not enough light in this room.

Love, please go on writing. Your letters will always reach me. You can write me in your real, your littlest script. I will hold it to the light. I will magnify it with my love.

THE DUMMY

Since my situation is intolerable, I have decided to take steps to resolve it. So I have constructed a lifelike dummy made of various brands of Japanese plastic simulating flesh, hair, nails, and so forth. An electronics engineer of my acquaintance, for a sizable fee, built the interior mechanism of the dummy: it will be able to talk, eat, work, walk, and copulate. I hired an important artist of the old realistic school to paint the features; it took twelve sittings to make a face that perfectly resembles mine. My broad nose is there, my brown hair, the lines on each side of my mouth. Even I could not tell the dummy and myself apart, were it not that from my peculiar vantage point it is quite obvious that he is he and that I am I.

What remains is to install the dummy in the center of my life. He will go to work instead of me, and receive the approval and censure of my boss. He will bow and scrape and be diligent. All I require of him is that he bring me the check every other Wednesday; I will give him carfare and money for his lunches, but no more. I'll make out the checks for the rent and the utilities, and pocket the rest myself. The dummy will also be the one who is married to my wife. He will make love to her on Tuesday and Saturday night, watch television with her every evening, eat her wholesome dinners, quarrel with her about how to bring up the children. (My wife, who also works, pays the grocery bills out of her salary.) I will also assign the dummy Monday night bowling with the team from the office, the visit to my mother on Friday night, reading the newspaper each morning, and perhaps buying my clothes (two sets—one for him, one for me). Other tasks I will assign as they come up, as I wish to divest myself of them. I want to keep for myself only what gives me pleasure.

An ambitious enterprise, you say? But why not? The problems of this world are only truly solved in two ways: by extinction or by duplication. Former ages had only the first choice. But I see no reason not to take advantage of the marvels of modern technology for personal liberation. I have a choice. And, not being the suicidal type, I have decided to duplicate myself.

On a fine Monday morning I wind the dummy up and set him loose, after making sure he knows what to do—that is, he knows just how I would behave in any familiar situation. The alarm goes off. He rolls over and pokes my wife, who wearily gets out of the double bed and turns off the alarm. She puts on her slippers and robe, then limps, stiff-ankled, into the bathroom. When she comes out and heads for the kitchen, he gets up and takes her place in the bathroom. He urinates, gargles, shaves, comes back into the bedroom and takes his clothes out of the dresser and closet, returns to the bathroom, dresses, then joins my wife in the kitchen. My children are already at the table. The younger girl didn't finish her homework last night, and my wife is writing a note of excuse to the teacher. The older girl sits haughtily munching the cold toast. "Morning, Daddy," they say to the dummy. The dummy pecks them on the cheek in return. Breakfast passes without incident, I observe with relief. The children leave. They haven't noticed a thing. I begin to feel sure my plan is going to work and realize, by my excitement, that I had greatly feared it would not—that there would be some mechanical failure, that the dummy would not rec-ognize his cues. But no, everything is going right, even the way he folds *The New York Times* is correct; he reproduces exactly the amount of time I spent on the foreign news, and it takes him just as long to read the sports pages as it took me.

The dummy kisses my wife, he steps out the door, he enters the elevator. (Do machines recognize each other, I wonder.) Into the lobby, out the door, on the street walking at a moderate pace—the dummy has left on time, he doesn't have to worry—into the subway he goes. Steady, calm, clean (I cleaned him myself Sunday night), un-troubled, he goes about his appointed tasks. He will be happy as long as I am satisfied with him. And so I will be, whatever he does, as long as others are satisfied with him.

Nobody notices anything different in the office, either. The sec-retary says hello, he smiles back as I always do; then he walks to my cubicle, hangs up his coat, and sits at my desk. The secretary brings him my mail. After reading it, he calls for some dictation. Next, there is a pile of my unfinished business from last Friday to attend to. Phone calls are made, an appointment is set up for lunch with a client from out of town. There is only one irregularity that I notice: the dummy smokes seven cigarettes during the morning; I usually smoke between ten and fifteen. But I set this down to the fact that he is new at his work and has not had time to accumulate the tensions that I feel after working six years in this office. It occurs to me that he will probably not have two martinis—as I always do—during the lunch, but only one, and I am right. But these are mere details, and will be to the dummy's credit if anyone notices them, which I doubt. His behavior with the out-of-town client is correct—perhaps a shade too deferential, but this, too, I put down to inexperience. Thank God, no simple matter trips him up. His table manners are as they should be. He doesn't pick at his food, but eats with appetite. And he knows he should sign the check rather than pay with a credit card; the firm has an account at this restaurant.

In the afternoon there is a sales conference. The vice president explains a new promotional campaign for the Midwest. The dummy makes suggestions. The boss nods. The dummy taps his pencil on the long mahogany table and looks thoughtful. I notice he is chain-smoking. Could he be feeling the pressure so soon? What a hard life I led! After less than a day of it, even a dummy shows some wear and tear. The rest of the afternoon passes without incident. The dummy makes his way home to my wife and children, eats my dinner appreciatively, plays Monopoly with the children for an hour, watches a Western on TV with my wife, bathes, makes himself a ham sandwich, and then retires. I don't know what dreams he has, but I hope they are restful and pleasant. If my approval can give him an untroubled sleep, he has it. I am entirely pleased with my creation.

The dummy has been on the job for several months. What can I report? A greater degree of proficiency? But that's impossible. He was fine the first day. He couldn't be any more like me than he was at the very beginning. He does not have to get better at his job but only stick at it contentedly, unrebelliously, without mechanical failure. My wife is happy with him—at least, no more unhappy than she was with me. My children call him Daddy and ask him for their allowance. My fellow workers and my boss continue to entrust him with my job.

Lately, though—just the past week, really—I have noticed something that worries me. It is the attention that the dummy pays to the new secretary, Miss Love. (I hope it isn't her name that arouses him somewhere in the depths of that complex machinery; I imagine that machines can be literal-minded.) A slight lingering at her desk when he comes in in the morning, a second's pause, no

more, when she says hello; whereas I—and he until recently—
used to walk by that desk without breaking stride. And he does
seem to be dictating more letters. Could it be from increased zeal
on behalf of the firm? I remember how, the very first day, he spoke
up at the sales conference. Or could it be the desire to detain Miss
Love? Are those letters necessary? I could swear he thinks so. But
then you never know what goes on behind that imperturbable
dummy's face of his. I'm afraid to ask him. Is it because I don't
want to know the worst? Or because I'm afraid he'll be angry at my
violation of his privacy? In any case, I have decided to wait until he
tells me.

Then one day it comes—the news I had dreaded. At eight in
the morning the dummy corners me in the shower, where I have
been spying on him while he shaves, marveling how he remembers
to cut himself every once in a while, as I do. He unburdens himself to me. I am astonished at how much he is moved—astonished
and a little envious. I never dreamed a dummy could have so much
feeling, that I would see a dummy weep. I try to quiet him. I ad-
monish him, then I reprimand him. It's no use. His tears become
sobs. He, or rather his passion, whose mechanism I cannot fathom,
begins to revolt me. I'm also terrified my wife and children will
hear him, rush to the bathroom, and there find this berserk creature who would be incapable of normal responses. (Might they
find both of us here in the bathroom? That, too, is possible.) I run
the shower, open both the sink faucets, and flush the toilet to
drown out the painful noises he is making. All this for love! All
this for the love of Miss Love! He has barely spoken to her, except
in the way of business. Certainly, he hasn't slept with her, of that
I am sure. And yet he is madly, desperately in love. He wants to
leave my wife. I explain to him how impossible that is. First of all,
he has duties and responsibilities. He is the husband and father to
my wife and children. They depend on him; their lives would be

smashed by his selfish act. And second, what does he know about Miss Love? She's at least ten years younger than he is, has given no particular sign of noticing him at all, and probably has a nice boyfriend her own age whom she's planning to marry.

The dummy refuses to listen. He is inconsolable. He will have Miss Love or—here he makes a threatening gesture—he will destroy himself. He will bang his head against the wall, or jump out of a window, disassembling irrevocably his delicate machinery. I become really alarmed. I see my marvelous scheme, which has left me so beautifully at my leisure and in peace the last months, ruined. I see myself back at the job, making love again to my wife, fighting for space in the subway during the rush hour, watching television, spanking the children. If my life was intolerable to me before, you can imagine how unthinkable it has become. Why, if only you knew how I have spent these last months, while the dummy was administering my life. Without a care in the world, except for occasional curiosity as to the fate of my dummy. I have slid to the bottom of the world. I sleep anywhere now: in flophouses, on the subway (which I only board very late at night), in alleys and doorways. I don't bother to collect my paycheck from the dummy any more, because there is nothing I want to buy. Only rarely do I shave. My clothes are torn and stained.

Does this sound very dreary to you? It is not, it is not. Of course, when the dummy first relieved me of my own life, I had grandiose plans for living the lives of others. I wanted to be an Arctic explorer, a concert pianist, a great courtesan, a world statesman. I tried being Alexander the Great, then Mozart, then Bismarck, then Greta Garbo, then Elvis Presley—in my imagination, of course. I imagined that, being none of these people for long, I could have only their pleasure, none of their pain; for I could escape, transform myself, whenever I wanted. But the experiment failed, for lack of interest, from exhaustion, call it what you will. I discovered that I am tired of being a person. Not just tired of being the person I was, but any person at all. I like watching people, but I don't like talking to them, dealing with them, pleasing them, or offending them. I don't even like talking to the dummy. I am tired. I would like to be a mountain, a tree, a stone. If I am to continue as a person, the life of the solitary derelict is the only one tolerable. So you will see that it is quite out of the question that I should allow the dummy to destroy himself, and have to take his place and live my old life again.

I continue my efforts of persuasion. I get him to dry his tears and go out and face the family breakfast, promising him that we will continue our conversation in the office, after he dictates his morning batch of letters to Miss Love. He agrees to try, and makes his red-eyed, somewhat belated appearance at the table. "A cold, dear?" says my wife. The dummy blushes and mumbles something. I pray that he will hurry up. I am afraid he will break down again. I notice with alarm that he can hardly eat, and leaves his coffee cup two-thirds full.

The dummy makes his way sadly out of the apartment, leaving my wife perplexed and apprehensive. I see him hail a cab instead of heading for the subway. In the office, I eavesdrop as he dictates his letters, sighing between every sentence. Miss Love notices, too. "Why, what's the matter?" she asks cheerfully. There is a long pause. I peep out of the closet, and what do I see! The dummy and Miss Love in a hot embrace. He is stroking her breasts, her eyes are closed, with their mouths they wound each other. The dummy catches sight of me staring from behind the closet door. I signal wildly, trying to make him understand that we must talk, that I'm on his side, that I'll help him. "Tonight?" whispers the dummy, slowly releasing the ecstatic Miss Love. "I adore you," she whispers. "I adore you," says the dummy in a voice above a whisper, "and I must see you." "Tonight," she whispers back. "My place. Here's the address."

One more kiss and Miss Love goes out. I emerge from the closet and lock the door of the little office. "Well," says the dummy. "It's Love or death." "All right," I say sadly. "I won't try to talk you out of it any more. She seems like a nice girl. And quite attractive. Who knows, if she had been working here when I was here . . ." I see the dummy frowning angrily, and don't finish the sentence. "But you'll have to give me a little time," I say. "What are you going to do? As far as I can see, there's nothing you can do," says the dummy. "If you think I'm going home to your wife and kids any more, after I've found Love—" I plead with him for time.

What do I have in mind? Simply this. The dummy is now in my original position. His present arrangements for life are intolerable to him. But having more appetite for a real, individual life than I ever had, he doesn't want to vanish from the world. He just wants to replace my admittedly second-hand wife and two noisy daughters with the delightful, childless Miss Love. Well then, why shouldn't my solution—duplication—work for him as it did for me? Anything is better than suicide. The time I need is time to make another dummy, one to stay with my wife and children and go to my job while this dummy (the true dummy, I must now call him) elopes with Miss Love.

Later that morning, I borrow some money from him to go to a Turkish bath and get cleaned up, to get a haircut and shave at the barber's, and to buy myself a suit like the one he is wearing. On his suggestion, we meet for lunch at a small restaurant in Greenwich Village, where it is impossible that he meet anyone who might recognize him. I'm not sure what he is afraid of. Of having lunch alone, and being seen talking to himself? Of being seen with me? But I am perfectly presentable now. And if we are seen as two, what could be more normal than a pair of identical adult male twins, dressed alike, having lunch together and engaged in earnest conversation? We both order spaghetti *al burro* and baked clams. After three drinks, he comes around to my point of view. In consideration of my wife's feelings, he says—not mine, he insists several times in a rather harsh tone of voice—he will wait. But only a few months, no more. I point out that in this interim I will not ask that he not sleep with Miss Love but only that he be discreet in his adultery.

Making the second dummy is harder than making the first. My entire savings are wiped out. The prices of humanoid plastic and the other material, the fees of the engineer and the artist, have all gone up within just a year's time. The dummy's salary, I might add, hasn't gone up at all, despite the boss's increased appreciation of his value to the firm. The dummy is annoyed that I insist that he, rather than I, sit for the artist when the facial features are being molded and painted. But I point out to him that if the second dummy is modeled on me again, there is a chance that it would be a blurred or faded copy. Undoubtedly, some disparities have developed between the appearance of the first dummy and my own, even though I cannot detect them. I want the second dummy to be like him, wherever there is the slightest difference between him and me. I shall have to take the risk that in the second dummy might also be reproduced the unforeseen human passion that robbed the first dummy of his value to me.

Finally, the second dummy is ready. The first dummy, at my insistence (and reluctantly, since he wanted to spend his spare time with Miss Love), takes charge of his training and indoctrination period, lasting several weeks. Then the great day arrives. The second dummy is installed in the first dummy's life in the midst of a Saturday afternoon baseball game, during the seventh-inning stretch. It has been arranged that the first dummy will go out to buy hot dogs and Cokes for my wife and children. It is the first dummy who goes out, the second who returns laden with the food and drinks. The first dummy then leaps into a cab, off to the waiting arms of Miss Love.

That was nine years ago. The second dummy is living with my wife in no more exalted or depressed a fashion than I had managed. The older girl is in college, the second in high school; and there is a new child, a boy, now six years old. They have moved to a co-op apartment in Forest Hills; my wife has quit her job; and the second dummy is assistant vice president of the firm. The first dummy went back to college nights while working as a waiter during the day; Miss Love also went back to college and got her teacher's license. He is now an architect with a growing practice; she teaches English at Julia Richman High School. They have two children, a boy and a girl, and are remarkably happy. From time to time, I visit both my dummies—never without sprucing myself up first, you understand. I consider myself a relative and the godfather, sometimes the uncle, of all their children. They are not very happy to see me, perhaps because of my shabby appearance, but they haven't the courage to turn me out. I never stay long, but I wish them well, and congratulate myself for having solved in so equitable and responsible a manner the problems of this one poor short life that was allotted me.

UNGUIDED TOUR

took a trip to see the beautiful things. Change of scenery. Change of heart. And do you know?

What?

They're still there.

Ah, but they won't be there for long.

I know. That's why I went. To say goodbye. Whenever I travel, it's always to say goodbye.

Tile roofs, timbered balconies, fish in the bay, the copper clock, shawls drying on the rocks, the delicate odor of olives, sunsets behind the bridge, ochre stone. "Gardens, parks, forests, woods, canals, private lakes, with huts, villas, gates, garden seats, gazebos, alcoves, grottoes, hermitages, triumphal arches, chapels, temples, mosques, banqueting houses, rotundas, observatories, aviaries, greenhouses, icehouses, fountains, bridges, boats, cascades, baths." The Roman amphitheater, the Etruscan sarcophagus. The monument to the 1914–18 war dead in every village square. You don't see the military base. It's out of town, and not on the main road.

Omens. The cloister wall has sprung a long diagonal crack. The water level is rising. The marble saint's nose is no longer aquiline.

This spot. Some piety always brings me back to this spot. I think of all the people who were here. Their names scratched into the bottom of the fresco.

Vandals!

Yes. Their way of being here.

The proudest of human-made things dragged down to the condition of natural things. Last Judgment.

You can't lock up all the things in museums.

Aren't there any beautiful things in your own country?

No. Yes. Fewer.

Did you have guidebooks, maps, timetables, stout shoes?

I read the guidebooks when I got home. I wanted to stay with my—

Immediate impressions?

You could call them that.

But you did see the famous places. You didn't perversely neglect them.

I did see them. As conscientiously as I could while protecting my ignorance. I don't want to know more than I know, don't want to get more attached to them than I already am.

How did you know where to go?

By playing my memory like a roulette wheel.

Do you remember what you saw?

Not much.

It's too sad. I can't love the past that's trapped within my memory like a souvenir.

Object lessons. Grecian urns. A pepper-mill Eiffel Tower. Bismarck beer mug. Bay-of-Naples-with-Vesuvius scarf. David-by-Michelangelo cork tray.

No souvenirs, thanks. Let's stay with the real thing.

The past. Well, there's always something ineffable about the past, don't you think?

In all its original glory. The indispensable heritage of a woman of culture.

I agree. Like you, I don't consider devotion to the past a form of snobbery. Just one of the more disastrous forms of unrequited love.

I was being wry. I'm a fickle lover. It's not love that the past needs in order to survive, it's an absence of choices.

And armies of the well-off, immobilized by vanity, greed, fear of scandal, and the inefficiency and discomfort of travel. Women carrying parasols and pearl handbags, with mincing steps, long skirts, shy eyes. Mustached men in top hats, lustrous hair parted on the left side, garters holding up their silk socks. Seconded by footmen, cobblers, ragpickers, blacksmiths, buskers, printer's devils, chimney sweeps, lacemakers, midwives, carters, milkmaids, stonemasons, coachmen, turnkeys, and sacristans. As recently as that. All gone. The people. And their pomp and circumstance.

Is that what you think I went to see?

Not the people. But their places, their beautiful things. You said they were still there. The hut, the hermitage, the grotto, the park, the castle. An aviary in the Chinese style. His Lordship's estate. A delightful seclusion in the midst of his impenetrable woods.

I wasn't happy there.

What did you feel?

Regret that the trees were being cut down.

So you have a hazy vision of natural things. From too much indulgence in the nervous, metallic pleasures of cities.

Unequal to my passions, I fled the lakes, I fled the woods, I fled the fields pulsing with glowworms, I fled the aromatic mountains.

Provincial blahs. Something less solitary is what you need.

I used to say: Landscapes interest me only in relation to human beings. Ah, loving someone would give life to all this . . . But the emotions that human beings inspire in us also sadly resemble each other. The more that places, customs, the circumstances of adventures are changed, the more we see that we amidst them are unchanging. I know all the reactions I shall have. Know all the words that I am going to utter again.

You should have taken me along instead.

You mean him. Yes, of course I wasn't alone. But we quarreled most of the time. He plodding, I odious.

They say. They say a trip is a good time for repairing a damaged love.

Or else it's the worst. Feelings like shrapnel half worked out of the wound. Opinions. And competition of opinions. Desperate amatory exercises back at the hotel on golden summer afternoons. Room service.

How did you let it get that dreary? You were so hopeful.

Rubbish! Prisons and hospitals are swollen with hope. But not charter flights and luxury hotels.

But you were moved. Sometimes.

Maybe it was exhaustion. Sure I was. I am. The inside of my feelings is damp with tears.

And the outside?

Very dry. Well—as dry as is necessary. You can't imagine how tiring it is. That double-membraned organ of nostalgia, pumping the tears in. Pumping them out.

Qualities of depth and stamina.

And discrimination. When one can summon them.

I'm bushed. They aren't all beautiful, the beautiful things. I've never seen so many squabby Cupids and clumsy Graces.

Here's a café. *In the café.* The village priest playing the pinball machine. Nineteen-year-old sailors with red pompons watching. Old gent with amber worry beads. Proprietor's granddaughter doing her homework at a deal table. Two hunters buying picture postcards of stags. He says: You can drink the acidic local wine, become a little less odious, unwind.

Monsieur René says it closes at five.

Each picture. "Each picture had beneath it a motto of some good intention. Seeing that I was looking carefully at these noble images, he said: 'Here everything is natural.' The figures were clothed like living men and women, though they were far more beautiful. Much light, much darkness, men and women who are and yet are not."

Worth a detour? Worth a trip! It's a remarkable collection. Still possessed its aura. The things positively importuned.

The baron's zeal in explaining. His courteous manner. He stayed all through the bombardment.

A necessary homogeneity. Or else some stark, specific event.

I want to go back to that antique store.

"The ogival arch of the doorway is Gothic, but the central nave and the flanking wings——"

You're hard to please.

Can't you imagine traveling not to accumulate pleasures but to make them rarer?

Satiety is not my problem. Nor is piety.

There's nothing left but to wait for our meals, like animals.

Are you catching a cold? Drink this.

I'm perfectly all right. I beg you, don't buy the catalogue. Or the postcard-size reproductions. Or the sailor sweater.

Don't be angry, but—did you tip Monsieur René?

Say to yourself fifty times a day: I am not a connoisseur, I am not a romantic wanderer, I am not a pilgrim.

You say it.

"A permanent part of mankind's spiritual goods."

Translate that for me. I forgot my phrase book.

Still, you saw what you came to see.

The old victory of arrangement over accumulation.

But sometimes you were happy. Not just in spite of things.

Barefoot on the mosaic floor of the baptistery. Clambering above the flying buttresses. Irradiated by a Baroque monstrance shimmering indistinctly in the growing dusk of the cathedral. Effulgence of things. Voluminous. Resplendent. Unutterable bliss.

You send postcards on which you write "Bliss." Remember? You sent one to me.

I remember. Don't stop me. I'm flying. I'm prowling. Epiphany. Hot tears. Delirium. Don't stop me. I stroke my delirium like the balls of the comely waiter.

You want to make me jealous.

Don't stop me. His dainty skin, his saucy laughter, his way of whistling, the succulent dampness of his shirt. We went into a shed behind the restaurant. And I said: Enter, sir, this body. This body is your castle, your cabin, your hunting lodge, your villa, your carriage, your luxury liner, your drawing room, your kitchen, your speedboat, your tool shed . . .

Do you often do that sort of thing when he's around?

Him? He was napping at the hotel. A mild attack of heliophobia.

In the hotel. Back at the hotel, I woke him up. He had an erection. I seated myself on his loins. The nub, the hub, the fulcrum. Gravitational lines of force. In a world of perfect daylight. Indeed, a high-noon world, in which objects cast no shadows.

Only the half wise will despise these sensations.

I'm turning. I'm a huge steering wheel, unguided by any human hand. I'm turning . . .

And the other pleasures? The ones you came for.

"In the entire visible world there is hardly a more powerful mood-impression than that experienced within one of the Gothic cathedrals just as the sun is setting."

Pleasures of the eye. It had to be emphasized.

"The eye can see nothing beyond those glimmering figures that hover overhead to the west in stern, solemn rows as the burning evening sun falls across them."

Messengers of temporal and spiritual infinity.

"The sensation of fire permeates all, and the colors sing out, rejoicing and sobbing."

There, in truth, is a different world.

I found a wonderful old Baedeker, with lots of things that aren't in the Michelin. *Let's.* Let's visit the caves. Unless they're closed.

Let's visit the World War I cemetery.

Let's watch the regatta.

This spot. He committed suicide right here, by the lake. With his fiancée. In 1811.

I seduced a waiter in the restaurant by the port two days ago. *He said.* He said his name was Arrigo.

I love you. And my heart is pounding.

So is mine.

What's important is that we're strolling in this arcade together.

That we're strolling. That we're looking. That it's beautiful.

Object lessons. Give me that suitcase, it's heavy.

One must be careful not to wonder if these pleasures are superior to last year's pleasures. They never are.

That must be the seduction of the past again. But just wait until now becomes then. You'll see how happy we were.

I'm not expecting to be happy. *Complaints.* I've already seen it. I'm sure it'll be full. It's too far. You're driving too fast, I can't see anything. Only two showings of the movie, at seven and at nine. There's a strike, I can't telephone. This damned siesta, nothing's

open between one and four. If everything came out of this suitcase, I don't understand why I can't cram it all back in.

You'll soon stop fretting over these mingy impediments. You'll
realize you're carefree, without obligations. And then the unease
will start.

Like those upper-middle-class Protestant folk who experience
revelations, become hysterical, suffer breakdowns under the dis-
orienting impact of Mediterranean light and Mediterranean
manners. You're still thinking about the waiter.

I said I love you, I trust you, I didn't mind.

You shouldn't. I don't want that kind of revelation. I don't want
to satisfy my desire, I want to exasperate it. I want to resist the
temptation of melancholy, my dear. If you only knew how much.

Then you must stop this flirtation with the past invented by
poets and curators. We can forget about their old things. We can
buy their postcards, eat their food, admire their sexual noncha-
lance. We can march in their workers' festivals and sing the "In-
ternationale," for even we know the words.

I'm feeling perfectly all right.

I think it's safe to. Pick up hitchhikers, drink unbottled water,
try to score some hash in the piazza, eat the mussels, leave the
camera in the car, hang out in waterfront bars, trust the hotel con-
cierge to make the reservation, don't you?

Something. Don't you want to do something?

Does every country have a tragic history except ours?

This spot. See? There's a commemorative plaque. Between the
windows.

Ruined. Ruined by too many decades of intrepid appreciation.
Nature, the whore, cooperates. The crags of the Dolomites made
too pink by the sun, the water of the lagoon made too silver by the
moon, the blue skies of Greece (or Sicily) made too deep a blue by
the arch in a white wall.

Ruins. These are ruins left from the last war.

Antiquarian effrontery: our pretty dwelling.

It was a convent, built according to a plan drawn up by Michelangelo. Turned into a hotel in 1927. Don't expect the natives to take care of the beautiful things.

I don't.

They say. They say they're going to fill in the canal and make it a highway, sell the duchess's rococo chapel to a sheik in Kuwait, build a condominium on that bluff with a stand of pine, open a boutique in the fishing village, put a sound-and-light show in the ghetto. It's going fast. International Committee. Attempting to preserve. Under the patronage of His Excellency and the Honorable. Going fast. You'll have to run.

Will I have to run?

Then let them go. Life is not a race.

Or else it is.

Any more. Isn't it a pity they don't write out the menus in purple ink any more. That you can't put your shoes outside the hotel room at night. *Remember.* Those outsize bills, the kind they had until the devaluation. *Last time.* There weren't as many cars last time, were there?

How could you stand it?

It was easier than it sounds. With an imagination like a pillar of fire. And a heart like a pillar of salt.

And you want to break the tie.

Right.

Lot's wife!

But his lover.

I told you. I told you, you should have taken me along instead.

Lingering. In the basilica. In the garden behind the inn. In the spice market. In bed, in the middle of the golden afternoon.

Because. It's because of the fumes from the petrochemical factories nearby. It's because they don't have enough guards for the museums.

"Two groups of statuary, one depicting virtuous toil, the other unbridled licentiousness."

Do you realize how much prices have gone up? Appalling inflation. I can't conceive how people here manage. With rents almost as high as back home and salaries half.

"On the left of the main road, the Tomb of the Reliefs (the so-called Tomba Bella) is entered. On the walls round the niches and on the pillars, the favorite objects of the dead and domestic articles are reproduced in painted stucco relief: dogs, helmets, swords, leggings, shields, knapsacks and haversacks, bowls, a jug, a couch, pincers, a saw, knives, kitchen vessels and utensils, coils of rope, etc."

I'm sure. I'm sure she was a prostitute. Did you look at her shoes? I'm sure they're giving a concert in the cathedral tonight. *Plus they said.* Three stars, I'm sure they said it had three stars.

This spot. This is where they shot the scene in that movie.

Quite unspoiled. I'm amazed. I was expecting the worst.

They rent mules.

Of course. Every wage earner in the country gets five weeks' paid vacation.

The women age so quickly.

Nice. It's the second summer for the Ministry of Tourism's "Be Nice" campaign. This country where ruined marvels litter the ground.

It says. It says it's closed for restoration. It says you can't swim there any more.

Pollution.

They said.

I don't care. Come on in. The water's almost as warm as the Caribbean.

I want you, I feel you. Lick my neck. Slip off your trunks. Let me . . .

Let's. Let's go back to the hotel.

"The treatment of space in Mannerist architecture and painting shows this change from the 'closed' Renaissance world order to the 'open,' 'loose,' and deviating motions in the Mannerist universe."

What are you trying to tell me?

"The harmony, intelligibility, and coherence of the Renaissance worldview were inherent in the symmetrical courtyards of Italian palaces."

I don't want to flatter my intelligence with evidence.

If you don't want to look at the painting, look at me.

See the sign? You can't take the boat that way. We're getting near the nuclear-submarine base.

Reports. Five cases of cholera have been reported.

This piazza has been called a stage for heroes.

It gets much cooler at night. You have to wear a sweater.

Thanks to the music festival every summer. You should see this place in the winter. It's dead.

The trial is next week, so now they're having demonstrations. Can't you see the banner? And listen to that song.

Let's not. I'm sure it's a clip joint.

They said. Sharks, I think they said.

Not the hydrofoil. I know it's faster, but they make me sick.

"The sun having mounted and the heat elsewhere too extreme for us, we have retired to the tree-shaded courtyard." It's not that I loved him. But in a certain hour of physical fatigue . . .

At the mercy of your moods.

Contented sometimes. Even blissful.

Doesn't sound like it. Sounds like struggling to savor.

Maybe. Loss of judgment in the necropolis.

Reports. There's a civil war raging in the north. The Liberation Front's leader is still in exile. Rumors that the dictator has had a stroke. But everything seems so—

Calm?

I guess . . . calm.

This spot. On this spot they massacred three hundred students.

I'd better go with you. You'll have to bargain.

I'm starting to like the food. You get used to it after a while. Don't you?

In the oldest paintings there is a complete absence of chiaroscuro.

I feel well here. There's not so much to see.

"Below the molding, small leafy trees, from which hang wreaths, ribbons, and various objects, alternate with figures of men dancing. One man is lying on the ground, playing the double flute."

Cameras. The women don't like to be photographed.

We may need a guide.

It's a book on the treasures they unearthed. Pictures, bronzes, and lamps.

That's the prison where they torture political suspects. Terror incognita.

Covered with flies. That poor child. Did you see?

Omens. The power failure yesterday. New graffiti on the monument this morning. Tanks grinding along the boulevard at noon. *They say.* They say the radar at the airport has been out for the last seventy-two hours.

They say the dictator has recovered from his heart attack.

No, bottled water. Hardier folk. Quite different vegetation.

And the way they treat women here! Beasts of burden. Hauling those sacks up azure hills on which—

They're building a ski station.

They're phasing out the leprosarium.

Look at his face. He's trying to talk to you.

Of course we could live here, privileged as we are. It isn't our country. I don't even mind being robbed.

"The sun having mounted and the heat elsewhere too extreme for us, we have retired to the shade of an oasis."

Sometimes I did love him. Still, in a certain hour of mental fatigue . . .

At the mercy of your moods.

My undaunted caresses. My churlish silences.

You were trying to mend an error.

I was trying to change my plight.

I told you, you should have taken me along instead.

It wouldn't have been different. I went on from there alone. I would have left you, too.

Mornings of departure. With everything prepared. Sun rising over the most majestic of bays (Naples, Rio, or Hong Kong).

But you could decide to stay. Make new arrangements. Would that make you feel free? Or would you feel you'd spurned something irreplaceable?

The whole world.

That's because it's later rather than earlier. "In the beginning, all the world was America."

How far from the beginning are we? When did we first start to feel the wound?

This staunchless wound, the great longing for another place. To make this place another.

In a mosque at Damietta stands a column that, if you lick it until your tongue bleeds, will cure you of restlessness. It must bleed.

A curious word, wanderlust. I'm ready to go.

I've already gone. Regretfully, exultantly. A prouder lyricism. It's not Paradise that's lost.

Advice. Move along, let's get cracking, don't hold me down, he travels fastest who travels alone. Let's get the show on the road. Get up, slugabed. I'm clearing out of here. Get your ass in gear. Sleep faster, we need the pillow.

She's racing, he's stalling.

If I go this fast, I won't see anything. If I slow down—

Everything. —then I won't have seen everything before it disappears.

Everywhere. I've been everywhere. I haven't been everywhere, but it's on my list.

Land's end. But there's water, O my heart. And salt on my tongue.

The end of the world. This is not the end of the world.

OLD COMPLAINTS
REVISITED

want to leave, but I can't. Each day I wake up and tell myself today I'll write a letter. No, better yet, I'll go around and let the organizer know in person that I'm resigning. My arguments are in order. I review them in my head. But his arguments are powerful, though I've heard them a hundred times. Meanwhile, acting stern without getting angry makes his cheeks sag, he sweats, his fingernails redden from gripping the desk—a dangerous strain for the old man. I break off, not sure whether I've been mastered by his words or am being considerate in view of his poor health. The organizer smells of death; and I'm rather a favorite, a protégé of his.

It's conceivable that I could talk him down, compel him to see my point of view.

Suppose I actually could secure his consent, or simply stride from his office, leaving him hissing, coughing with rage—that's only the beginning of my ordeal. Even armed with the organizer's permission, I still have to confront my fellow members.

I dread their eyes more than their words. How well I know—from having worn it myself—the characteristic expression that comes over their faces when dealing with delinquent members: the expertly blended look that becomes in turn indignant, envious, contemptuous, mournful, indifferent. No special merit exempts me from their reproaches. Why shouldn't my colleagues rage if I desert them? What right have I to be free if they're not?

No, I get a better idea—always the same better idea. I'll move abroad. Lee, with a brand-new promotion at the hospital, won't want to go, especially now, with the war on. I'll insist. I'll sulk. I'll weep. I'll explain. Luckily, we both renewed our passports last month, our modest savings could be withdrawn from the bank any weekday morning, and a translator (I'm good at languages) and a doctor can find work anywhere. But then (this is the next thought), if I leave, how could I face them? I don't mean now the local members—there's a sizable branch here, while in the tropical country I have in mind for Lee and myself and our daughter to emigrate to, members are sparse and leaderless—but the dead ones: those I'd meet when I died and went to wherever it is one goes.

(Don't smile when I say I do believe in an afterlife of some kind.)

They would crowd around me as I entered diffidently, washed and nicely dressed for my funeral, my lungs un-gassed, unmarked by bullet or whip or fire; and they would parade their implacable faces and mutilated bodies before me. Martyrdom is a hard legacy to disown. Sisters and brothers! I shout. I sink to my knees and stretch out my arms, pleading for their forgiveness, explaining that it wasn't their sacrifice that I'd repudiated. But they would refuse to pardon me. They would say, how could you? When we were steadfast unto death, how did you dare to leave?

———

You'll interrupt impatiently. Then it's fear that detains you. Fear of their arguments, their disdain, their reproaches, their pathos. Fear of the gray mouths; fear of the organizer's rheumy, uncertain eyes, focusing doubtfully, straying, slipping back into focus, coming to rest the blade of guilt against your throat. Confess yourself a coward and stay. Go on being the good member, the slave of seriousness, disciple of virtue, duty's fool. Haven't you observed that not everyone's destined to be free?

Don't be impatient. Oh, if I were just a coward. But it's worse. Let's leave the dead out of it; I'm being literary, as the old man might say. As for the living members—how could I be afraid of them, since they have so little power as power is generally conceived? Those outside the organization suppose that we wield tangible power; indeed, they're convinced that we're becoming more powerful all the time. But I know, everyone who belongs to us knows, how weak we are. Retaliation, in the form of physical harm or irreparable damage to my career, is either contrary to members' principles or beyond their powers. Even the humiliating procedures of expulsion, which used to be practiced on those who left us, have fallen into disuse. And in the unlikely event that I should be threatened or harassed, there would always be nonmembers to protect me. I have only to be discreet and slip away quietly to be safe. Why, my departure might scarcely be noticed (except by the organizer, who would have to get a new translator for his books) so long as I didn't make a public scandal—denounce the organization in letters to the newspapers, reveal our secrets on television talk shows or on the college lecture circuit. What prevents me from defecting isn't just fear.

It's that, really, I'm convinced by them. Phoenix-like, my allegiance resurrects itself each time I imagine I have killed it—because that isn't a murder; it's a suicide. And one's feelings, contrary to the de-plorable idea rife among members, can't commit suicide. However much I recoil from what the organization enjoins, in my heart I remain a member. Though I know they're wrong, I can't help feeling that it's a privilege to be a party to their error. I find it a glorious error.

Better wrong with them than right with the others.

That's a quotation, I think. ("Better wrong with us than right with them"?) My skull is crammed with quotations.

Understand, I don't believe all that. I can't. Stripped of every flat-tering excuse and extenuating circumstance, my dilemma seems absurd. And, like you, I see its absurdity.

One way out. (The rewards of candor.) By setting down my feel-ings in all their shameless illogic, I've vaulted outside the charmed circle of those feelings. By declaring that what I believe is false, and truly meaning what I say, I've broken the spell of credulity. Liberated, by the white magic of reason. I might feel about the organization, about myself, as I've explained. But I can't believe any longer in what I feel.

No, not so simple. Try again.

The Translator Seeks a Showdown with a Long-standing Problem. A brief message. Or perhaps the title of a book.

First paragraph: the organizer's accent. He was born abroad, and all his relatives were consumed in some purge or massacre. I translate his books, and live between his language and mine. I do other books as well. (And it's soothing to translate books that are not essential, mere entertainments: novels, studies predicting the future.) Of course, I say I have to do them to make a living. The old man's books have never sold enough to support him, so you can imagine how tiny a sum is the small percentage of his royalties that accrues to me. He smiles indulgently at my other activities. He says he doesn't have time for "literature." That, too, is for the others—the nonmembers.

You can't imagine how enfeebling it is to be a translator. But I'd hardly be better armed, more lucid, if I'd written my own books about the organization.

Look, this is how it is. We are a very old organization. And, as you know, while in one sense we are a secret organization, we are also well known to the general public. Many books and articles, of both a scholarly and a popular nature, have been written about us. Though any account written before the present century is bound to be unreliable, recent histories of the organization are at least likely to be based on solid source material. Many original documents were salvaged from the Second Purge, when the old archives were shredded: confidential memoranda drawn up by past presidents and their subordinates, minutes of plenary councils, manifestoes, petitions, privately circulated tracts, correspondence between branches, and biographies of leading members. As an accredited translator, I can get permission to consult these arcane yellowing pages in the lead vaults where they're stored. But to use these sources it's not necessary to have access to the new archives. Thirty years ago, in an uncharacteristically humble gesture toward improving our stormy relations with the outside world, the organization put on microfilm an edited selection of these documents, which may be found in any well-stocked municipal or university library.

A dog is barking in the neighboring apartment. Louder than the ambulance siren in the street below. Louder than the shouting children on the staircase.

At the turn of the century, some members charged that all these records, those kept for the eyes of authorized members only as well as the ones made available to the public, were forgeries. (One of their arguments: the papers were too well preserved, too legible; documents of such antiquity should be partly undecipherable.) These dissidents claimed that not even our most highly placed members know the truth about our origins. But they have to keep up the pretense that they do, because origins are very important to us. Origins are, in fact, the pride of the organization; all members are given to boasting about how we began so long ago, and under such glorious auspices.

This heresy has died out in recent years, since the last purge. Few think it worthwhile now to contest the received version of our origins. Even if the canonical account were mere guesswork, or a lie, it seems to matter much less today. Our members have hallowed this account by generations of unbroken belief. Were it not true to begin with, it is true now. And it becomes still truer, probably, as our point of origin recedes further into the past. (Certainly, it becomes heavier.)

Once, I said as much to the organizer. "Right," he answered, a gracious smile twisting his withered face. "It's truer." Wheezing, he hauled himself out of his oak swivel chair, hesitated before the book-laden shelves behind his desk, took down a heavy old folio, and read aloud a gloss—with which I wasn't familiar—on the Commentator's gloss on the Seventh Lesson that was right to the point. (I must explain that the seventh of the Eight Lessons has been thought to treat the topic of retroactive truth.)

We're more sophisticated now. Even the cleverest and most contentious among us agree that a retroactive truth is enough.

Indeed, we are altogether less concerned with origins. Now it is our history—above all, the history of our sufferings—that absorbs us; and of the veracity of these accounts there can be no dispute. The movement's unhappy history is the first item to be laid before new members, even before the four-volume *Commentaries* and the reading of the anthology of quotations *What Must Be Done.*

Lee will be home soon from the hospital, and then it will be time for dinner. Our daughter, who is built like a tiny jockey, is laboring over her homework in the living room and watching a basketball game on television. I mention this so you can visualize how plainly I live.

Dissent must be set off from dissent. I dissent differently.

Far from wanting to dispute the details, or accuse our leaders of ignorance or of deceiving us, I want to challenge our very involvement with history. That our origins are debatable (possibly), remote (certainly), is not the problem. The sheer continuity of the organization is. It seems to me far from enough that our movement is so old, that we have survived so much misunderstanding and vilification and injustice.

Understand me. I am not objecting that the movement has not been more successful, or urging that in all this time it should have accomplished more, won more members than it has, infiltrated more institutions, taken over territories, ruled cities. Our successes, whose real scope only highly placed members know, are hardly negligible. (Prudently, the organization minimizes this sort of thing.) And I see how a more visible success might have imperiled the very idea of the movement, which depends on its remaining small and closely knit, however dispersed our adherents. It is just that I doubt if our successes are worth the price we've paid for them— unless the organization was designed simply to demonstrate the power of human perseverance in the face of crushing obstacles. But even our bitterest members wouldn't claim that.

It's too late to go to the typewriter repair shop to pick up the other machine.

I don't claim that the organization is without taint. Plenty of shady deals have been closed in its name: our history does have its disreputable chapters. And I will admit that certain charges made against us—snobbishness, exclusiveness, our deliberate cultivation of differences from others—are, to some degree, true. It's not our faults that trouble me. It's our virtues.

Consider the genuine glories of the movement. The varied ways in which it retains the allegiance of the members. The subtlety and flexibility of its teachings. The loftiness of its ideals. Finally, what all this amounts to is the creation of a certain type: the member. Far from conspiring to overturn society, as many people suppose, the movement operates mostly upon itself, not upon the world. And for what end? To knit together ever more tightly those who belong.

What justifies this endless self-perpetuation? That we possess a secret of which the others, the nonmembers, are ignorant? But they do know it, in part. We've made it available to them. And they have founded larger and more ample organizations that imitate ours and draw upon our doctrines. Why do we continue, then? For the residue of our truth, which they haven't yet adopted? But they'll never adopt it, never. What they have left us, unimitated, is our truth alone.

My fingers are often print-stained. I own between five and six thousand books and periodicals. Lee has almost as many, a third of which are medical books. The roaches like to breed in the books. Our daughter doesn't like to read.

Someone is knocking at the door of the neighboring apartment.

In this city, you can tell the exact age of a building by the thickness of the walls. The knocking is getting louder.

We disdain outright proselytizing among nonmembers, but members seem to need continual reproselytizing. (Privately, our leaders admit that many members are lax in their duties, unmindful of the exalted responsibilities of belonging to the organization.) After the initial enthusiasm, which lasts, typically, for several years, the majority of us tend to use the movement mostly to make social and business contacts, to strike up a deal or find a trustworthy lawyer or select a mate. Our members have a tradition of suspecting nonmembers. For good reason, I readily admit: we have in fact been cruelly persecuted. Our membership gets regularly thinned by massacres, in which the loyal and the disloyal, the zealous and the lax, are treated with equal severity; the others do not distinguish among us. Finally, neither do we. For we don't hold to any clearly identifiable doctrines, and even the Eight Lessons are best known for the latitude of their interpretations. What unites us is rather what we reject.

I could compile a new anthology of quotations: *What Must Not Be Done.* Perhaps the real title was a mistake.

What unites us is a certain specialization of character, which draws the members together in the bonds of familiarity. We know what to expect from members; and while we can be harder on each other, more acerbic in our contempt for ourselves than nonmembers ever are, we usually end by making allowances. These unifying characteristics also make us easily recognizable to nonmembers. We are recognized everywhere by our distinctive customs, vows, energies, scruples, even (people say) by a common physiognomy and posture.

How many demented prejudices still exist against the organization! Obviously, we can't all look alike—since our members are drawn from several races and are citizens of many countries (we are indeed staunchly internationalist); further, it's not even common for membership to stay long within the same family. Take my own case. Lee is a member, of course. But our younger daughter has so far shown neither the temperament nor the interests that indicate a future member. We're a little disappointed, to be sure— Lee more than myself. I, in my present mood, should be rejoicing at my daughter's good fortune.

A small mercy. At least no one is born into the organization! To have such a choice assigned to one by birth, to have one's childhood paralyzed by such morbid predilections, would be too oppressive. There is this much humanity in our leaders' otherwise rigorous severity: they leave us to find the organization ourselves.

———————

Lee is late today. Maybe I should start the dinner.

Whatever induces anyone to join, you ask. Idealism—which goes without saying. And other motives that are less noble, but not ignoble, either. For some, it is the social advantages I've mentioned. A member knows he or she can present our credentials to another member anywhere in the world and be offered aid and hospitality, for members consider that they constitute one family. That's no small asset, the world being the dangerous place it is, to have helpful relatives to call on wherever you find yourself. For some, it is the number of distinguished writers, scholars, scientists, actors, political figures, and so on, who have been members; those who join us feel they are entering a select society. For some, it is the moving story of our hardships; suffering has great prestige among those who are drawn to us.

What attracted me, I think, was all these reasons. Even as a child, I had the psychological predisposition that marks a potential member. From the age of nine, I wanted to be a writer. Since I never did find the freedom to write with my own voice, I entered a profession that puts me at the service of other writers. Service, being useful to the community and to the highest ideals, has always seemed to me what made life worth living. But no vocation—not even that of the writer, exalted as was the conception I had of it— seemed to exhaust my hunger for the truth, my wish to lead not just a good but a morally intense life.

Also, as I remember, I was fascinated by the idea of being different. Dozing off in the grade-school civics class, I longed to have been born a Jew; I fancied myself left-handed; I imagined myself, grown up, as a homosexual, as a monk or a nun, as a bomb-throwing revolutionary; I dreamed about Robin Hood. While still young, I'd heard vaguely of the organization. (Here, where branches are numerous, who hasn't?) But I never thought of joining until I was nearly grown, mainly because I'd never actually met a member: personal recruitment, of course, is the chief method by which the movement gains new adherents. People rarely make application to join us on the basis of reading or hearsay alone.

Sometimes one's first contact with a member—if he or she is disagreeable or stupid—drives the prospective candidate away. This nearly happened to me, for the first member I met, a plaintive-voiced, sandy-haired man with spectacles who had recently married my father's young sister, was the dreariest kind of member, the kind who turns up regularly at meetings and pays his dues, as if nothing more were to be expected of him. Uncle George's lack of seriousness was already suggested by his very willingness to marry into a family of nonmembers. My well-off suburban parents, who prided themselves on being enlightened, had promptly yielded when my aunt brought home her fiancé. They even swallowed comment on his table manners and short-sleeved sports shirts. He thought he was honoring us; the family thought it was being very modern and spirited in accepting him. Eager at the prospect of knowing a member (I was fifteen), I besieged him with questions. He evaded them all with a trite boast, a complacent shrug. I decided that he must be bound by a rule of secrecy or afraid to confide in me, thinking I was a spy for my family, sent to interrogate him. Later, disillusioned, I realized that the most likely explanation of George's vagueness was that he took his membership lightly.

Once, I described George to the organizer, berating policies so slack that such a person could have been admitted. A naïve complaint:

typical of the mentality of members. Even after belonging for many years, my pride in the organization, my wish or belief that members must be better than other people, remained intact.

I was almost eighteen when I met my second member, a professor at the university where I was enrolled. Long before knowing anything about him, I was drawn to Cranston. He wore three-piece suits with leather elbow patches and had a peculiarly arrogant manner on the lecture platform, for which, with the pathos of youth, I admired him. He was balding fast. Though at the time he must have been twenty-eight or twenty-nine, he looked to be in his early forties at least. This internationally acclaimed expert in his abstruse field came from a poor and uneducated family of butchers, dressmakers, and cops. Years of near-starvation, while he was putting himself through college and graduate school by his own efforts, had left him extremely thin. And when, through a classmate's gossip, I found out that he was a member, I thought I'd divined the secret of his austerity and dedication.

Of course, I didn't immediately dare bring my personal interest in the organization to Cranston. I was shy. And I wanted to offer him something more serious than curiosity. Before approaching him, I read up on the history of the organization. Being uninitiated, I understood little of what I'd read; but on the basis of that, I proposed doing a term paper on the organization's tenets of belief in the early nineteenth century. Cranston's assistant reluctantly approved my topic. The next step was to get to see Cranston himself, no easy matter, since he always hurried away after his lectures. I tried to devise a suitable question I might put to him—I mean, a question that was neither distasteful in its ignorance nor impertinent in its maturity.

———

"Would you agree that the reason the organization's members cluster together is not snobbery or clannishness but to be able to aid each other in the most difficult circumstances?" I blurted out at Cranston in the corridor one day after class. My pretext was still that paper for his course. "We preach a universal brotherhood," he replied drily. I'd been rebuffed, and I respected him for that. I came at him again, undiscouraged, a week later. This time I'd typed out a list of questions, which I thrust into his hands. "All this for a term paper?" he said, frowning. He had long, thin fingers with beautiful pale, tapering nails.

"Not exactly, sir," I said. "It's really more of a personal interest. And I thought that since you . . . I mean, I've heard that you . . ."

I suppose another reason I was drawn to the organization (I should mention them all) is that my mother so disapproved of my joining. It was all right for my aunt to marry George, she was no bigot, etc.—so she said. I knew that it was because she had never liked any of her in-laws. Convinced that she'd married down in settling for my father, she thought it fitting for her husband's sister to marry even further down, by choosing George; but not for her spoiled, precocious only child—who was going to be a great writer— to get mixed up with that tawdry, suspect, clannish crew. And besides, it was dangerous. Weren't some of their activities illegal? I enjoyed defying her; at last she had a reason to worry about me. (I'd been a far too docile child.) Years later, she herself became a member. This embarrassed me.

I could see, to my surprise, that Cranston had taken a sudden liking to me. He seized my elbow awkwardly. "What's your name?"

Cranston invited me to his one-room apartment near the university, and started to make some instant coffee on the hot plate. Then the cord broke. We talked for several hours that day, the first of many conversations. He took down rare leather-bound books from the seventeenth century and showed them to me. (One was called *Oceania*.) How flattered I was! Here was a man such as I had imagined members of the organization to be—dignified, articulate, reserved, yet (nobody can hide that sort of thing) inflamed with a great passion.

I hadn't yet met the type of member, all too common, who becomes ashamed of belonging to the organization, and conceals it.

Cranston smiled—for what that was worth. His almost-handsome, skeletal head was handsomer when he didn't smile; when he did, you noticed that he had trouble with his gums. He started to tell me a little about the organization. Unlike my uncle, Cranston didn't boast of his affiliation with the movement. His remarks were detached, factual. To him, I was still an outsider, and he wasn't interested in proselytizing. I sat in a broken armchair, spellbound by his sense of purpose, and longed to share in what inspired him.

———

I'd better pass over the stages of my entry into the organization, for I feel myself sliding back into the mood of grateful reverence that brought me into it. Since I'm trying to assemble my reasons for leaving, I should be explaining these—and perhaps, in the telling, fortify my resolution.

I suppose the main reason is that, despite the close camaraderie that membership supplies, I do feel isolated. It's difficult to explain, for there are members all around me, and from the organization

I have drawn friendships, love affairs, professional contacts, and, nine years ago, a marriage. I'm never alone. Although our movement is numerically very small, no more than the tiniest fraction of the world's population—in many places the organization has never gained a foothold—it often seems to me that the world is populated only by members. Everywhere I go, and I've traveled on three continents, I meet them. Perhaps this is a delusion, part of the special mentality, the unique way of looking at the world, that one adopts upon becoming a member—a kind of protective myopia conferred by initiation. How often has it happened that when I strike up a conversation with a stranger whom I assume to be a nonmember (never, I must admit, without the definite awareness that he is not one of us, an awareness that sometimes heightens our intimacy but often inhibits it), my new acquaintance turns out to be a member. Perhaps he's concealing it, for reasons of personal convenience, or because he fears some new persecution is afoot.

Or perhaps he is a lapsed member—at any rate, one who has stopped paying dues and attending meetings. But even so, I can't help treating him as a member in full standing. For it's one of the peculiarities of our movement that while we are (or claim to be) scrupulous in screening candidates and admitting new members, we never regard someone as really having left. Even after expulsion, disgraced members are kept track of. They are watched carefully and with a certain solicitude.

Once, I asked the organizer why the movement remains so attached to its former members. Sentimentality? "We're well rid of the disaffected," I said, "the ones who no longer contribute anything to us." It would be better, I argued, to have clear standards of misbehavior and reliable procedures for severance—as marriage, also a permanent and binding contract, is compatible with the possibility of getting a divorce.

———————

This conversation took place four years ago, before I was aware of feeling anything other than pride in the organization. The old man had just recovered from his first heart attack; I was polishing my translation of his third collection of polemics. Now it occurs to me that my questions were not disinterested: that I was pleading, in advance, for myself—for the possibility of my own exit.

I'm not saying it's not possible to be thrown out of the organization. It is. But only after committing definite, public, and outrageous acts. Some hold that joining another organization is sufficient grounds for expulsion. For others, it's moving to a country where there are no members—not even a small cell, an embryonic branch. (A minority consider this second tantamount to the first.) Others would expel anyone who denounces the organization or reveals its secrets to nonmembers—while remaining notably indulgent toward indiscretions that don't carry beyond the movement's roster. Still, one can't commit any of these treasonable acts with certainty that expulsion will result. On many occasions, the organizer has surprised rebellious members by his leniency. That's one reason—not the only one, of course—why I still hesitate to take any particular step. It would be easier if there were precedents to guarantee that at least some steps I might take would have consequences.

You've noticed, I hope, that I'm digressing. The reasons why it's difficult for me to leave are not identical with the reasons that prompt me to leave; and it's those I want to explain.

I mentioned the sense of isolation from which I suffer, despite the nourishing proximity of members all around me. I can't describe this isolation more accurately than by saying that I have a keen sense of being cut off. But from what? After only twelve years of belonging to the movement, I hardly remember what it was like not to belong. Understand, I'm not denying for a moment the advantages and strenuous privileges of membership. But I know that I lost something upon joining, something I probably couldn't ever recover if I left, for the organization leaves its mark on you (our teachers proclaim), and besides, I am twelve years older, no longer exactly young. I have, probably, given the best years of my life to the movement.

To be fair, I must explain that the organization makes no secret of the sacrifices demanded of its members (quite apart from the risk of martyrdom—never quite real to me, since I'm a citizen of a country mercifully untempted, so far, by such a crime). "Merit through suffering" is one of the organization's slogans, which every applicant is instructed to ponder. ("Deeper and deeper into the books" is another, more obscure slogan, which is studied by some members only, at a later stage of initiation.) Still, I think the organization does minimize some of the sacrifices that membership entails. We are exhaustively instructed about the world's disfavor and about the high moral demands that the organization's traditions make upon the members. But no word about the rest of our sacrifices. Have these been overlooked in the discussions? Or concealed? I think not. (Whatever my other complaints, I'm not accusing the leadership of hypocrisy or bad faith.) No, I think that most of our presidents, along with the rank and file, are not even aware of them. The bitterest truth of all.

I mean, for example, the narrow mode of living that membership fosters. Although our movement was founded by recluses living in underpopulated regions, it has appealed almost exclusively to inhabitants of large cities. It's as if dry solitude, as in the desert, had been necessary to formulate the ideal or have the experiences that gave birth to the movement, but damp crowding, as in city life, is needed to perpetuate it.

The elevator has broken down again, so Lee will have to walk up sixteen flights of stairs. The dog has stopped barking in the next apartment. Our neighbors are cooking dinner. Someone nearby is practicing the violin, accompanied by a reckless piano tuner.

Our members vacation in the country, and occasionally live in barns. But they rarely feel at home there. They dislike working the land, or exploiting nature for purposes of pleasure. In part, this may be explained by the organization's rule (more a tradition, really) of nonviolence. But it's not only hunting and fishing—as well as farming and raising animals—that members abjure. All sports, involving as they do an intolerable degree of thoughtlessness and yielding to the body, are, as it were, instinctively avoided by most of us. Members who do go out for football or hunt foxes or sail or parachute-jump or race stock cars or dance the tango or grow wheat seem to be engaged in some astounding, unconvincing, laborious affectation.

And yet it's not instinct. For these same persons once—at least as children—boxed and rode horseback and played tennis as freely as anyone else. It's the style of character produced by membership (more by example, through contact with other members, than by explicit rule) that results in these aversions. The proof is that we're even proud of our incapacities; we learn to retort, "That's for the others."

It's the same with the food preferences shared by many of our members. Undoubtedly, when they were young, future members ate spinach and brussels sprouts and cabbages just like everyone else. But after joining, most turn up their noses when a plate of such stuff is placed before them. "Grass," they sneer. I can vouch for the fact that it's not because of some old superstition about the color green—one of the sillier beliefs about us held by nonmembers. Nor is it a lingering religious taboo. The reason we're a meat-eating group who shy away from vegetables is that we associate a herbivorous diet with mental dullness. And yet, as if to compensate for this aversion, members have a tendency to overeat, and our meals in common are often festive.

Have you noticed that the reproaches leveled against us, even when justified, are quite contradictory? Some say we're dirty; others that we're neurotically clean. (Members will rarely leave a sink full of dirty dishes.) Some say we're priggish; others that we are too sensual. (We love food. We admire sex.) That's the genius of the organization: that we are at once so dispersed and so unified, so similar and so disunited. Only this way, probably, could we have survived so many persecutions.

Well, you may say, go to the country then. Lie in the sun, tan your pale body, do calisthenics, commit adultery, scuba dive, ride a motorcycle, raise dogs, eat lettuce. But it's not so simple. I do, I do many of these things—without being ostentatious about them in front of other members. But they remain exotic to me. I feel I lack permission. And even if I could give permission to myself, something is wrong as long as I need permission.

Unfortunately, I've never gone off to the country without taking my typewriter along. I always have such a backlog of work.

Even more stupid than not wholeheartedly enjoying the rural and the carnal is performing these things on principle, with effort.

(Effort should be reserved for the struggle to elevate one's mind and perfect one's principles.) Still, I continue discreetly to pursue my pathetic projects. I've started a garden on our apartment-house roof, where—despite the polluted air—I manage to grow string beans.

When I arrived at my mother's apartment last Saturday, she was absorbed in a book about the war. Her eyes were bloodshot; she rubbed them frequently. I felt prosperous, healthy, at ease with myself. "You were always a bit stuffy," she muttered. "That's why the organization appealed to you." She looked down at her arthritic hands. "We're full of well-meaning prigs." I didn't mind her insults, if they made her feel better. And I marked that "we."

"Listen," she said, putting down the book. "There's another organization." I think her speech was slurred. "What?" I exclaimed. "You heard me," she said.

"You mean one of the rival groups?" I asked cautiously. "No, I mean another one like ours," she muttered. "But more enlightened. You'd like that one better." She leaned back in the chair and closed her eyes. "I'm not shopping," I said, almost gaily. The terror was underneath.

If only I could commit a crime, and be done with it.

Members in this country have started watering down the rules. If there have to be rules, I prefer them to be stricter.

————

Perhaps I should say something about the structure of the movement. We have a loose hierarchy, with an organizer in each locality where members are numerous. Members in some countries use the Central Committee system; in others, they elect a president. There's no written constitution. Attempts to set up a permanent international headquarters were abandoned generations ago as too risky, and it's customary to hold the annual conference of organizers in a different country each year. The most striking evidence of our lack of centralization are the several schismatic groups who continue to call themselves chapters of the organization, and whose adherents (who insist on calling themselves members) send a sizable annual contribution for the upkeep of the central archives. And there is the long-rumored existence of entirely secret chapters, such as a sect in southern India that compiled its own anthology of quotations and *Commentaries*. Besides the academy for training advanced members, the only regular institution in each locality is a court. The duties of the court (which is composed of ten senior members) require that it convene whenever a persecution of the movement seems imminent, to draw up plans for safeguarding the members' lives and properties. The decisions of the court, when it functions in the usual, judicial sense, don't require a unanimous vote. I might explain that nothing is ever unanimous in the society.

The court also screens candidates for membership and supervises the education of new members. At the court of the local branch, disciples and counterdisciples of the old man hold frequent classes on our history and teachings. (He is housebound now, because of his illnesses and because he is preparing another book.) After a lecture, the class is thrown open to discussion. The movement has traditionally placed great faith in lengthy and free debate. Members are not a particularly quarrelsome lot. At least, the quarrels practically never lead to physical violence. But we are notorious among outsiders for being word-drunk and loquacious. Our weekly meetings, scheduled to break off at midnight, often go on until three in the morning. After a meeting is adjourned, a few members can usually be found outside, continuing the discussion until dawn.

Are these discussions a device whereby we perpetuate ourselves? In my twelve years of belonging to the organization, I don't remember that anything has ever been decided at a meeting. Words with us seem to be ends in themselves. We spend altogether too much time talking.

Perhaps that's why the bodies of most members strike me, now, as underdeveloped; why so many of us who inhabit northern climates exhibit an uncommon sensitivity to the cold, and often seem a bit overdressed alongside nonmembers. When I see the members standing outside the meeting hall in the early hours of the morning, the steam rising from the manholes in the empty streets, disputing some fine point in the discussion, I see them in my mind's eye mostly in turtleneck sweaters and long overcoats—whatever the season.

Perhaps I exaggerate.

In the tropical country to which I imagine moving with Lee, we could complain all the time about the heat. Our daughter would grow up a familiar of piranhas. She would swim naked with village children in the local stream. She would sleep under mosquito netting. I would sweat over my typewriter; and when it broke down there would be nobody to repair it. Lee would be out in the bush, dispensing quinine pills and treating scabrous infants and examining the feet of water carriers for jungle rot. Every few weeks I would take a raft downriver to the nearest post office to send off my proofs or collect a small check for the last book or receive a new manuscript—perhaps in a language studied in college but from which I've never before translated.

Lately, I've been trying to train my body against the cold. I just opened the window. The papers are fluttering on my desk. That may be the sound of a fire engine. The children on the staircase are romping like wolves.

In the tropical country to which Lee and I might emigrate, the mail takes three weeks to arrive; and the postal service is erratic. Lee and I might hear of a right-wing coup d'état in the capital. We won't even be indignant. We'll be foreigners, and it's none of our business.

But we may have to work even harder in that green distant village than we do here, to stifle the feelings of strangeness. (I'll have to translate still more books. Lee will have to deliver more babies, comfort more dying people.) Members tend to become despondent when they are away too long from other members—from the family-like shelter of the organization. Even if we enjoyed nature as children, we grow to feel uneasy there. It's none of our business.

Not even a twinge of indignation? But have we heard how bad it really is? Will the news reach us among our banyan trees that ten thousand union leaders, journalists, students, and other supporters of the former government were penned up in the new modernistic soccer stadium without food ten days ago, six hundred of whom have been maimed by torture and then carried out and immediately propped up against the cement wall inside the Municipal Park and shot by military firing squads?

It's obvious why members of the organization tend to cluster in cities. That's where we can do the most good. Cities are where things happen, where (we feel) we are needed. In the cities, art is made and power is wielded. The decisions that affect everybody, for good or bad, are reached in cities. The countryside may seem beautiful to us, but it also seems morally empty. It is a place to exercise the physical but not the moral will. It's not for cultivating any degree of moral intensity. The country is amoral. The city is either immoral or moral.

Part of the manuscript of the organizer's new book has been blown onto the floor. I'm closing the window.

Need I talk some more about the moral will? Last summer, I almost left Lee for someone else. Sometimes when I said I had an appointment with an editor or was conferring with the old man, I had actually gone to a painter's studio downtown. In bed with Nicky, I suffered all the pangs of guilt. Monogamy is rather more strictly observed among members than nonmembers; and we are known for the warmth and stability of our family life.

The Translator Is on the Verge of Talking About Sex.

Instead of going on about the moral will, I'd rather talk about sex. But there's an obstacle here—of my own making. I have told you I am married. I have mentioned an adultery. But I don't want to go into too much detail. I'm afraid of your losing the sense of my problem as a general one.

That's why I have made a point of not making it clear whether I'm a man or a woman. And I don't think I will—because, either way, it might subtract from the point of what I'm trying to explain. Think about it. If I'm a man, the problem stands but I become a type. I'm too representative, almost an allegorical figure. If I'm a woman, I survive as a singular individual but my dilemma shrinks: it reflects the insecurities of the second sex. If I tell you I'm a woman, you'll write off my problem—still the same problem!—as merely "feminine."

Assume I'm a man, if that makes it easier for you to understand the problem as a general one. A man, say, in his mid-thirties, tall, good-looking, sallow, thickening in the waist, etc., who usually wears a suit and tie. Lo and behold, Everyman. And Lee and Nicky are women. Nicky is probably a blonde, chews gum, and takes a larger-size bra than Lee. Nicky reads rock magazines and smokes pot; Lee wears glasses. But it doesn't have to be like that. I could be an adolescent-looking woman in my mid-thirties, with long straight hair, small breasts, fair skin, and nail-bitten hands, who wears jeans and button-down shirts. If I am a woman, Lee can be my overworked, gently reared, soft-spoken husband; and Nicky my proletarian, paint-bespattered, beer-swilling, rough-talking lover. In either version, you'll assume, the sex is livelier with Nicky than it is with Lee. Unfortunately, I have to agree with you.

As a translator, I'm aware that this may be the only language in the world that allows me to leave the matter open. (Except for having to steer away from a telltale "his" or "her," it shouldn't be hard.) All other languages I know are saturated with gender. A little triumph. I have the pleasure of writing, myself, something that *can't* be translated.

Not that this is the only difference between this language and the others. Think of how many ways one could translate the following words: *pariah, onslaught, inbred, insurgent, fear.*

I am reluctant to describe myself at all, for fear that too many particularities will make you take my problem less seriously. But I can describe Nicky to you, and that way I'll also, by inversion, be describing myself. Nicky has many qualities that I signally lack— for example, an unwillingness to judge others. Nothing makes Nicky indignant.

In bed this steamy summer, I tried to arouse Nicky's sympathy for my longing to quit the organization. All I got for an answer was a smile, although not a callous smile. (It was certainly not the typical response of a nonmember, glad to hear the bad news about us.)

Actually, what I wanted to be—when I was a child—was a saint. With the full awareness of how ridiculous this was. People who want, desperately, often want to be either angels or saints. Unfortunately, angels are not saints. And saints are not angels. Nicky (fortunately?) was an angel.

Once, Nicky explained to me how it was possible to get through the day without judging. The art is in not letting any time elapse between events and one's acting upon them. A judgment, said Nicky, is a cry of impotence. When people can't do anything to change a situation, what's left but to judge it? But isn't judging necessary in order to act, I asked, when we are acting rationally? Isn't there, in all our acts, at least an implicit judgment? "No," Nicky replied. Judgment is no more implicit in acts, according to Nicky, than impotence is implicit in potency.

As for judging oneself—one of my favorite occupations—you can imagine what Nicky thought of that.

The portrait Nicky started painting toward the end of our affair did not judge me. It observed me, it recorded me—in my mid-thirties, tall and well formed, etc., or with long hair and small

breasts and nail-bitten hands, it doesn't matter. (It's very important to me whether I am a man or a woman. But whether most of
you know isn't important at all.) I kept wanting Nicky to add
something. "What more do you want?" Nicky asked. "It's the face,"
I replied. "I'm not as calm as you portray me."

"Do you want me to paint doubt?" asked Nicky. "Grief?" As
Nicky left the canvas to get a beer from the refrigerator, I shook
my head. "I want you to show someone in the process of becoming
someone else. But do it without making the portrait any less linear
and figurative. Don't let the paint drip or smudge or blur."

"You can't become other than what you are. Only more or less
what you are. You can't walk over your own feet."

"I can, I can, Nicky," I murmured. "That's just what I have
to do."

Nicky was right, of course. But that didn't prevent me from returning to Lee. It wasn't guilt that brought me back. It was a very peculiar kind of homesickness: a longing for the word. Nicky and I
could have a certain kind of laconic, aphoristic conversation. But
the full-blooded verbal union that I had with Lee finally counted
for more. Returning to Lee, I was plunged back into the warm
bath of talk that I'll never be able to do without.

Never mind the pleasures of the body that I had enjoyed with
Nicky. In the end, the life of members is founded on the word.
Talking becomes an addiction—like alcohol (which members tend
to shun) and work (to which they are particularly addicted).

I feel how verbal we are as I reread what I've written up to now.
But I can't see the alternative. If I could be silent, maybe I could
walk over my own feet. Maybe I could even fly. But if I'm silent,

how can I reason? And if I can't reason, how can I ever find a way out? And if I can't talk, how can I complain, accuse, sum up? I need words for that.

———

A summing up. "I accuse the organization of depriving me of my innocence. Of complicating my will.

(I don't deny that it has improved my mind, taught me to see the world in a truer, less falsely expectant way. But what use is truth if it makes you despise other people? In despising others, you only despise yourself.)

I accuse the organization of depriving me of my commonness. Of instilling me with false pride.

(I don't deny there is altruism in all this. I'm ambitious not for myself but for the glory of the organization—to be a credit to them. But what use is altruism if it makes one more vain?)

I accuse the organization of depriving me of my strength. Of teaching me to fear those who are not members. I accuse the organization of depriving me of my stupidity. Of making me solemn, heavy, judging . . ."

Are you with me? Have I surprised you? A gasp of admiration, anyone? One short round of applause?

I'd deserve it, had I actually said these things at one of our weekly meetings. But I've done nothing—except to adopt a certain evasiveness in my gaze when I listen to my fellow members. I am silent more often at meetings, although when I do speak it's with an unaccustomed fervor. I used to be quite a capable orator. Largely because of that talent, I attained my present modest rank in the organization's hierarchy. But when I get up to speak now, I feel my face flush and even my eyeballs seem hot. I stammer, I gesticulate at inappropriate moments, I go on too long and have to be gently reprimanded by the old man.

All this inner tumult, while I am voicing sentiments of the most irreproachable orthodoxy. But it's shame that makes me ardent, for all the while I know I'm deceiving my credulous fellow members, betraying their trust. Instead of expounding with my old certitude the Eight Lessons and the other doctrines, I ought to have the courage to make a clean breast of my doubts. "Look at me!" I ache to say. "I'm no good to you any more. Truths in my mouth are lies. Don't listen to me. I don't believe what I'm saying. I'll infect you, you'll begin to doubt, too. Teach me. Demote me. Expel me." Of course, I haven't said anything of the kind. I fear the laughter that might greet me, or the resentful smiles, or the patronizing gestures of sympathy as for someone temporarily deranged.

Or maybe I'm afraid that the membership would take me at my word, and expel me, after which I should suffer all the pangs of exile. Habituated to the battles, the sectarian controversies, I would find the world empty. I'd be struck from the organization's mailing list. I would no longer receive monthly publications and private memos. There would be no calls during the night for emergency meetings. No meetings at all. Alone.

I don't want this decision forced on me by an impetuous, irrevocable act that I should undoubtedly regret. An act of bravado, some histrionic gesture, would be bound to backfire. I want my leaving the organization to be my decision, not theirs. Though I don't expect or hope to be cajoled into remaining (do I lie to myself now?),

I should like my departure to be imposed on my fellow members, against their will.

Enough of rhetoric. Only an important deed can do the trick. But even then there is the possibility that the leading members of the local branch will refuse to recognize that I have left and continue to treat me as a member.

One idea: when I resign I will get someone else (an equally devoted and trusted member) to resign with me; and perhaps, by that calculated doubling of the offense, I shall at least guarantee my own expulsion.

Maybe my private discontent isn't enough to make anything happen, which would accord very well with the central doctrines of the movement—just as the old man's personal qualities and defects do not impugn or even describe his right to be the Old Man. For instance, his fingernails, the back of his neck, and so forth, are dirty. Tufts of hair sprout from his ears and nostrils. His tie is often egg-stained. His fly is usually open. Each time I have to bend over him, to show him a passage in a manuscript of his I'm translating, I am assailed by the smell of his sour breath. I can't look at the paintings on the walls of his apartment, dreadful in their ugliness and lack of taste. I hate the way he badgers his wife. But what does my private squeamishness matter?

The dignity of his office, the values he symbolically upholds, have nothing to do with the large mole on his chin.

The last time I went to see the organizer was Wednesday evening, at his apartment. Lee had given him his bimonthly checkup the day before, and told me that his cardiac condition appeared stable.

He did indeed seem more robust than he had been when I'd seen him earlier in the month; but with fragile health like his, one never knows. When I arrived, he started complaining about his lumbago. I expressed my sympathy; he brightened and, in the midst of telling me what a good doctor Lee is, called out for his wife and told her to bring two glasses of tea laced with whiskey. I was surprised, not just because I'd never seen the organizer drink but because, as is well known, the organization enforces a rule of strict temperance. Lee should have a word with him.

My mother has always been a heavy drinker, though you might not actually call her an alcoholic. This is one of the reasons I would never have expected her to be attracted to the organization. (She was already a tardy forty-one when she joined.) If she drinks now, as I suppose she does, she has to do it in secret. She must be ashamed. Poor struggling, unhappy woman. To feel still guiltier than she already did!

To take the glass from the organizer's hand, I had to come within the borders of his sickly breath. He seemed to be in a particularly expansive mood. We went on talking.

I was hovering near my customary theme. I wanted the organizer to explain and justify the movement to me—without letting on how serious were my own doubts and dissatisfactions. Yet, as always, I felt embarrassed to appear to be questioning what this frail, venerable man had devoted his life to, the cause for which all his relatives (before he arrived in this country) had been executed.

The knocking next door has started again.

———

Instead of actually talking about the organization, I alluded off-handedly to my own restlessness. The old man caught some under-current of my questions. He urged upon me the necessity of giving up private distress. "All that's irrelevant now," he said. From his point of view, he's right. My problem is, indeed, small—compared to the suffering that the organization knows about, sufferings of all humankind, of history itself. That, finally, is our secret. For that, we carry ourselves so portentously through the world. For that, we are endowed with our fabled sense of humor, our mordant gaiety. We do know about suffering. "Guard the secret!" he shouted after me, as I got up and rushed toward the door.

Was he drunk? That can't be good for his heart. I must tell Lee.

Secret! What secret? That each human being suffers? But every-body knows that. And if there are some people who don't, blessed be their ignorance. And cursed be my own knowledge, which connects me with the pain of so many people, living and dead—from people I've never known to that dirty old man whom it repels me to touch. Cursed be the memories of centuries of suffering that are not mine, except as I am by temperament predisposed to ac-knowledge them. Cursed be millennia of isolation and complaining. Cursed be the paper chains that bind me.

"Deeper and deeper into the books." I miss Lee.

———

I'll begin again. Although I don't yet know how to leave the orga-nization, I know what would help me to find my way. I need some-one with whom I can share my perplexity, someone who harbors similar rebellious discontents. It would be no good, of course, to confide in a nonmember. (What a disappointment it was with Nicky.) Don't suppose it's because I think a nonmember is not astute or warmhearted enough to help me with my problem. In principle, I'd like nothing better than to place my entire confidence in some nonmember, if only to show that I do not completely share that habit members have of looking only within the movement for friends—thinking that members are automatically smarter, more virtuous, quicker than nonmembers. Unfortunately, I can't. But my reason is quite different: my loyalty to the organization. However much I may esteem the intelligence and humanity of many nonmembers, I can't bring myself to confide in one. Hearing my own criticisms seconded by a nonmember would probably make me want to defend the organization. Despite what makes me long to resign, I still feel the most intense loyalty to it.

If some new persecution were to erupt tomorrow, and the members of the organization were summoned from their modest dwellings, offices, libraries, to report to the police station, and from there dispatched to prison and executed, I know that without a moment of doubt I, wherever I was, ill even, with whatever excuses of disaffection or lapsed participation in our rites, would hasten to dress, descend in my elevator, and march through the street, singly and unescorted but with as much speed as if I were being hurried along by the butt of a rifle, to appear at that police station, sign my name to the bottom of the list, and share proudly the doom of my fellow members.

I'm not boasting. Of course, my behavior is fairly predictable. For this is just what the organization teaches: how to die for the organization, as well as how to live (apart). Will I ever find the courage to be a traitor? I would have to stop thinking that I was someone special. I'd have to stop needing to feel that.

It's for this reason that I need to pour out my heart to a fellow member, one who feels the tug of the same irrational pride and loyalty. Only a member's seconding of my own disenchantment will make sense to me. I'm bound to write off any criticisms of the organization from nonmembers as unfeeling prejudice.

My daughter is standing at the door of the study, munching on a celery stalk. She wants to know when Lee is coming home.

Oh, it's easy enough to criticize the organization from the outside. We are always being attacked: for our stubbornness, our vanity, our exclusiveness. I flinch when I realize I'm now echoing these judgments. I tell myself that when I, a member, say such things, it's different. After all, I've felt the lure of the organization's ideals, have submitted to its discipline. To make such criticisms costs the others nothing while it costs me a great deal. But does it, actually? What price do I pay, besides the agony of knowing myself to be a damned hypocrite? For I've yet to do anything—even speak my mind.

And if I were to speak up, suddenly bursting out in a meeting and denouncing the organization, is it likely that they would let me go? After all, criticism of the organization is one of our members' most cherished occupations. The last time I saw the old man, when I touched ever so lightly upon the defects of the organization and some of its members, he quite agreed. Of course, we're pretentious and corrupt, he said.

He'd been drinking tea laced with whiskey. Maybe he was drunk.

I still don't see the way out. The Translator Reaches an Impasse.

That's why I need a confidant. But who? Not Lee. Any complicity with me would be too easily explained as conjugal loyalty rather than independent conviction. Besides, Lee's given no sign of ever regretting belonging to the organization, or being dissatisfied with its regimen. The prospect of approaching any of my friends here in the local branch fills me with apprehension. I don't dare. Better to make a stab in the dark.

That's why I am writing this, and will have it photocopied tomorrow.

I promise you who are reading this that only members have it in their hands. Nonsense, you'll interrupt.

I agree that what I've written may seem destined to be read by nonmembers. Otherwise, why would I have painstakingly explained matters well known to everybody who belongs to the organization? But don't be deceived by appearances! How could I have seriously considered sending this to nonmembers? (That would be too vast a treason.) I shall have no confidant who is not herself or himself a member.

I am mailing copies to a hundred members living here and abroad. Apart from Lee, who has a right to know what I'm thinking; the scholar (not Cranston) who actually initiated me, the third member I ever met; my mother, etcetera, most of the names on my list are members I don't know, chosen at random from the archive files. Let anyone who cares to answer it.

I anticipate my answers.

Someone, perhaps Cranston, will write me. "Your problem is mediocre, and therefore has no solution. It is the problem of a mediocre person. The liberty you seek is mediocre, as is your view of the bondage you are trying to escape. Who the hell cares about your small problems? What do you know about wisdom?"

What will I do then? Perhaps it's true that I don't know much about wisdom. But credit me, at least, with this: that a love of wisdom was one of the main reasons I joined the organization and have for most of these twelve years been such a zealous, passionate member.

And if my notion of constraint and of liberty is mediocre, that still creates a real problem, one at least dimly sensed by millions of people: the invention of liberty.

Several people will write to denounce me in much less eloquent terms, as a renegade, a coward, a weakling. Perhaps one of these letters will come from my mother.

"Whatever put this idea in your head, anyway?" another letter will begin. "Don't tell me it was slow discontent ripening over the years. There must have been something specific, some experience, a conversation with someone that set you off."

"Yes," I will reply. "There was . . . an experience of sorts. But I don't want to talk about it." Why not? "Because it's my business," I'll answer firmly. "Because I couldn't describe it," I'll add. "Because," I'll conclude, "it's not a reason for quitting the organization. Only a spur."

Someone, a rather high official in the organization, who perhaps will turn out to be George, will write me. "You never understood me. You thought I was just that gum-chewing advertising executive with thirty pairs of moccasins who married your aunt. Actually, I was carrying out an important secret assignment in your be-nighted community, and had to adopt this persona as a cover. Now it's your turn. You've never understood anything, for all the confidences to which you've been privy. It's never occurred to you that the organization, as you have described it, is only a *front*. Stop carping, stop wailing, stop thinking only of yourself. Believe me, it's a good cause, the best there is. And right now it's in grave danger." Then follow instructions designating me the assassin of a cabinet minister of a neighboring country who is about to start a lethal persecution of our membership there, using mobs of ignorant local patriots. A plane ticket and a phony passport are enclosed. I am supposed to leave on my dangerous mission tomorrow, furnished with credentials from the highest international council of the organization.

What will I do then?

Someone, perhaps a colleague of Lee's, will write me. "You've got everything backward. To you the organization is just a cumbersome set of obligations. But I can testify to its value as a source of consolation. First of all, in history. Second, personally." The letter goes on to recount the story of her marriage, and how her husband abuses and neglects her. "How can you want to leave," she adds, "once you've invested suffering in the organization?"

Someone, perhaps the organizer of a branch in another city, will write. "I have sent my instructions to the Central Committee naming you my successor. You are the new organizer."

———

One answer could come from Morgan, a school friend I haven't seen since we were in our teens, who became a member two years after I did. (I have consulted Morgan's dossier in the organization's files; her living in the country seems to me a good omen. But what I don't know is that Morgan was expelled in a secret ceremony eighteen months ago, and that it was only after her disgrace that she bought the abandoned farmhouse and restored it.) What I will receive from Morgan is not a direct answer but the mirror image of what I have written here. It begins: "I want to return. But I can't."

And so on. I try to imagine the variety of responses I might receive. The outcome is unpredictable, for not all the responses are caustic. Some are sympathetic.

Wouldn't it be strange if I learn that I am not unusual—that the confidant I seek, far from being unfindable, exists everywhere? Perhaps wanting to leave the organization is a not uncommon trait in a member and there are thousands of complaints similar to mine in circulation throughout the world. If that is the case, should I stay?

Not unless it comes from the organizer himself. (To whom I'll also send a copy of this.) That may seem unlikely, but who knows? From his mouth anything is possible.

A story is told about an organizer in another country, adjudicating a case in the presence of a favorite disciple. First he hears one side of the dispute, reflects for a while, and tells the plaintiff, "You're right." The woman goes out, and her enemy comes in. The organizer listens gravely to her version of the grievance, pauses, and

then says, "You're right." The second plaintiff departs, equally satisfied that a just verdict has been rendered. As soon as the organizer
and the young disciple are left alone, the disciple breaks out: "But,
sir, the two stories are completely contradictory, and you told each
one of them she was right. That's wrong, that's impossible. You've
made a mistake." The organizer ponders for a moment, and then
says to the disciple, "You're right."

I remember the old man's brilliant essay on the principle of contra-
diction, the topic of the Third Lesson. Although I can more easily
imagine him telling me off, berating me for my insolence and super-
ficiality, I can also imagine him agreeing with me.

Perhaps I shall get a letter from the organizer, saying that he
wants to leave too. He has always wanted to leave, and never dared.
To hell with his murdered relatives. To hell with his responsibilities. Even though he's very old, he wants to have fun—dance and
chase young girls and go surfing and play the alto sax. He proposes
that we resign together.

   Should I discover that this is the case, then I shall stay.

———

I've just reread what I've written so far. Consider that I have noted
its limitations. (As a translator I have a certain knowledge of texts.)
I squirm as I reread it. For I recognize that I am incapable of inves-
tigating my plight without embodying it. That leaden, bloodless
tone of the true member! Anyway, other members will recognize
my voice. It's my certificate of identity, like a thumbprint.

Oh, if I could change my style. (Then I wouldn't need to think
about changing my country.) Jump out of my own skin. When

Nicky said, "You can't become other than what you are," I murmured, "I can, I can, Nicky. That's just what I have to do." If I could stay—with the strut of commitment. Or really leave.

Perhaps if I rewrote what I've written here, it would be more convincing. If I could be lyrical! Unpredictable! Concise! In love with things as they are! But, alas, this thin, overscrupulous voice is mine. And if I could change my voice, have written this differently, I would not be the person I am. I would not have the problem I have.

The Translator Indulges in Some Generalizations.

My problem is identical with my language. I mean, if I didn't have this language, I wouldn't have this problem. If I didn't have this problem, I wouldn't have this language. I wouldn't need your help.

It's because I am the sort of person to whom only this language is available that I'm forced to plead for your help and sympathy. But it may be that this very language is not capable of evoking sympathy—at least, not in anyone I could respect.

You should be honest with me. Have I forfeited all claim to your sympathy by the way I write? Have you written me off as passionless? Unspontaneous? Too unspecific? Disembodied? But I have a body, I assure you. If I don't tell you more about myself and the kind of body I have, it's only because I know my problem is a general one.

I'm trying not to lose my calm. I'm trying not to become hysterical.

This fabric, this bolt of language, belongs to whom? To me, yes. But I disavow it. I'm more than my voice. If I've written about my dilemma with this high-handed treatment of details and lack of concreteness, hiding behind a stiff, somewhat old-fashioned voice, it's because I'm embarrassed, shy—and afraid. Because I'm not free. Because I am what I am. Because I'm a member. But even being what I am, I can want to be different. You'll admit that, I imagine.

My profession has perhaps also contributed to deforming my language. I work between two (or more) languages. But that seems appropriate, somehow—since my problem lies between two (or more) problems. If the sentence structure and diction that comes naturally in writing this is not fully grounded in one language—my own beautiful, rich, native language, which offers so many words and rhythms I haven't used—but contains constricting echoes of other languages, it is apt, since my problem contains echoes of other problems.

The language in which I tell you all this is a language floating a few inches off the ground. As my problem (the one I've related to you) is a problem located a few inches off the ground. The language may be poor. I will not go far in defending it. But the problem is real, even if it's a familiar story. An Old Complaint. A Heretic's Nostalgia. A Dissenter's Apology. A Traitor's Pathos.

Knowing that my dilemma is perhaps contemptible, imagine how I feel. Imagine what that does to my writing: how it deforms my idiom and inhibits my voice. Please don't judge me too quickly.

If I began again from the beginning, would you understand better? Don't laugh.

I've heard there are members of the organization who never open their mail. They're too busy talking or reading. Or sighing. Or chopping the air with their hands. Or breeding children who they hope will be future members. Or bettering themselves and improving the world. Or stroking their beards. Or running away from their would-be murderers. Or staying and getting killed. Or writing books. Or making money. Or looking ironically about them with their expressive, melancholy, heavy-lidded eyes. None of that is an answer. I can do those things, too.

Speak to me! Answer me!

I shall wait for your answers.

BABY

Monday

What we decided, doctor, was that it would be best to lay our problems before a really competent professional person. God knows, we've tried to do the best we could. But sometimes a person has to admit defeat. So we decided to talk to you. But we thought it would be better not to come together. If one of us could come Monday, Wednesday, and Friday, and the other on Tuesday, Thursday, and Saturday, that way you could get both of our points of view.

A few debts. Not many. We try to live within our means.

Of course we can afford it. We don't want to spare any expense. But, to tell the truth, we picked you because your fee was more reasonable than some others. And Dr. Greenwich said you specialized in problems of this sort.

No, we're not doing anything right now. Just riding out the storm.

Certainly not. That's what we're here to find out from you.

How much background do you need to know?

Yes, we've both had physical checkups within the past year.

Both born in this country, good native stock. Why, did you

think we were foreigners? You're a foreigner, aren't you, doctor? You don't mind questions like that, do you?

At the beginning, you can imagine, we felt very sure of ourselves. With a good income, a house with no mortgage, membership in three—

Sometimes. Sure. Doesn't every couple? But they blow over. Then we usually celebrate by seeing a movie. We used to take in the plays at the Forum, too. But we don't have much time for that any more.

Oh, we dote on him. After all, when you have an—

Pretty regularly. Once, twice a week. Thank God, there's nothing wrong with that side of things.

No, it was the group that suggested we consult you. We're not claiming all the credit for ourselves. But probably we would have thought of it anyway.

All right, sure. We do. But what's wrong with that? We really get along very well, considering the difference in our educational backgrounds.

Perhaps our problem seems ridiculous to you.

No, no, we didn't mean it that way.

All right.

That door?

Tuesday

It's really Baby who's the problem, doctor.

What?

Oh, complete sentences right off the bat. He just started right in.

We take turns. It's not far.

He likes to. After the alarm rang, every morning, Baby used to bring us cups of steaming hot coffee in bed.

We try not to interfere. Baby's room is full of junk. We offered him the bigger bedroom, but he insisted—

We took a camping trip last spring in Big Sur for two weeks. We wanted to take Baby along, but he wouldn't go. He said he had to study for his exams.

Sure, he's perfectly able to take care of himself, cook his own meals. Still, sometimes we do worry.

He loves to.

But we're afraid Baby is ruining his eyes. He doesn't want to play with the other kids.

Comic books, Poe, Jack London, the encyclopedia, it doesn't matter to him. After we turn the lights off at nine, he reads under the covers with a flashlight. We've caught him several times.

Just sitar lessons.

No, we don't try to influence Baby. Whatever he wants to be when he grows up is all right with us.

We don't believe in the old kind of family. Everybody living on top of each other.

We've talked about taking our vacations separately. It's good for people to get away from each other once in a while, don't you think?

Like when we go to Sunday meetings of our group, we usually don't sit together.

No, we decided not to have affairs. Lying would be awful, and since we both have a jealous nature, it seemed best not to.

You have a pretty cynical view of human nature, doctor. Maybe you spend too much time with people with problems.

That's right. From the beginning. We don't find being honest as complicated a business as some people do. All it takes, after all, is a little courage. And self-respect. But perhaps we're old-fashioned.

A dream. Anything you say, doctor. But it'll have to be for the next session.

Wednesday

You've probably had a lot of parents who brag about their children. But Baby really is precocious. When he was little, we tried to keep him from knowing how much smarter he was than the other kids. We didn't want him to get conceited.

Perhaps if we were younger . . .

Not what you'd call an accident. No. But he wasn't planned, either.

We don't believe in abortion. As far as we're concerned, even a fetus has its rights. Despite what you doctors say.

No, we never thought of adopting another child.

Baby is quite healthy.

It wouldn't be the same, would it?

Of course, sometimes we wish Baby were athletic. Truth is, he can't even swim. Even in the Doughboy pool he just flounders around. Hardly makes it worth while to get a real swimming pool.

Isn't that a rather conventional idea, doctor? Maybe there aren't many athletes with high I.Q.s, we'll grant you that. But we don't see why a brainy kid has to stay indoors all the time and refuse ever to go to camp.

You bet we encourage him.

He's always had real guts. And stick-to-itiveness. He likes challenges. And he's curious, too.

He likes to collect things. Old things. Baby loves the dinosaurs in the County Museum.

You know, we both remember the night Baby was conceived.

No. He's always brought all his little problems to us.

One spanking was enough. We haven't had that kind of trouble since.

The maid.

Yes, he used to bite his nails. But not any more.

We're thinking of moving to a better neighborhood. It's probably more than we can afford. But the kids from Cudahy that Baby
has been running around with are rough. And the other Sunday,
when we were out driving in Topanga Canyon, we saw this split-
level hacienda—it wouldn't cost much, just the down payment with
a twenty-year mortgage—that would be just right for us. It has a
three-car garage that Baby could use part of for his chemistry lab
and his ducks and six chickens.

Two ducks.

Laurie and Billy. Sounds ridiculous, doesn't it?

No, he hasn't given names to the chickens.

Straight A's this semester. We promised him a bicycle if he
made the honor roll.

Oh, it's a fine school. High standards. Old-fashioned discipline.
And they take all the necessary precautions. Baby came down with
the measles yesterday. And his homeroom teacher called the house
this morning, around 10 a.m. That school is very careful, they have
to be. Since they had a kidnapping two years ago.

No, we don't discuss what you say between us. You told us not
to, didn't you? Neither one of us is deaf, doctor.

Already?

Thursday

We found a box of condoms in the drawer in Baby's night table.
Don't you think he's a little young for that, doctor?

Baby's teacher came to the house. She wanted to know what
was wrong.

Maybe Baby ought to see a doctor, too.

Baby's handwriting is very strange. Should we bring you a
sample?

Just say the word.

Baby keeps a journal. Under lock and key, mind you.

We wouldn't dream of it. That would be one hell of a fast way to lose his confidence, wouldn't it, doctor?

We couldn't agree more. Young people are so pretentious.

It's nice of you to say that.

Arithmetic is his weakest subject. Penmanship, that's not even worth mentioning. Atrocious.

History. And chemistry.

Not much. He has such a good memory, he doesn't have to. But we'd like him to read more.

Everything. He remembers last year's supermarket prices, smog readings, the dialogue from a TV show, closing averages on the stock exchange. He knows all our friends' telephone numbers. At the end of a day, he can reel off the license plates of every car we passed on the freeways. We tested him. He's a regular garbage can of useless information.

He's waited hours outside The Greenhouse because Steve McQueen has lunch there sometimes.

Basketball. He's good at volleyball, too.

Well, of course, he is tall for his age. It runs in our family.

Regular measles, mumps, tonsillitis, the usual, when he was little. Braces for three years.

He snores when he sleeps. He's had his adenoids out twice.

You know something odd about Baby? He laughs at four every morning. He must be dreaming. But if you try to wake him up, he doesn't remember anything funny.

No, you don't understand. Always at four, exactly. Even when we went to Hawaii, where it's a two-hour difference. Still 4 a.m., right on the dot. How would you explain that?

Honestly! You can set your clock by it.

He has a wonderful laugh. Wonderful. It makes us feel warm all over, in the next room, just to hear him.

Actually, we did try once. We stood at the door to his room, waiting for 4 a.m. As soon as we heard the laugh, we rushed in and shook him awake and asked him what he was dreaming. He was so sleepy, poor kid. At first he didn't say anything. And then, you know what he said?

Guess.

You'll never guess.

"Fish." His eyes were closed, mind you. Then he laughed some more and repeated "Fish." And then he went back to sleep, snoring.

We asked him in the morning. But he didn't remember a thing.

One other time. But we didn't actually wake him up. It was when we were camping out in Big Sur last spring, sharing the same tent. Sure enough, the laugh went off at 4 a.m. exactly. We checked our watches to make sure. And we just called out, very softly, "Baby?"

And you know what he said? In his sleep, of course. He said: "Napoleon in a sealed train going to Elba." And then laughed and laughed. Pretty smart, don't you think? Even when that kid dreams, he dreams smart.

Maybe it's stupid to worry so much about a child. Is that what you mean, doctor?

We've tried to give him every advantage, but—

Yes. Sometimes. Not often.

You think we were wrong?

Good. That's what we thought. Anyway, it was the maid who caught him.

Oh. Juanita loves Baby. Everybody who meets Baby knows he's special. Especially kids.

We were wondering if you shouldn't meet Baby yourself. Then you'd see what we mean.

Friday

Baby got a bloody nose in school yesterday.

The pediatrician says he's quite healthy except for his adenoids. Do you think he should have another checkup?

We think protein is very important.

But some things are physical. You do agree, doctor?

Using Dr. Greenwich's guidelines, we tried to cope ourselves. But it didn't seem fair taking up too much time at group sessions for a personal problem.

Perhaps you've never had a case exactly like ours.

Of course, we've tried to get him to see a therapist. But he refuses. You can't force someone to go, can you, doctor? People have to want to be helped.

Exactly. That's why we thought we could help Baby by talking to you.

That wouldn't help. We raised Baby's allowance last week.

With green stamps. But he'll never make it.

Baby says he wants to be a priest when he grows up. He sleeps with a Gideon Bible under his wooden pillow.

From The Wigwam in Barlow. It's a motel in the shape of a wigwam.

Awfully hot. You know what Barlow's like in the summer. We almost suffocated. But Baby doesn't mind the heat.

We were probably crazy to go there in June. But when we get to feeling cooped up, sometimes we just have to get into the car and drive someplace.

You don't mind if we turn up the air-conditioning, do you? Aren't you hot?

That way, oh. Thanks.

Baby is very mechanical, you know. He fixed the TV in the den the other night, when it jammed just as we were expecting eight for dinner.

Sometimes we regret he leans so much toward science. It's a bit like having Dr. Frankenstein Jr. around the house. And no matter what they say, you have to admit that science hardens the heart.

For instance, when Mickey, his best friend, died of polio last summer. They'd been in surfing camp at Seal Beach the year before. We tried to keep the news from Baby, because we were afraid he'd be too upset. But when we told him, he didn't seem sad at all.

No, not you, doctor. We're sure you're a regular torrent of sympathy. But then, we wouldn't call what you do exactly a science. Would you?

Oh. Well, that isn't what Dr. Greenwich says.

You really want us to ask him? What if he doesn't agree?

Do you know, doctor, that's the first time since we've been coming here that you've smiled. You ought to smile more often.

It's a deal. Why didn't you say so in the first place?

Saturday

Sharper than a serpent's tooth, and all that. You don't mind our being a little corny, do you, doctor? It's such a relief to talk about it.

We wanted him to have piano lessons.

No problem with hair.

Well, that depends what you mean by drugs, doesn't it?

No.

Only at school.

A little, small doses, but he swears that he's stopped.

Never, thank God! That just ruins your mind for good, doesn't it?

What makes things difficult is that Baby holds grudges.

Wait a minute. Has Baby tried to see you, behind our backs?

Why not? Listen, you don't seem to understand how clever he is.

Baby says he was born on Krypton and that we're not his real parents.

Well, what do you think of a kid only five years old who announces that he's going to win the Nobel Prize? And that we would be proud then to have known him. He said it to the maid.

In chemistry.

The first time he ran away? Yes.

With an air rifle.

No, not very far.

A tempura vendor in Ocean Park got Baby to show her his school-bus pass and telephoned us. She saw Baby going on the roller coaster for four hours straight.

The police was only the third time. We hated calling the police, but there didn't seem anything else to do.

Everyone has an unhappy childhood, don't they, doctor? At least, everyone seems to think so. You must have a lot of people trooping in here to tell you that. What did we do that was especially wrong? Of course, nobody has any respect for the family nowadays. We knew the ideas Baby would pick up at school. But in the home we tried to provide some balance, to teach him—

No, he doesn't like any of his cousins. Of course, they're not as bright as he is. But even so . . .

His cousin Bert was accepted at Caltech.

He's always liked to be treated as a grownup, rather than a

child. He beams when you give him little responsibilities and tasks. You know, Baby's more punctual than we are. That's pretty unusual in someone his age.

Whenever he feels we're treating him like a child, he has a tantrum.

The first time Baby had his adenoids out, we stayed by his bed in the hospital all night. But this time—don't you think?—he's old enough.

Not strict, no. We haven't the heart. But sometimes we have to be stern, for his own good.

Well, you do have to give him credit for that. We know it's necessary for him to rebel against us.

That's not the same.

Do you have any children of your own, doctor?

Anyway, a precocious child is different. You're not going to tell us that an eight-year-old who's reading Schopenhauer could possibly be easy to handle.

Maybe.

All right. We'll try to find out for tomorrow.

That's right! Hey, how are we going to manage for a whole day without you?

Of course, we'll do it without asking him directly. You really take us for idiots, don't you? Just like Baby.

Monday

We had a fight last night, after the group meeting. And bang in the middle, we caught Baby listening at the door in his sleep suit.

We couldn't.

In the morning, we found he'd wet his bed again.

Oh, we did. And we tried sleeping in twin beds. Baby has a habit of crawling into bed with us on Saturday and Sunday mornings.

Sometimes we have affairs. We don't feel we ought to take each other for granted. But we tell each other everything.

Listen, everybody's got to live their own lives.

Sure we've thought of having other children. But it never seemed to be the right moment. You have to plan these things.

Maybe it's too late now. And we haven't done so well with the one we've got, let's face it.

He never says. He prefers older children. His best friend is eight. Her name is Thelma DeLara, but he calls her Bloomers. She calls him Vanilla. They're so adorable together. He told us he's going to marry her. Those two can sit in the front-hall closet together giggling for hours.

Thelma baby-sits for us when we go down the street to the Turnells' to play bridge. Generally on Thursday nights. They have a boat just like ours.

The Turnells. They're friends, doctor.

No, they don't belong to the group. They're not the type.

What do you mean? Who the hell told you that?

Oh. Well, it's not true. We're not interested in that kind of thing. We don't object to it, of course. Other people can do what they want.

Why are you asking so many questions about us, doctor? Nothing in our friendship with the Turnells will help you understand better the problem with Baby.

Baby doesn't even know the Turnells. They don't have children his age.

Sure it makes a difference. Raising children is an art, you know. We see so many parents around us who don't take it seriously. Even you'd be shocked, doctor. You don't know the half of what goes on!

Tuesday

Are most of your patients members of some group, doctor?

Just curious.

We did once. We decided to get a divorce, but we couldn't go through with it. Baby would have been so unhappy. He's too small to understand.

First, to teach him how to take care of himself. Baby is so trusting. He's ready to go off with any smiling stranger who promises to drive him to Disneyland.

We take turns walking him to school. It's only six blocks away, but with the neighborhood what it is now, you can't be too careful.

What part of town do you live in, doctor? This isn't your apartment as well, is it?

Oh, you're lucky. It's so hard these days to find a good house.

Baby got mugged in Griffith Park, where he went to fly his kite. Three Mexican boys.

He was carrying seven dollars.

Just a knife.

No, he wasn't hurt.

When he first got the chemistry set, it was really adorable. He said he was going to find a magic formula so that we could live forever.

No, that was the odd part. Just the two of us.

We worry occasionally that we can't be as close to him as other parents because we weren't all that young when he was born. Not that the generation gap is all it used to be. But still . . .

Of course, youth is a state of mind. Don't you think, doctor? And we do keep fit. We jog. And we don't smoke.

Us walk around naked in front of Baby? Certainly not! Not that we have anything against it. But Baby is so beautiful.

We're saving Baby's first lock of hair. Yesterday we took him to an Italian barber in Westwood. Baby hardly cried at all.

Sometimes we have a sinking feeling of time passing by so quickly. He's changed so much already.

You can see it in the snapshots we take each month to record his growth. That album is probably worth more than all the words we're spilling out here put together.

That's a strange thing to say, doctor. You know perfectly well what we want.

Wednesday

Reason with him? That's all we do. But he's so withdrawn.

Last year he refused to eat breakfast any more. And now he's stopped drinking milk. We've warned him it's bound to stunt his growth. Actually, it hasn't. But it still doesn't seem healthy.

Cheez Doodles, Banana Chips, Squirt, Fritos, pizzas, tacos, you know the kind of junk kids stuff themselves with.

Mostly he stays in his room. We have to ask him ten times before he'll help with the dishes.

Baby says he disapproves of hobbies. Imagine! But, of course, he has them. Just like every youngster.

Model airplanes. But Baby refuses to buy the plastic ones you get now. He made his own parts out of balsa wood and worked out an ingenious propeller and tail strut with Popsicle sticks and rubber bands. The damn thing looks as if it could really fly.

Of course, we know about glue sniffing. Doctor, please! We weren't born yesterday.

Listen, Baby cares too much about his child-prodigy brain ever to get involved with drugs. Also, he's too unsociable. We wonder if he ever even talks to the other kids at school.

Perhaps it's just as well. You should see that school. It's a mess.

No supervision. The kids can do anything they want. The teachers are simply afraid of them.

Maybe the Chinese have the right idea. Not that we'd want to live over there. But at least people are honest, they have a real sense of community, there are neighbors, marriages stay together, children respect their parents. Of course, people don't have any material comforts and they aren't allowed to think. But we could do without the three cars and the pool and all that. A lot of good it's done us, when you come to think of it. And as for heavy thinking, look where that's gotten Baby.

You don't believe that, do you, doctor? That's a smug look you've got on your face. You think you've got us pegged, don't you? Maybe you'll realize now we're not as typical as you think. We're really radicals, though we don't show it.

Baby thinks we're radicals.

He's going through a conservative period, like a lot of kids nowadays. We don't criticize him. We just hope he'll outgrow it.

Baby has a Confederate flag over his bed.

Last Christmas, we gave him a record of Pete Seeger singing anti-war songs. His first phonograph, you know, very sturdy. He couldn't break it. He could just manage to hook the record on the spindle with his pudgy fingers.

He used to play those songs for hours. And sing them in the bathroom, while he played with his rubber ducks.

Now he just wants cash for Christmas and his birthday. We don't know what he spends it on.

Oh, we don't stint. Listen, the kid has to have a normal life. But that doesn't mean that we don't feel excluded. And sometimes, when we see him doing something stupid, we really have to bite our tongues.

But he doesn't seem to like fun, like other kids. Always studying. Worrying. He's so stern.

Baby got a crew cut, doctor. And what's even worse, you know what he says?

He says he knows it's the least flattering hair style in history. And that's why he likes it. He says it's meant to deflect attention from the surface to the inner man.

Strange to think of Baby being such a puritan.

We begged him to grow his hair long, like the other kids.

Your hair is sort of short, isn't it, doctor?

Thursday

He did it again! Played hooky yesterday. You see what we're up against. Probably went to the movies. At least, we hope so.

Baby has seen *The Great Escape* with Steve McQueen thirteen times. Would you say that the film represents—

Oh, you haven't seen it.

Do you go much to the movies, doctor?

Never. Even when he brought girls to his room, we closed our eyes to it. After all, we hardly have the money to set him up in an apartment of his own. Not at this stage of the game. But we thought he shouldn't be penalized for that. Our problem.

Then one day we caught him stealing.

Oh, no. He doesn't know we caught him.

No, you couldn't exactly say he was accident-prone.

He did get a nail in his foot in camp last summer. The counselor said he was quite brave.

All his shots.

But he never tells us when something is wrong. That's why we have to worry so much.

After Baby had his wisdom teeth out all at once, we took him down the Colorado. We were in a dinghy with the other tourists, all wearing heavy black slickers. He started to bleed on the rapids. A lot of water came into the boat. Baby's face was wet and the blood ran out of both sides of his mouth. But he didn't say a word.

No, that was his decision. He's got to learn to make decisions on his own. And not come to us for everything.

Baby wants a motor bike. But we told him it's too dangerous, what with city traffic. Not like the Valley in the old days.

His cousin Bert had a dreadful accident and was laid up for eight months in St. John's. Both ankles shattered, three operations. He still limps a little. Probably will for the rest of his life. And Bert was lucky! We've heard of some really gruesome accidents.

You know kids. They never stop wanting things.

He's always wanted a dog, but we don't think he has enough sense of responsibility. He's too young to walk the dog each night. And he's already late every other morning for school. So you can imagine if he had a dog to walk first.

In a few years, maybe.

Getting him to accept responsibility has always been the hard part. He thinks we're here just to pick up after him.

But you should see Baby's room. He never throws out anything. All his torn issues of the *National Lampoon* and *Penthouse* and *Rolling Stone.* Jars of pennies and God knows what else, movie stubs, Dodgers score cards, dirty Kleenexes, cigarette butts, old candy wrappers, empty matchbooks, Coke cans, his clothes all over the floor. Not to mention what's hidden.

Baby has a swastika in his top bureau drawer, beneath his underwear.

Baby draws obscene comic strips.

We used to go in and pick up after him, as soon as he left for school. But he would be furious when he found something missing. Now we don't touch anything.

If he wants to live like a pig, he'll have to find out how unpleasant it is.

Some of them, we admit. They turned out to be collector's items. Of course, Baby won't sell them. But you're not going to tell us that Baby's keeping six years' worth of *TV Guide*s is ever going to amount to anything.

People have to choose, don't they, doctor?

Friday

Do you think a gradual gain of weight is a sign of anything wrong, doctor?

The past six months.

Not more than usual.

No, he doesn't smoke. Thank God for that. As a matter of fact, Baby's always kidding us about smoking. He's rather hypochondriacal. Since he was small.

Baby is afraid of germs. He's started wearing a white-cloth mask over his mouth, like the Japanese.

Of course we've tried to give up smoking. Hasn't everybody?

Does this smoke bother you? Come to think of it, we just assumed, because you have all these ashtrays around—

Good.

Maybe he's afraid we'll die before he grows up.

Pretty long-lived, on both sides. But we can't talk about longevity to Baby, just mention the idea and he goes wild. It only seems to remind him about death.

Sure he knows. Every date. Baby made a genealogical chart and hung it over his bed, beside the Confederate flag. You wouldn't believe the questions he asked.

Imagine, he wanted to know if we were first cousins.

Enough is enough, we said to him. Trying to make a joke out of the whole thing. And he actually seemed disappointed.

The best part about Baby is just holding him. We feel inadequate sometimes, answering his questions. But when he shows his need for us more directly, then it's all pleasure.

If only he'd laugh more often. He has such a wonderful laugh.

Baby loves spinach. And lamb chops. Those are his two favorite dishes. He won't let us set him in his high chair unless we call him Baby Lamb Chop.

Baby's teeth are coming in crooked. He was born with an abnormally high palate, the obstetrician told us.

No, but that's what's causing the trouble with the adenoids. It was predicted right then.

And a bluish mark in the small of his back, called a Mongolian spot. Funny. We certainly don't have any Oriental blood, that's for sure. The obstetrician said it was very rare in Caucasian babies.

Have you ever heard of the Mongolian spot?

At least up to then. Until puberty, he used to run all around the house naked. We dropped some hints, but when he kept on doing it, we stopped. We certainly didn't want him to feel that we—

Perfectly normal.

Fifteen. No, that's wrong. Fourteen and a half.

Well, we assume so. Naturally, we haven't seen him naked since.

He does like clothes, yes. You could say he's rather vain. He can take an hour to make up his mind whether he's going to wear the Mr. Natural or the Conan the Barbarian T-shirt to school in the morning.

Sometimes he stays in the sauna for hours. It isn't as if we don't give him his privacy.

We always feel that Baby is hiding something from us. That he's ashamed. Particularly the crush he had on his journalism teacher, Mr. Berg.

Baby is editor of his high-school paper. He was junior-high-school paper editor, too.

Of course, it's normal, in a way. You don't need to tell us that. But you can understand we were a little apprehensive.

We just didn't want Baby to be hurt. We saw what happened when Berg didn't praise one of his editorials. Baby was in a tearful sulk for days.

No, we wouldn't object if he turned out to be. One thing we've learned, doctor. Any way you can be happy, you're already ahead of the game.

That doesn't mean that when Baby got married, we weren't relieved. We'll be honest with you.

We don't believe in early marriages, either. Young people have to find themselves first.

Her father is a systems engineer at Lockheed. We should tell you about her. It's too late to start this time.

Saturday

Leaving something behind means we didn't want to go at the end of the last session, right?

It looks broken.

No, here. Look.

Never mind, it doesn't matter. We have another one at home.

Perhaps we could double the sessions. We could both come on the same day. One in the morning, one in the afternoon.

Naturally. But starting Monday?

Well, it doesn't seem to be getting any better.

No, not worse.

No. Why should we be pessimistic, doctor?

We're not pessimists by nature. We're just trying to be realistic.

Going to group gives one a certain confidence, you know. Perhaps we were too confident.

Laurie died.

The duck. Remember? We told you.

In the back yard. By candlelight.

Not very. Surprisingly enough. If Baby could cry when he learned that George Washington is no longer alive, the least we thought he'd do was cry about Laurie.

We offered to get him another duck, but he said he'd rather have a snake. There's some snake store out in Culver City, where he went after school last Thursday with a friend. He wants us to come with him, but we put it off. Spoiling him, giving him everything he wants, won't help, will it, doctor?

Fish, turtles, a macaw. No, first the macaw and then the turtles. They died. Baby forgot to feed them. Then the chickens and the two ducks.

It's funny that Baby likes snakes now. He used to be so terrified of being bitten by a rattlesnake when we had the house on Doheny Hill.

He's afraid of policemen, too. It started when he was three.

We pretend we don't notice the pot smell in his room. And he pretends he doesn't know we're pretending not to smell it.

Of course, the windows were open.

He buys an awful lot of pornographic books and sex manuals, it seems to us. You'd think he'd learn enough about all that in school.

Baby wears earphones when he plays his cassettes. We don't take it personally, mind you. But it is another way in which he shuts us out. And the look on his face when he's listening to music is almost indecent.

Are you recording what we say? Funny, we never thought to ask you that. There's no tape recorder on your desk. But, of course, that doesn't mean anything.

Lots of doctors do. Dr. Greenwich does. We don't mind. It's probably a very good system, especially if you don't have an excellent memory. Go right ahead.

Are you sure?

In fact, it might even be helpful for us to listen to ourselves. You could play back parts of the sessions and we could comment on them.

Really, you ought to think about it, doctor.

Monday

What pressure?

When he dropped out of Occidental, after one year, we didn't insist that he get a job. We told him that his room was always there, waiting.

He hung around.

That was later, after he did try something.

Right. Then we forked out for flying school in Long Beach. It's supposed to be the best in the country. But he flunked out because of his nose.

Three adenoid operations. But there's still something wrong with his nose.

Have we? Every specialist known to God and man.

Sure, we're going to try again. We can't let the kid go around breathing through his mouth for the rest of his life.

You should see what happens when we go to the movies together. People near us change their seats, his breathing is so loud. They can't at a play, because the seats are reserved.

Oh, one thing. Before we forget. At the meeting last night, they asked us to report on our work with you, doctor. You don't mind, do you? Perhaps we should have asked you first.

Dissatisfied? Certainly not.

Sometimes, though, to tell the truth, we have the impression that it's you who are dissatisfied. With us.

Well, impatient, then. Isn't that true, doctor?

Listen, if you think we have any interest in prolonging this, you're sadly mistaken. Not to mention the money that's going down the drain.

Okay, but imagine how impatient *we* are. We have to live with the problem every day, round the clock. You get to sit there, listen to us, and then you can forget about us after we leave.

Of course, we have moments of joy. Have we ever denied that?

Baby got a new tooth today. Don't think that doesn't give us pleasure. But it doesn't cancel everything else out.

How? We don't just live from moment to moment, like the lilies in the field, doctor. Much as we might like to. We have memories and hopes. And fears.

Afraid of you? Why should we be afraid of you, doctor?

Feelings are one thing. But sound advice is another. Dr. Greenwich vouches for you. We're sure the group is going to give you a clean bill of health.

We're afraid of Baby.

Monday

Why shouldn't we look grim? He's started drinking again. Mescal. Southern Comfort. And some vile stuff called Georgia Moon.

Since he's of age, how can we?

Moral force? That's easier said than done.

Baby has a will of his own, doctor. That's what you don't grasp. A terrible will. Trying to stop him only makes him do it more. He'll do anything to defy us.

Even cause himself pain.

We had to put bars in front of the portable grill after Baby inched all the way across the dining-room floor in his playpen, rocking it back and forth, and laid his palms on it. He knew what he was doing. He knew it was hot.

A terrible burn. He's got both little fat hands bandaged up over the wrists, like gloves. But the pediatrician says it won't leave any scars.

One day he's really going to hurt himself. That's what worries us.

We're not sure he even knows any more what causes him pain. Or else—and this is worse—Baby has made himself into someone who just feels less and less.

When Thelma DeLara moved away, Baby was inconsolable. He cried for weeks. You remember our telling you about Thelma. His best friend in first grade.

Now he's gotten cold and hard.

Whatever we want to do, he's against. What we cherish, he spits on.

Last night he hung a big black flag from the television aerial on the roof. We almost broke our necks getting it down.

Patient! What do you think we've been all these years? You've heard of the limits of patience, haven't you, doctor?

We've been shopping around for a special school. Not an institution, of course. He wouldn't feel locked up or anything like that. Just some place where people would know how to handle him.

It's only reasonable, don't you think, doctor? To admit defeat when your back is against the wall.

What would that accomplish? What's done is done, isn't that right?

But we *are* still trying. Why the hell do you think we came to see you in the first place? Isn't it evidence enough of good faith that we've—

Already?

Tuesday

Do you have a cold, doctor?

Sounds like a cold. You'd better take care of yourself.

It's off the subject, of course, but we're curious to know your opinion. Do you believe in massive doses of vitamin C?

Baby does. He's a regular health nut these days.

Anyway, it's better than becoming a Krishna freak like his cousin Jane. Painted all blue and everything.

Not Bert's sister. Bert's cousin. Baby takes fifty vitamin C pills a day. But he still gets colds.

Squeamish about some things, yes. Baby threw up eating a soft-boiled egg because the white was runny. And he refuses to kiss his Aunt Rae—Bert's mother—because he says she has a black mole on her cheek.

No, he isn't imagining it. She does have one. The kid's not a basket case, for God's sake.

But we don't think that was the real reason.

Rae's a good-hearted gal, but you have to know how to handle Baby. You have to win his confidence first. He's not delicate but he's high-strung, like all precocious kids.

You can't just charge at him and grab him. You have to kneel down, get down to his level and talk to him first. Before you can touch him.

Baby's never been the sort of kid who likes to be hugged and kissed just like that, or jumps in your lap, the way Bert is. Every kid is different. And they understand a lot more than you think, even before they can talk. We learned that.

You know, doctor, what you've just said is a little surprising to us. If there's some misunderstanding, we better clear it up right now. Baby isn't crazy.

We don't have your clinical experience. But we know the difference between crazy and not crazy.

Sure, we can give you an example. Baby told us recently that for the past two years, every time he is about to board the bus that takes him to school, he hears a voice. The voice says, "Sit on the left side. Or you will die." Or, "Sit on the right side. Or you will die." And he never knows, each morning, which command the voice is going to give.

Right. But wait till you hear the rest. We were very upset, of course. The morning Baby told us this, quite casually, as he was eating breakfast before he went off to school, our hearts sank. Once you start hearing voices, and voices that say you're going to die if you don't obey them, it's pretty serious.

But then we thought to ask Baby a question. Has it ever happened, we asked, that when you got on the bus, the side that the voice told you to sit on was completely full? So you were forced to sit on the other side?

"Sure," Baby answered. "Lots of times." And then what happens? we asked. Wondering if Baby had noticed that, despite having disobeyed the voice's command, he hadn't died.

"Oh, then," Baby said cheerfully, "then the voice says: 'Today it doesn't matter.'"

What are you thinking, doctor?

Well, it's obvious. You couldn't come up with a neater example of the difference between psychosis and neurosis, we'll bet, if you practiced your dubious profession for a hundred years. You know what we mean? A psychotic is someone who doesn't hear a voice at the last minute saying, "Today it doesn't matter."

Don't you agree, doctor?

It's not that we're asking you to give us much hope. But he's not crazy. That's not what's wrong.

Maybe it's worse.

Tuesday

Baby's become a vegetarian. We're humoring him. He'll outgrow that, don't you think?

Cottage cheese and fresh pineapple. And lots of raw peas. He always has some in his pockets.

And his pockets always have holes. If you want to sum it up, there it is.

He never takes care of his things. Clothes are to wreck, as far as Baby is concerned.

He's stopped wearing underwear. Is that a fashion these days among junior-high-school kids, doctor?

Baby likes to hold his breath under the water in the bathtub. He's got a stop watch.

Baby hasn't washed in two months.

1-Y. He was all ready to go to Canada, he said. We were beside ourselves. But it turned out the adenoids were good enough. Of course, we'd feel safer with a 4-F. But Baby says they're really the same now and that we shouldn't worry.

He doesn't respect any of the conventions any more. At his high-school graduation, when they played "Land of Hope and Glory," we cried. Baby didn't even go.

Don't think we're feeling sorry for ourselves. We're probably better off than most parents. Two of Baby's friends have OD'd. One suicide. And his best friend in high school is doing one to five in San Quentin for holding up gas stations.

He's certainly holding his own.

Maybe we expected too much of him. The way you do with an only—

All we hope is that some of the damage can be undone. That's not too much to ask, is it?

If he would only confide in us, tell us some of his problems. Then we could help him better. He knows we know it's not easy to belong to his generation.

We both had hard lives. Nobody gave us a head start, and we've had to work to get where we are now. But at least we could take certain things for granted.

The family.

Poor Baby! You've got to help us help him. We'll never forgive ourselves if we don't.

His life is just beginning, ours is at least half over. It isn't fair, doctor!

We'll do anything.

But what more can we do?

Wednesday

Baby has asked more than once how babies are made. We tell him, but he always forgets and asks again in a few weeks.

It must be that he can't connect it with anything in his experience. We feel awfully silly explaining it over and over.

But if we don't answer his questions, he's liable to think there's something shameful about the whole business.

He's quite dexterous. He learned to tie his shoelaces on a wooden shoe in one morning flat.

A friend of ours gave Baby a Marine flak jacket for his birthday. Of course, it's much too large now. He'll have to grow into it.

Ronnie Yates. He runs the heliport in Venice West. He got stuck on helicopters during the war. Baby loves to hear Ronnie's war stories.

Baby wants a set of barbells and an exercise machine. It seems to us he gets enough exercise already. Sheer narcissism, that's what it looks like to us.

He's always chinning himself.

Baby wants to get a tattoo. A black sun between his shoulder blades, larger than a silver dollar.

Yes, but if he ever gets tired of it, he won't be able to have it taken off. They say it's awfully painful to do that.

He may be stoical, but he's not that stoical.

Everybody has their limit of pain, isn't that so, doctor?

Of course, he's healthy. That isn't the point. No matter how many times the pediatrician gives him a clean bill of health, we can see with our own eyes.

Baby has found a guru. Doctor, he looks so awful with his hair long. Sickly. The guru lives in a dune buggy parked by the San Pedro marina. Baby is planning to go with them on an expedition to Guatemala, gathering medicinal herbs.

Threatened and threatened him. We told him right away we'd cut off his allowance. But they had warned him that would be a part of his initiation.

But we hate to think that our authority over Baby finally rests on the simple fact that we're still supporting him.

His wife apparently doesn't want to go. That's our only hope. She's scheduled to give some noon and midnight poetry readings at Farmers Market in April, and she doesn't want to pass up the opportunity.

Yes, but it all depends on whether Baby really loves her.

Frankly, we don't think Baby knows what love is. That's his problem.

Wednesday

What we're afraid of, doctor—it's an awful thing to have to say—is that Baby is poisoning us. We discovered him trying to synthesize parathion in his lab in the garage the other night. When we asked him what he was doing, he looked scared and didn't answer at first.

You're right. We should have told you before. But there are some things that are just too painful to face. Even the bravest of us become ostriches from time to time, isn't that so?

We've heard that three drops is enough.

Did we mention that he won the citywide Bausch & Lomb Science Award in high school? And it was he who founded the chemistry club in his high school.

Astronomy, too. Baby asked for a telescope for Christmas.

Of course, we wish he'd read more. Literature, that is. He must take after one of us that way. You can't get him near a book that isn't some manual all full of charts and formulas. Still, it's more practical to be interested in science.

Did you ever want to be anything other than a doctor when you were a child?

What a strange ambition.

Baby is so single-minded. Once he decides something, you can't budge him. You wouldn't believe how stubborn he is.

Sure, everybody hates to be wrong. But Baby takes it much harder than most people.

Changed the subject? How?

But what can we do? We don't have any proof. We can't call the police.

Oh, we threw it out. When he wasn't looking. He hasn't said anything about it yet.

Well, we certainly aren't sleeping as well as we used to.

With the lights on.

Of course, we're keeping our date with the Turnells tonight. If we don't, Baby is sure to get suspicious. We can't let on that we know.

That's the only advantage we have right now. He thinks we're dumb. That we haven't noticed a thing.

No, how could Dr. Greenwich help? He's never even met Baby.

Well, if we don't show up for tomorrow's sessions, at least you'll know, doctor.

You hate wisecracks, don't you, doctor? Listen, if we were serious about this all the time, we'd go crazy.

Look, don't worry. You want us to give you a call around midnight, just so as you'll know we haven't received our forty and forty-one whacks, respectively?

No. Baby's supposed to go to a yo-yo tournament with Bert at the Wilshire Ebell Theatre.

Baby has fantasies of omnipotence.

No. Much more specific. What it is is that he thinks that everyone he sees is blessed, something like that, because he looks at that person. If only just for one second, in a crowd. So he has to travel around as much as possible, so his glance will catch the greatest number of people.

He says it's his responsibility.

Well, not exactly blessed. But their lives become different, once he has looked at them. All the people he's seen will get what they deserve. The good will be rewarded. And the bad people will be punished, eventually.

We think so too, doctor.

No. He says he hasn't decided whether the look works for people he only sees in photographs or on TV.

That would give his powers a much wider scope, wouldn't it? Perhaps we should be encouraged that he's at least hesitating there.

Justice! What's justice got to do with it? That's the last thing in the world that interests Baby.

He wants to make us feel bad. He wants to make us feel unwanted in our own home.

Thursday

What are you being so aggressive for, doctor? If you don't think you can help us, we can see someone else.

Defensive, then, if you like.

Well, of course, everything is relative. Isn't it, doctor?

We want Baby to be more independent.

He's devious. That's the word. He never tells us anything.

A water bed. We have to keep Baby off or he'd wreck it.

He wants to make us feel like outcasts.

We're bleeding. Can't you see, doctor? Help us.

Are you a medical doctor?

Yes. Much better.

Oh. Did we tell you that Baby has a gun in the closet? He's an N.R.A. junior marksman.

Then you do think it's possible to make poisons with a Chemcraft set. A big, expensive one.

He has everything set up in the garage. That limits the damage, at least. Like when he burned himself with his Bunsen burner.

Baby got gassed at an anti-war demonstration at the Long Beach Naval Base.

He was always a natural pacifist. When he was four, we read him a child's version of the *Iliad* and he wept at the death of Patroclus.

We're hiding the book from him until he's older.

Baby carries a picture of Steve McQueen in his wallet. That's the sort of person he admires now.

He's trying to grow a mustache.

Maybe he got tired of being a sensitive child. But don't you think he's gone too far in the opposite direction? We never asked him to be a genius and we never asked him to be a slob.

Baby's teacher came over this morning and told us he beat up a little kid in his class and took away his lunch money.

We wouldn't be surprised if he joined the Hells Angels. Or worse.

If they'll have him. Baby's not as tough as he thinks.

Oh, doctor, it's terrible to want something from a child. Baby is right. We should be treating him like a visitor from another planet. We shouldn't care what the hell he does. We should be taking care of ourselves, for a change, instead of throwing good money after bad.

Not you, doctor.

Thursday

We had to cut Baby's right hand off. It was the only way. He kept playing with himself.

We made a little wheelchair for Baby. And a bed with sides, so he doesn't fall out.

We had to cut his left foot off, because he tried to run away again.

All we wanted for him was to be happy, make a living, rear a family, contribute to society, and stay out of trouble.

Do you believe everything we tell you, doctor?

That's not really an answer. Maybe it's part of your profession to be evasive, but for once we're asking you a direct question. Why don't you answer?

Of course, we're telling you the truth.

About the foot?

That's right.

And the hand.

But we *told* you it was a terrible situation, doctor.

Maybe you see too many people who have to exaggerate in order to get your attention.

If you want to know the truth, our problem is that we tend to minimize things. We like to face life with a cheerful point of view. There's enough horror in the world without inventing more, don't you think, doctor?

Sure. Of course, you probably have an overly sad view of life. Since you spend most of your time listening to people complain. We've always felt that the more positively you confront a situation, the more likely it is to turn out well. At least to your advantage.

Because even disasters can be a blessing, can't they? They teach you something. You become wiser.

What doesn't kill you makes you stronger.

Exactly. That's how we try to approach the situation with Baby.

Baby says what doesn't kill you leaves scars. He's right, too.

Sure, it's horrible. That's what we've been trying to tell you all along.

Didn't you believe us?

For God's sake, doctor. Now's a fine time to tell us that—after all these weeks. And then calmly look at your watch and say it's the end of the session. Put yourself in our place.

All right. Maybe we've accomplished something today, after all.

Friday

It was Dr. Greenwich who saved our marriage. Before joining the group, we were so caught up in the rat race, we'd completely lost touch with each other. Just going to their meetings once a week—

Sometimes.

Yes.

You're right.

It's a relief to talk about ourselves for a change. We envy your other patients, doctor.

Well, back to work.

Of course, we do. Isn't that natural?

He could get work part-time in the post office or drive a truck. Jim Turnell offered him a job as a data shipping clerk in his Van Nuys warehouse. But he says he doesn't want to do anything.

We've offered Baby the summer in Japan, Mexico, if he promises to take a job in the fall, when he comes back. But he says he doesn't like to travel. Isn't that awful, at his age?

Not blasé, exactly. All the kids of his generation are a little blasé. But it's not that.

He seems angry.

Sometimes it just doesn't seem worth it. Neither of us ever had much chance to travel when we were young. But he just doesn't seem to appreciate that.

Have you traveled much, doctor? Apart from being born abroad, that is.

When?

That soon?

You're probably hoping you can finish the work with us by then, aren't you?

Doesn't matter.

Listen, we've been thinking. The financial burden of the two sessions daily is a bit more than we can bear. We're going to have to cut back to one a day.

No, Dr. Greenwich didn't say a thing. We decided by ourselves. You didn't expect that, did you?

Tomorrow?

Saturday

About travel and enjoying life while you can—

Don't you remember? What we were saying yesterday. Some things are just wasted on some people.

Not you, doctor. Baby.

Baby thinks he's going to live forever. We don't want to disillusion him. It's great to be young and not know what the world is about.

Maybe somebody should tell him he's not going to live forever.

No. He wouldn't believe it coming from us. It should be some older, wise person. If he knew someone like you, doctor, you could tell him.

Tell him he's not going to live forever. Tell him that we aren't, either. Tell him that one of us has to die first and that we've made a new will. Tell him not to hate us. Tell him what we've done was meant for the best. Tell him we couldn't help it. Tell him we're not monsters. Tell him how monstrous he's been to us. Tell him he has no right to judge us. Tell him we don't have to all live together, if he doesn't want to. Tell him he's free. Tell him he can't leave us alone. Tell him he's killing us. Tell him he can't get away with it. Tell him he's not our Baby, that he was born on Krypton. Tell him we hate him. Tell him we never loved each other but only him. Tell him we didn't know any better. Tell him we've gone away forever and the house and the station wagon are his and the spare set of keys is under the door mat, and that we've remade the will entirely in his favor and disinherited Bert. Tell him he'll never find us. Tell him we'll be waiting on the patio by the fountain in the cute little house in San Miguel de Allende. Tell him we'll get him an arithmetic tutor so he won't flunk fourth grade again. Tell him he can have a dog—Malemute, old English sheep dog. Samoyed, Saint Bernard, whatever, as big and stupid as he wants. Tell him we did try to get an abortion, but the doctor was in Acapulco. Tell him we met Steve McQueen last year and didn't ask for his autograph. Tell him we poisoned Laurie: Billy too, but it didn't work, that's why only Laurie died. Tell him we threw out his collection of old issues of *Rolling Stone* and *National Lampoon* behind his back, not the maid. Tell him to wear underwear, because it's disgusting not to wear underwear. Tell him to take his vitamin pills, and the yeast and the rose hips. Tell him Thelma DeLara's mother is a dyke. Tell him he's not any better than we are. Tell him we should never have had children, but we thought we ought to. Tell him we never wanted him to be like us. Tell him it's too hard to bring up a child, especially an only child, and he'll see that one day when he grows up. Tell him he's got to drink milk. Tell him he looks ridiculous with a mustache. Tell him not to take out his braces at night or his teeth will never get straight. Tell him to blow his nose. Tell him the dog can shit all over the living-room rug for all we care. Tell him he got ripped off and the stuff he's hoarding in the Skippy jar is birdseed and oregano. Tell him he'll understand us one day when he has children of his own. Tell him we were born on Krypton and were just pretending to be his parents, but we've gotten tired of concealing our superpowers beneath this meek, mild-mannered exterior and have flown away. Tell him he'll miss us when he has to manage on his own. Tell him to feel guilty. Tell him to come off it and burn his Superman suit. Tell him he's not going to win the Nobel Prize; or if he ever does, by then he'll be so old he won't care any more. Tell him how proud of him we always were, and are. Tell him how he intimidated us. Tell him we know he stole the money. Tell him to clean up his room. Tell him to write Aunt Rae the thank-you note for the roller skates. Tell him he has to renew his registration and that he can't drive the Toyota around with one headlight. Tell him how we lied. Tell him how sorry we are. Tell him we're victims, too. Tell him our childhoods weren't any better than his. Tell him how we wept with joy when he was born. Tell him when he was born we started to die. Tell him that we tried to kill him. Tell him that we knew what we were doing. Tell him that we love him.

Oh God, doctor, why did our Baby have to die?

DOCTOR JEKYLL

J ekyll is thinking. Somewhere else, Gabriel Utterson is examining Jekyll's dossier, a thick, somewhat soiled tan folder with the doctor's surname followed by the initial "H." neatly printed in purple ink on the flap. Jekyll lies on the sloping beach, under-used for a Saturday in May, searching his mouth with his tongue to expel some sand. His toddler lurches along the water's edge, his wife has gone up to the station wagon to change from her wet bikini into a dry one. With his back pressed against the scorched sand, his belly flattened under the hot sun, Jekyll is thinking about the war, Utterson is perched on a high old-fashioned architect's chair (one that doesn't swivel), thinking about Jekyll, and between these two points a line might be drawn, a physical link between them like a long nylon thread. It might run from the gaudy cowboy belt that Utterson has put on today, to confound extra-pious disciples in town, straight to Jekyll's right ankle here in East Hampton. Utterson is wearing tinted bifocals. Were Jekyll to tug hard on his end, or make any sudden violent movement, Utterson might be jolted out of his chair. If he falls, his spectacles might be broken.

Jekyll looks at his white toes, flexes them. Could messages using words be sent along this thread? In code, of course. Or is only violence transmissible? Jekyll's right ankle begins to itch. The idea of sending messages suggests a problem that Jekyll has been chewing over for months. Clearly Utterson has sources of information to which Jekyll is denied access. Jekyll's handsome leg begins to tremble: he'd like to get these messages, too. Is there a circuit he could plug into? A sand crab nips his toe. Jekyll jerks his right foot viciously.

Inside the cabin the Jekylls rent in Labrador for the whole of June, the good doctor, nerves strung tight by the long hours he puts in all year at the clinic, doesn't take advantage of his vacation to unwind. He is thinking about Utterson. The walls are fragrant and rough to the touch. The bed sheets smell of camphor. Fir trees filter the crisp northern heat, and the mountains rising on all sides make the days short, too short; the sun doesn't surface until eight in the morning and has slid behind a snowy peak by five.

Outdoors, thoughts of Utterson spring less frequently to mind. Other risks become more attractive. Jekyll saunters through the woods, as carefree as he's ever likely to be, the astringent taste of liberty in his mouth. By three, breaking a halfhearted promise to his wife not to attempt anything dangerous in the way of mountaineering, he is almost to the top of a steep mountain. This climb would normally be no grand exploit for Jekyll, a competent Alpinist since his year as a postgraduate medical student in Vienna. What does make a mishap possible is that Jekyll is taking someone much less experienced up with him: Richard Enfield, his wife's cousin, who is sharing the cabin with them for the first week.

Jekyll advances nimbly, hand over hand, with Enfield following, dogged will power firmly in control of his neglected suburban body. Glancing below, Jekyll spies Enfield absorbed in a duel with a boulder, slowed to a crawl. Jekyll stops instantly, to maintain the right degree of slackness in the rope tying them together. Sure that his cousin-in-law is not in serious trouble, Jekyll isn't going to embarrass Enfield by pointing out an easy way to clamber past the obstacle, and turns away, splendidly vertical.

Jekyll inhales joyously. His torso is free as long as his left elbow stays braced in a crevasse in the rock face. His feet feel reassuringly heavy, sure, the soles of his climbing boots secured, almost welded to the narrow ledge on which he stands, waiting for Enfield to heave his other leg over the boulder and scramble up beside him. He checks the tautness of the rope that rises from his waist to the loop he's thrown to a cornice above, then yanks hard. The loop holds. He looks upward. The sun is still high. Dry-mouthed, contemptuous of his craving for a cigarette, Jekyll pulls more clean air into his long, robust body. He is not thinking of Utterson. He would be, though, if a substitution could be made, if Utterson were in Enfield's place, tied waist to waist to Jekyll, equally inept. For then Jekyll could imagine cutting the rope and letting Utterson fend for himself during this last, most strenuous part of the ascent. But he would be unlikely to go so far as to imagine Utterson panicking, losing his grip, scraping the air, shrieking like a flayed pig, hurtling from rock to rock down to the fjord below.

Tanned and fit, back from his Canadian holiday, Jekyll is loitering on an empty street below the North Tower of the World Trade Center. He's waiting for Hyde, who is supposed to bring a message. Hyde is usually late, but not this late. Jekyll has skipped lunch to keep this date with Hyde, who, by insisting on meeting at the World Trade Center, which is out of everyone's way, and on a Sunday, shows that he hasn't lost his yen for the picturesque rendezvous. Utterson, who drove into town this morning with a sample entourage and has not skipped one meal in the past thirty years, is midlunch at the Russian Tea Room. He is sucking on an unlit pipe, hungry-eyed, truculently waiting for his second order of borscht

and pirojkis. It is possible that a line extends from the flattish back
of Utterson's head to Jekyll's striped tie or the laces of his new ox-
fords. But Jekyll doesn't consider this possibility. He's too preoccu-
pied with Hyde.

The young man Jekyll expects to materialize at any moment
no longer makes it into town often; today, if he comes, it's as a special favor to his respectable would-be alter ego. Also, if he comes,
he won't look the way he is usually pictured. In the old days, the
days of his citified wickedness, Hyde got the reputation of being
big and hulking. But this was a fantasy concocted from nineteenth-
century middle-class nightmares about the immigrant urban poor,
and diffused in our own century by Hollywood monster movies. The
truth, which once perplexed Jekyll, is that Hyde is small, sickly,
and younger than he is. "Naturally," Utterson has explained. "The
evil part of your nature is less developed than the good part."
Jekyll is not convinced by Utterson's allegorical view of their physical disparity. For one thing, he finds it too flattering to himself,
too dismissive of Hyde. Jekyll has not been all that good. And
hasn't Hyde been delinquent enough? Jekyll suspects that Hyde's
dwarfish stature and feeble stamina have a more banal, simply
physical cause: a bad case of childhood rheumatic fever that was
misdiagnosed by the school pediatrician and neglected by his ignorant parents. Hyde looks more underprivileged than monstrous.
His fanglike teeth are not so much bestial as bad, despite extensive
dental work done in his early twenties, which Jekyll paid for; and
he still suffers from bleeding gums. The quantity and distribution
of Hyde's body hair have also been exaggerated. It's true that Hyde
is hirsute and Jekyll is, for a Caucasian male, relatively hairless.
However, while Jekyll has a well-barbered head of thick brown
hair with no white hairs showing, which hasn't begun to recede at
the forehead and temples, the younger man's greasy black shoulder-
length hair is already starting to fall out. Utterson is bald, entirely

bald. Jekyll is not wearing a hat, for if he were it would be blown
away.

Jekyll steadies himself against the unseasonable July wind to
keep from being pushed over to the tower wall. Perhaps a hurricane is blowing up prematurely from the Caribbean. Just as he is
about to give up and go home, he glimpses the puny figure of his
old protégé, who still affects the black cape he stole years ago from
an East Village boutique, stumping along at a good walk. Jekyll
waves. Hyde hurries near, then nearer, then speeds right past him—
as if he didn't see him at all. "Wait!" Jekyll shouts, grabbing for the
billowing black cape. Hyde breaks into a lope, but Jekyll catches
up with him at the far corner.

"I'm in a jam," Hyde whines. "I can't stop."

"I must talk to you," says Jekyll.

"Then come on up to my country place," Hyde barks hoarsely.
He seems winded. "This dude is waiting for me now—"

"It's Utterson. Right?"

"Hell, no! Stop hassling me!" Hyde feints, eludes Jekyll's grasp,
and lunges around the corner. Disappointed, Jekyll lets him escape. He crosses the street thoughtfully, enters a cafeteria, sits at a
window table, and asks for an iced coffee. At the moment the waitress arrives with his order, he sees the bony figure in the cape veer-
ing around the block again, panting, but still keeping the same rapid
pace. Jekyll lights a cigarette, then stubs it out (he's almost quit
smoking), sips his coffee, and waits. The drink is two-thirds ice, most
of which he removes with his fingers and drops into the ashtray. A
few minutes later, Hyde rounds the corner again.

Jekyll is willing to suppose that Hyde will keep circling the
block all afternoon, and feels like watching a while longer. But
the waitress has come over and presented him with the check so that
he will vacate his table. Indignant, Jekyll points out that the cafeteria is almost deserted. She won't be budged. "One beverage is worth

fifteen minutes," she recites. "It's a rule of the management. I don't make the rules around here."

"But you can break the rules," Jekyll says.

"How can I do that?" she answers.

Jekyll pauses, debating whether he should stick to his principles or order another undrinkable iced coffee. It is conceivable that, with the cord that might extend from the harness of a parachute that Jekyll could be wearing (in case he might be so foolish as to be tempted to leap from the top of the World Trade Center) to Utterson's left wrist, provided that at this moment Utterson is at the estate out at Oyster Bay (but he isn't; he is noisily drinking his third bowl of borscht and munching his eighth pirojki in midtown Manhattan), something could happen that would stop Hyde dead in his tracks. For if the rope were properly tied and Utterson were in the place where he usually is, which would put him north-northwest of the cafeteria where Jekyll sits, then he, Jekyll, could trip Hyde the next time he rushed around the block. But for this feat he would need Utterson's help, and Jekyll is never sure how well disposed toward him Utterson really is.

"What's happened to your confidence in me?" That's Utterson speaking. It is the first word he has directed to Jekyll since Jekyll took a seat at the long oval table in the pseudo-medieval refectory out at Oyster Bay. Utterson is entertaining a Mr. Carew, ambivalent admirer and prospective pupil, who, being a senior trade-book editor at an important publishing house, is arranging for the paperback reissue of Utterson's long-out-of-print, thousand-page summum, *The Strange Case of Cain and Abel*; and Jekyll, along with three staff members and a handful of pupils in residence at the Institute, has been convened for lunch. Utterson is in his usual chair. Toward the end of the meal, he has been garrulously calculating the huge royalties the book is going to earn and lamenting his debts. Jekyll sits in one of the straight-backed chairs designed by Utterson for his pupils.

"My boy, I'm going to tell you something that, really, you are not eligible to know. Only those who are more developed, who have advanced further in the Work, know it." Two pupils lingering at the table stare avidly at Utterson, enviously at Jekyll. Without glancing at their side of the table, Utterson instructs one to wait for him in the Study House and the other to mow the front lawns, and doesn't continue until after they push back their chairs carefully, get up, and leave. "I receive messages from the future."

Even when frustrated by Utterson's habit of claiming anterior knowledge of everything that others tell him, Jekyll can't be as skeptical as he might like, because Utterson has so often demonstrated cool, inexplicable powers of clairvoyance. But he has never heard Utterson state his claim so impudently.

"Well?" says Utterson.

"I'm flattered . . ."

"You think too much about the body, Henry," Utterson says impatiently. "That feels natural to a doctor, but it's one-sided. You've never grasped a spiritual truth."

Jekyll bows his head at Utterson's reproach, while stubbornly continuing to think it unjust. This position gives him a mild cramp in his shoulder muscles, so he straightens up. "And the secret?" he says.

Utterson is sitting cross-legged on the raised platform in the center of the circular Study House, addressing some pupils. "Do what you will," he says, "and you'll find out how little you *can* will."

To English, which isn't his native language (as Utterson was not his name), he imparts a solemn and musical intonation. "Only a tiny part of your life is under your control," he declares. "As you are, you have no will."

He also says: "Try to know what you're feeling." He explains: "Observe yourself, yes. But as if you were a machine. You are nothing but your behavior."

Changing the metaphor, he adds: "And your behavior, your words are all aped."

And later: "Introspection is bad. You have nothing to look into."

And still later: "Begin with the body. It's the only tool you have."

Meanwhile, having finished his afternoon stint at the clinic, Jekyll is down to sweat pants and shower clogs and is working out in a private gym on Lexington Avenue. From the other side of the room, the Nicaraguan coach compliments him on his skill with the punching bag. With each punch that he throws, Jekyll feels the blood circulating more happily in his body. He thinks of Hyde, who was rarely able to overwhelm his victims by sheer physical force, but usually had to use some nasty weapon; and, even then, needed first to weaken them with the shock of his tense, misbegotten face, his stooped, undernourished figure, his outlandish, neo-diabolical garb. He had always expected Hyde to fill out, to become bigger, taller— if not simply with passing time, then as the result of gymnastics ("movements," Utterson calls them) that Hyde did when he was briefly in residence at the Institute. Spiritual gymnastics is not enough, Jekyll concludes, hardly for the first time, throwing a last vicious right hook at the punching bag. Utterson, his broad face turning brick pink from an hour's nonstop talking in the Study House, ducks slightly, rubs his shiny hard scalp, then sways with laughter. He, in his turn, concludes that he is getting careless. And that from now on he'd better give more thought to Jekyll.

As Hyde takes Jekyll for granted, the indifference of the ugly to the genteel, Jekyll envies Hyde, the envy of the almost middle-aged for the young. In spite of his confident, responsive body and a driving schedule of work, Jekyll regards himself as low in vitality ("fifty watts," Utterson once jeered behind his back); no matter how exemplary a physician he becomes, he accuses himself of a chronic deficit of initiative. Hyde agrees. Utterson's Institute for Deprogramming Potential Human Beings attracts far too many people of this type.

Hyde, of course, so far as he could be counted as having passed through Utterson's hands, would be an exception. Despite his frail build and chronic colds, Hyde is someone who always finds his second wind. He has always been enterprising. When he first came to Jekyll's attention, referred to the clinic for a skin disease by a psychiatrist at the High School of Industrial Trades, Hyde already seemed grown up, though he was only stealing cars then, and was just assembling his lucrative stable of thirteen-year-old boy and girl prostitutes. Raised in an impoverished family (his father is a janitor) with many children, he had to learn early to fight for whatever he wanted. Jekyll comes from a prosperous home (his father still commutes every day from Darien to Wall Street) and has one sister, who is an eminent biochemist, and no brothers. Utterson, who long ago changed his name to Gabriel Utterson from Gavril Uniades, claims to be a foundling. He denies indignantly that he could have had any sisters or brothers (other than his spiritual brethren in faraway Tibet, where he studied Transcendental Medicine forty years ago) but is given to boasting on almost any occasion about the swarm of illegitimate children he's fathered in the State of New York. Jekyll assumes that Poole, the very young pupil trembling on the brink of puberty, who sleeps on a cot in the hall outside Utterson's door and acts as his valet, is actually one of these bastards.

Cleaning up after Utterson occupies most of Poole's day, which starts when, each morning, Utterson shouts for him to enter, and Poole does, to find the bed in violent, wet disarray. There are acrid, heavy stains on the other furniture and on the carpet. There is

excrement on the walls of his dressing room. As for the bathroom!—
Poole has visions of great involuntary physiological epics enacted
nightly in the dressing room and bathroom. Or Utterson may be
aiming consciously to destroy these rooms—perhaps to test the development of Poole's will, his "true will," as Utterson would put it,
as the boy labors in his service. But either way, there would be no
point in beginning the actual cleaning until Utterson has finished
his breakfast, which is always taken in bed, for merely drinking
coffee can produce a holocaust: coffee spattered all over the room
as well as in the bed. When, as he sometimes does, Utterson takes
his late-afternoon coffee in his room in the presence of members
of his staff and a few pupils, the bed must be remade with fresh
sheets a second time. Though often questioned by the irreverent
and the curious, Poole—conscious of the great honor of serving
Utterson—refuses to describe the exact state of Utterson's quarters. And it is doubtful whether the details would give much preci-
sion to the persistent rumors that far more goes on there than
the consumption of coffee and the denouement of Utterson's diges-
tive dramas. All that Poole could truthfully testify to—from the
evidence of each morning's disorder, its variety, its thickness—is
that almost any human activity could have taken place there the
night before.

Utterson is being served eggs, steak, and coffee on a tray. Someone is lying next to Utterson, buried under the heap of blankets
and befouled sheets, but Poole can't make out who it is. Well trained,
he does not guess. The boy goes into the dressing room and sur-
veys the walls to see if he'll need a stepladder this morning. Meanwhile, Jekyll gets out of bed delicately so as not to wake his wife,
tiptoes across their bedroom, and goes through the apartment to
the kitchen to make breakfast. He is walking barefoot not for fear
of disturbing Utterson in Oyster Bay, who's already awake anyway,
gulping his coffee directly from the battered old thermos bottle,

but because he, Jekyll, revels in the feel of the pile carpet under his feet.

Sweating, white-lipped, Jekyll is jogging in Central Park. It's just twilight. A thin clay-colored pall lowers over the trees, but the wind is continually slicing into and redistributing the smog, so that Jekyll runs metronomically through many degrees and hues of twilight, some black, some dark green, some reddish-brown, all back-lit by the cubes of electric brightness multiplying minute by minute on the stolid ramparts along Fifth Avenue. Jekyll continues, paralleling the Reservoir. The gravel sounds under his sneakers, and it would be foolish to think that someone is following him; other people jog in the park, too. It's in the park that Hyde used to lurk, preying on strollers, crazies, baby nurses, and joggers. But Jekyll will stroll or jog here at any hour. He is not afraid. Ultimately, Jekyll has learned, one is only afraid of oneself. He has mastered the terror of Hyde, he has mastered himself. In Jekyll's schedule, as in the normal schedule of any alert city dwellers, there are always slots for danger. Jekyll keeps jogging. Then the voice speaks to him.

Is this a voice in my mind, Jekyll asks himself.

Once there were other voices that came and accused him, but Jekyll had decided—after a complex procedure in which he demanded that each voice accredit itself—that all these voices were interior voices. He dismissed them. They went. Now, with this one, he is not so sure.

Jekyll slows down. He has glimpsed a pair of feet in high heels between two bushes. Run! No, stop. He retraces his steps, grim-mouthed, his pulse leaping. Face down behind the bushes, moaning, is a black woman in a tight red skirt and pink satin blouse. Jekyll kneels next to the open purse lying at her side, and turns her over. She looks about forty-five, shows the usual signs of Cushing's syndrome, and is bleeding from a ragged cut on her face and a deep slash on her left arm. Jekyll stands and steps back onto the path, looking about to see if there is anyone to assist him. The woman moans. The twilight is advancing languidly into darkness. Nobody is in sight.

Stooping, Jekyll gathers the woman into his arms, then falls to his knees, then manages to stand up. Since recently he has lifted patients as heavy as she with ease, Jekyll wonders if he is getting out of condition. Still, he is doing better than Utterson would, if Utterson were here, stooping beside a bush, trying to pick up a heavy body. Utterson looks strong, but that's mainly because he's fat. And the carbuncle embedded in his right side must pain him sometimes. Should Utterson, because he likes to show off, be trying right now to lift one of his docile pupils above his head, he'd probably keel over, Jekyll thinks with tense pleasure. Jekyll slowly makes his way to the road with his inert burden, looking for a squad car or a taxi.

Jekyll is sitting to one side of the twelve-foot-high fireplace (under the bogus heraldic arms) of the great hall—the main building of the Oyster Bay estate being a Languedoc castle built in the 1920s by a Long Island faucet millionaire, and the rent for the whole property being a sum paid annually by one of Utterson's most generous admirers, a Texas oil magnate's widow now living in Bermuda. Utterson, in dinner clothes and a starched shirt, his haunches filling the big upholstered chair opposite Jekyll, is toying with a water pistol. In the far shadows of the room, under an Art Deco stained-glass window depicting the Grail saga in ten panes, a pupil is taking notes. Jekyll has come out to complain about being spied on. He's sure that his phone is tapped and his mail is being opened.

Utterson, who never expresses astonishment at anything

others tell him, and rarely disagrees, smiles ironically this time. "Perhaps you've done something to get you in trouble with the civil authorities. Your views on the war, for instance. Or some irregularity in your practice, like prescribing illegal drugs, or not doing enough to prolong the life of a patient with terminal cancer, or—"

"No." Jekyll shakes his head. "Nothing like that. I'm sure it's being done by people from the Institute."

"Wouldn't I know about it, if that were so?"

"Would you?" asks Jekyll.

"If I can see into the future"—glancing at the pupil in the corner bent over his notebook, Utterson winks at Jekyll—"you might assume that I can see into the present, too."

"And you don't see any danger, anyone shadowing me, keeping track of my movements, trying to scare me into giving up what I'd like to do?"

Utterson lets fly one of his celebrated scornful looks. "What about your friend Hyde? I've told you he's dangerous company for you."

"Nonsense," says Jekyll. "I never see Hyde any more. And besides, you know what he's become now. Why, he just"—he pauses—"just goes round and round in circles."

"Don't grin like an idiot. You didn't say anything funny."

"I did," says Jekyll.

"I, I, I," Utterson roars. "Do you hear yourself?" He aims the water pistol at Jekyll. "Who has the right to say 'I'?" He slams it to the floor. "Not you! Do you hear? That's a right that has to be earned!"

Jekyll stares back at him defiantly. "And Ed Hyde?" he says. "Can Hyde say 'I'?"

"Why not?" Utterson replies. "As long as he keeps—as you say—going around in circles. You understand now?"

Jekyll doesn't understand. Something better than understanding has happened. Utterson has put an idea in Jekyll's head. But since it's not an idea he intended to put there, it doesn't make his large bald head any lighter; it only makes Jekyll's head heavier. If Jekyll bounded out of his chair, flung himself onto the upholstered chair with the man in it opposite him, and knocked his heavy head against Utterson's—but he must do it right now, while the balance of physical forces has tilted ever so slightly in his, Jekyll's, favor— it is conceivable that Utterson's head might crack open, all his ideas spill out, and Jekyll, not Utterson, possess the secrets of the harmonious development of humankind. But Jekyll is not sure he wants the responsibility of having all that wisdom in his keeping. Look at the repulsively contradictory, heathen creature it's made of Utterson: someone both taciturn and voluble, mercenary and ascetic, glib and wise, plebeian and princely, obscene and pure, indolent and energetic, cunning and naïve, snobbish and democratic, unfeeling and compassionate, impractical and shrewd, irritable and patient, capricious and reliable, sickly and sturdy, young and old, empty and full, heavy as cement and light as helium.

Utterson once said, "I am a human being without quotation marks." Jekyll holds no such exalted view of himself. It's enough that Jekyll has pilfered his new idea about Hyde; and, in back of that, in case the first idea fails, another idea. About Hyde.

Jekyll is visiting his sister, who works at Rockefeller University, with his first idea. It's to ask if she and her colleagues can devote some of their spare time to developing a formula (to be ingested as a pill, capsule, suppository, or syrup) that would sack the very fortress of identity. What he has in mind is a formula that would enable him occasionally to become his young friend Hyde. Become Hyde physically, he means. For Jekyll is willing—from time to time, when he thinks it might be useful or stimulating, or simply when he senses that he's languishing—actually to inhabit Hyde's runty body. The prize is the increment in energy: the different species of energy from his own that Hyde possesses. And he is willing, in a most brotherly spirit, provided that the length of the exchange be settled in advance, to let Hyde borrow his own intelligent, solid body. Nothing less than a real exchange would be fair, though Jekyll doesn't intend to let Hyde put his hairy hands, with nicotine-stained fingers and nails chewed down to their moons, upon his beloved wife.

Understandably, it is the scoundrel of some years ago whom he wishes to become: Hyde of the prodigious crimes, Hyde before he was rehabilitated or lost his nerve, Hyde before he was tamed by Utterson, Hyde before he moved to a rural slum upstate. Certainly Hyde before he fell in love, with a redheaded ex-go-go dancer recently turned respectable who was a stewardess on Mohawk Airlines and who, two years later, fatigued by Hyde's amorous abuses, left him for a Volvo dealer in Great Neck. Jekyll supposes that Hyde's unexpected fall into love—invulnerable, lascivious, jaded, heartless Hyde, in love!—was what finally broke his spirit, and not the ministrations of Utterson, as is so often claimed. Jekyll longs to see the old Hyde again, careering through the dark dockside streets of Chelsea on his Harley-Davidson, grinding his teeth, gunning his motor, an Andean Indian woman's bowler on his small head, his ridiculous black cape blowing behind him in the wind, bearing against his slight back the weight of some leather-jacketed apprentice hoodlum with three switchblades who hugs him around the waist, running down old ladies, delivering dope, tossing Molotov cocktails through the windows of anti-war organizations.

Jekyll is explaining how much preliminary work on the potion he's done in his own laboratory, why he is unable to push his research to a conclusion, and exactly how his sister, who has the newest and best technology for genetic code-breaking at her disposal, can help. His sister, wearing a white smock, her firm back (like Jekyll's) aligned with the metal doorframe of her shiny laboratory, is turning him down cordially. With the new Defense Department grant, the team is too busy now. She looks pretty, reminding Jekyll that good looks run in their family. He lingers a moment longer, more chagrined by the nature of his request than by her refusal, hoping to cover it with a joke. "Professor Guest. My brother Dr. Jekyll," she murmurs as one of her assistants squeezes past them through the doorway, bearing a rack of test tubes filled with reddish, dark purple, and watery green liquids. While shaking Guest's free hand, Jekyll remembers that he has promised to drop by to see Lanyon and give him a quick examination and a shot before checking back at the clinic. In Lanyon's midtown office thirty minutes later, bending over the elderly lawyer with his stethoscope, he imagines it is Utterson's heart that he hears thumping.

Somewhere else, in a suburb of London, a once famous opera singer is explaining Utterson to a skeptical friend. "Though he could make one frantic, furious, miserable, whenever there was a real contact everything seemed justified."

"But he's a pig! My God, when I think of that appalling story you told me about his asking you to—"

"Yes, yes," the ex-pupil interrupts. "I know it's hard to understand . . ." She sighs. "How can I explain? From the beginning . . . the first time I ever saw Mr. Utterson, I sensed a deep bond with him, a bond that grew stronger with the years. It was never a hypnotic tie, believe me. Mr. Utterson's teaching helps one be free of suggestion. This inner tie (I suppose you could call it a magnetic tie), this invisible bond with him, made Mr. Utterson the person *nearest* to one, in the true sense of the word. That proximity was . . . painful, much of the time. Once in a while, one got to see the 'real' Mr. Utterson, with whom one wished to stay forever. This was not the 'everyday' Mr. Utterson, who sometimes was gentle and sometimes very disagreeable, and whom you often wished to run away from."

"A clown," her friend interjects. "A drunk. A sadist. A charla—"

"But even then," continues the ex-pupil, "one stayed with him, because one's Work depended on it."

"But finally you left," says the friend.

"Mr. Utterson made me leave. He said I had enough energy now, and that I wasn't likely to have any more."

"You miss him."

"Of course," says the ex-pupil fiercely. "But I never want to see him again as long as I live."

Meanwhile, on another day, Utterson is sitting in the great hall of the Oyster Bay estate, giving fifteen minutes to Ron Newcomen, a former Weatherman who has recently surfaced from underground and has hitchhiked with all his possessions on his back from the Coast to the Institute in the hope of being admitted as a pupil. Utterson is refusing to take him on, telling him he is not fit for the Work: "You'll go only so far and then you'll quit." Without giving Newcomen time to bleat out his protests and promises, Utterson continues. "Don't plead with me. And don't tell me you're unhappy."

"But I am! I'm desperate."

"You'll be much more unhappy if you start the Work with me. Right now you are sitting in a chair, comfortably."

"I'm not comfortable," shouts Newcomen.

Utterson waves his hand impatiently. "If you get up from the chair without being able to do this method's Work, it is better not to get up. You'll never get back to that first chair once you leave it. You'll be standing all your life."

And on still another day, in the same impressive room, a disciple—a journalist who lives in Washington, D.C.—is telling

Utterson that he needs to put off his scheduled term of residence at the Institute until he finishes his book. "Forget about the book," Utterson says, frowning. "If you don't come now, later will be too late. Next spring you won't be able to come any more than you can kiss your own elbow."

At the same time, in the midst of examining a sobbing child in the emergency treatment room of his South Bronx clinic, Jekyll feels a sharp twinge in his elbow.

Pounding the floor with his bare feet, Jekyll stands in a circle with nine other disciples near a small door at one end of the vast, bare, lofty room known as the Exercise Hall. Built with trusses, it resembles an old airplane hangar. Beyond the door is a cubbyhole with a bed and a small window that allows a cheerful view of the orchard, where, years ago, a much-acclaimed Lithuanian poet spent the last months of her short life. Already, before coming to live at Oyster Bay, in an advanced stage of the tuberculosis she contracted during her years in Dachau, she was first assigned by Utterson to the cowshed; but when she became too weak to work, she was moved here, and the solitary beatitudes she experienced before her mouth completely filled with blood constitute one of the Institute's most precious legends. Utterson, whom some dissident disciples held responsible for her death, still mentions her occasionally in his Wake-up Talks. "Remember our lost sisters and brothers," he says. But Jekyll has no way of learning if her physical, as distinct from spiritual, health was really neglected. She died before he met Utterson or ever heard of the Institute.

The slow percussive rhythms continue. Jekyll (taking a weekend refresher at the Institute) is in a pantomime play that Utterson has devised, "The Struggle of the Magicians," whose story calls for the ten participants to be divided into five Bad Magicians and five Good Magicians. Everyone works in absolute silence. The movements are not strenuous—the opposite of the exercises Jekyll does at the gym with punching bag and barbells, of which Utterson disapproves. At the far end of the room, Utterson sits on a folding chair. He is wearing his tinted bifocals, which diffuse the impact of his pale blue eyes. What kind of magician is he?

Jekyll, who is playing one of the Good Magicians, feels that Utterson is making fun of him. Jekyll wonders how good he really is. Speaking for goodness are all his good deeds, his coherent dignified habits, his dedication as a doctor, his delights as a husband and father. Speaking for at least a vicarious unworthiness is his undeniable complicity with Hyde. Inside the citadel of virtue that Jekyll has built for himself is a romantic, banal longing for life untrammeled which has even brought him to the point of covering for Hyde's crimes. Jekyll curses the weakness that prevented him from loving his own virtue and has made him for so many years hanker after the thick-lipped siren's call.

"That's enough," Utterson calls out softly. He gets up, walks across to the group, and puts his hand on Jekyll's back. "You're working too hard. Let your feet stay with the floor." An eerie peace invades Jekyll's body.

Utterson goes to a plump, solemn girl, puts his arm around her waist, and murmurs a few words against her cheek. She bursts into tears and smiles. As Utterson moves away, the other eight crowd around her and touch her tentatively. Jekyll longs for Hyde to be here, so he could wrap him in some heavy fraternal embrace. They lift the sobbing girl, carry her to the center of the floor, lay her down, and sit around her. Someone begins to hum. Jekyll gazes at the girl's radiant face. He pardons Hyde, he pardons himself. Utterson stands behind him.

Jekyll has not always felt so haunted. It was when he stopped working regularly with Utterson that he began to lose his nerve. He could not cut himself completely free from Utterson, either.

But he has a horror of confinement, and most of Utterson's pupils end up content to linger in one room. They come to Utterson to expand their energies, but the old man puts some kind of spell on them. Jekyll is struggling to free himself from the magician's spell; but he needs help, he needs love, he needs touch.

In the stone bathhouse recently constructed on the precincts of the Oyster Bay estate, Utterson is telling dirty stories, an evening custom—and calling for more. His embarrassed disciples are doing their best to amuse him, their custom. In their apartment near Lincoln Center, Jekyll is gazing tenderly at his wife. He presses his moist face into her long blond hair. "I love you," he gasps. "Have you any idea how much I love you?"

They lie interlaced on the living-room couch; the children are asleep. In the bathhouse a band of male pupils, under Utterson's direction, have finished spreading their bodies with a special clay imported from Turkey that removes all hair and leaves the skin elastic and soft. Naked except for the towels around their hips, they file into the steam room. Loving means getting fat, Jekyll thinks. And loving means getting very, very thin.

Jekyll feels the energy leaking out of him. Then this is love, too. This slow but unremitting leakage, this sensation of lying with veins open in a bathtub filled with warm water. He gets up and dries himself. Meanwhile, Utterson whips one of his older pupils across the buttocks with his damp towel and breaks into volleys of laughter as the gray-haired, flabby man stumbles backward with the unexpected pain. "That's what you've never learned," shouts Utterson boisterously. "How to play!" The bewildered man, of a generally trusting nature, hovers in the steamy corner, not sure whether he's about to laugh or to cry. "Don't be so serious!" Utterson yells, brandishing the towel above his bald dome like a cowboy's lasso. "Play!" Jekyll fidgets, then sits down again on the edge of the couch. As he unbuttons his wife's blouse with one hand, he would like to grab hold of that towel with the other hand, pull with all his might, and send Utterson sprawling face down onto the warm planks.

Lying down, heart's ease, body's home, floating, sleeping, touching, sliding, climbing. The darkness, the dazzle. Warm smells, worn sheets. But it doesn't last.

In bed with his wife, Jekyll is seized by a fervid absence of mind. Needless to say, it is signaled by an absence of body. His wife, at first bemused by the failing rhythm of his embraces, adapts herself, and for a few moments it goes well this way, too. She clasps him tightly, gratefully. But Jekyll doesn't seem to understand, and slows down even further. Now his wife is disheartened. Sighing, she whispers his name, then pulls his earlobes. "Where are you, darling?"

Utterson is straining over his nightly push-ups by the side of his enormous bed. For a man of his age and bulk, who eats and drinks as immoderately as he does, he's in better shape than he ought to be, as Jekyll has often noticed. Jekyll cannot imagine who lies in the freshly made bed, waiting for Utterson.

"Darling!"

Jekyll, diffident now, smiles. "I thought I heard something," he whispers.

"The baby?"

"No. In my head. Doesn't matter." He goes on smiling.

"But it does."

"It's only that I'm always thinking about you," Jekyll says despondently. "Even when I'm near you."

"But that's just it," she says. "You're not close to me."

Utterson, feeling sudden nibblings of pain on the left side of his chest, hastily climbs into bed. The figure under the covers rolls over expectantly, unfurling the blankets. Jekyll switches on the reading lamp and checks his watch.

Jekyll is thinking of the uncanny ability that Utterson has to transmit energy from himself to others. Jekyll has experienced this famous power several times, as well as witnessed Utterson practicing on others.

Flashback, to less troubled days—days in which Jekyll found Utterson's conversation extremely funny, when it was not breath-stoppingly wise. Once, years ago, when Jekyll was severely depressed, possibly suicidal, he drove out—without telephoning first—to Oyster Bay. Utterson, extraordinarily gentle, fatherly that day, received his visitor in his bedroom. Seeing him, Jekyll felt excited, feverish; his head began to pound, as it's doing tonight, in bed with his wife.

"You're sick." Utterson put one arm around Jekyll's shoulder. "Don't talk." He put Jekyll in a chair. "I'll give you coffee," he said, all imaginable tenderness in his voice. "Drink it as hot as you can."

Jekyll remembers sitting at a table while Utterson poured coffee into a saucepan from the old thermos he used to keep beside his bed and put the saucepan on a hot plate. Jekyll remembers being unable to take his eyes off Utterson, and realizing that Utterson looked desperately weary: he'd never seen anyone look so tired. Jekyll remembers slouching over the table, sipping at his coffee, when he became aware of a sudden uprising of energy within himself. It was as if a violent electric blue light flowed outward from Utterson and entered him. But as Jekyll felt the tiredness leach out of him, Utterson's preposterous heavy body sagged and his face turned gray as if it were being drained of blood. Jekyll looked at him, amazed.

Jekyll remembers Utterson muttering, an urgent tone in his

voice: "You're all right now. I must go." Jekyll remembers leaping to his feet to help him, and Utterson waving Jekyll away and hobbling slowly from the room.

Jekyll remembers waiting for Utterson, blankly savoring an exquisite sense of well-being. He was convinced then (and is convinced now) that when Utterson transmits energy from himself to others, it can be done only at great cost to himself. But it became obvious that Utterson knew how to renew his own energy quickly, for Jekyll remembers being equally amazed by the change in him when he returned to the bedroom fifteen minutes later. Utterson looked almost like a young man, alert, smiling, and full of good spirits. He said that this was a fortunate meeting, and that while Jekyll had forced him to make an almost impossible effort, it had been a positive experience for both of them. He then announced that he and Jekyll would eat together, alone: an enormous lunch, for which he would break open his best bottle of fine old Armagnac.

Jekyll remembers that as they ate this lavish meal, Utterson told Jekyll to talk about whatever had been troubling him. Jekyll remembers finding it difficult to begin, for at that moment he felt he had no problems at all. He had never felt better in his life. And Jekyll remembers that when he finally managed to explain his griefs and fears, Utterson listened without comment and said finally that what Jekyll had told him was of no real importance, nothing to worry about. End of flashback.

Jekyll feels weary now, as he holds his wife. Conceivably, he could throw a line to Utterson that would run from his solar plexus to Utterson's burly right hand. He would tug on that line, a signal of distress, and Utterson, wherever he is—in Oyster Bay or in the city—would feel the pressure, would realize that Jekyll is in trouble, would turn on that violent electric blue light, whose rays would be transmitted along the cord straight back to Jekyll's chest, and he would feel a new, pure uprising of energy, he would feel wonderful, he would feel that his problems were of no importance. But for this to happen, Utterson would have to be not too busy with whatever he's doing, sacred or profane, right now. And he would have to understand the exact sense of Jekyll's signal as well as who it was from, who among his many rebellious ex-pupils. And Utterson would have to be willing, at least for a while, to imperil his own forces. To be himself, at least for a while, very very tired.

Still in his surgeon's overalls, Jekyll tilts backward in a chair in the third-floor staff lounge of the clinic, having just come from two hours in the operating room that have saved his patient's life. He allows himself one cigarette. While somewhere else a war is going on, bombs are falling, flesh is being punctured and burned, hospitals with bamboo walls and thatched roofs are being targeted for more bombing, Jekyll looks at the backs of his capable hands, at the short pale hairs sprouting from each pore, at the intricate tiny lines connecting each pore that make a web, like an aerial map— or a game.

While a nurse brings Jekyll the latest report on the patient's condition (good) and stays long enough to flirt with him, the war goes on—an ache in the bones, an ache in the gut, an ache in the heart. To supplement the televised daily doses of atrocity, tours by helicopter are available for civilians to observe it at first hand. Countless small-boned, fine-featured people, the men with smooth hairless faces, the women with black hair down their backs, still youthful-looking in middle age, carrying rifles and spears, get massacred day after day. How are they replenished?

Jekyll, monogamous as ever, thinks about his wife's legs and decides they are not just shapelier than the nurse's but may be the prettiest legs he has ever seen. The nurse leaves the room with

instructions about 5 cc. of a new medication for the patient still lying unconscious in the recovery room.

Utterson declares that it is a waste of spirit to fret about the
war; that human folly will always persist; that most people being
idiots who sleep through their lives, the sole duty of the few who
struggle to awake is self-cultivation. For the treatment of melan-
cholia brought on by thinking about the war, Utterson recom-
mends several strenuous exercises, spiritual and physical, and a
rereading of chapter 109 of *The Strange Case of Cain and Abel*.
Deciding that he is tired of trying to tune his aching instrument
of a self, Jekyll also decides that even if he can't be Hyde, he can
still seek his help.

"Hey, look who's slumming!" Hyde shrieks gaily through a broken
windowpane, as the taxi deposits Jekyll next to the mailbox by the
road, just outside of Plattsburg, New York. The gaping mailbox,
flag down, is crammed with ads and brochures. Jekyll strides across
the large square of crabgrass, gains the porch, then steps over a
heap of wet newspapers, each folded and held together by a rubber
band, decaying into one another at the threshold of the blistered
front door. Another windy day, and rain in the wind.

Hyde spins about at the open door (equipped with neither bell
nor knocker), seizing Jekyll's gabardine raincoat and flinging it
onto a hook next to his black cape in the corner of his seedy lair.
When Hyde slams the door shut, Jekyll half expects to hear the
clank of a lock and chain.

"Let's take a look at you, buddy," Hyde growls. "Just as good-
looking and uptight as ever. You haven't changed a bit!"

Jekyll can't return the compliment, if it is a compliment. In the
three months since Jekyll last saw Hyde, trotting around and around
the World Trade Center, the younger man has aged fearfully. More
of his thinning stringy hair has fallen out. Right this minute, with

several days' growth of beard on his haggard face, he looks as old as Jekyll actually is. Jekyll feels a pang of paternal concern.

With extraordinary quickness, Hyde shoves Jekyll onto the top of a packing crate, then pours some orange juice into two tall bluish glasses, lacing both with what Jekyll soon discovers to be gin (it comes from a turpentine bottle), then crouches gleefully on another crate.

"What's up, doc?" he cackles.

Those two bluish glasses placed on a broken rattan table strike Jekyll as odd. As Jekyll knows, Hyde has lived alone since his girl-friend walked out on him; the glasses suggest that he was expect-ing someone. Himself? Jekyll has neither written nor wired Hyde (who has no telephone) about his visit this evening. Could someone have informed Hyde that he was coming?

Jekyll, taking a sip of his drink, asks about Hyde's house.

"You didn't come all the way up here to rap about my crummy house!"

Jekyll wonders if living in the country bores Hyde, after the glamorous dangers of city life: the thrill of pursuing his victims, the excitement of being chased by the cops. "Don't rush me," says Jekyll.

"Sorry, man," Hyde croaks. "I guess I'm just bouncing off my own peeling walls, panting to hear what's on your mind."

"You're acting as if you already knew what it was," Jekyll ventures—in case Hyde should have acquired some of Utterson's gift of clairvoyance.

"I do."

Jekyll fights down his anxiety. "Then you've no reason to be impatient."

"Shit, that don't mean I know every last word," Hyde squeaks plaintively.

"I'm still wondering why you stay up here," says Jekyll.

"Don't knock it, man. You should have seen this dump when I moved in." Hyde sounds almost wistful. "I did all the work myself, just like at the Institute. With my own two hands."

"I know," Jekyll murmurs distractedly, gazing at Hyde's corded, predator's hands, their backs sheathed with dusky fur, and noting that the tranquillity of country life has not helped Hyde to stop biting his nails.

"See," Hyde croaks, a triumphant gleam in his small eyes. "You know everything, too."

"Considering my problem," Jekyll retorts gloomily, "that wise-crack is in awfully bad taste."

"Bad taste"—Hyde's voice becomes strident—"is my specialty, man." He clenches his shrunken fists. "Want to make something of it?"

"No," says Jekyll.

Bad taste is Utterson's specialty, too. But whereas it seems natural with Hyde, given his slum background and his aggressive lack of aspiration to virtue, Utterson's case presents a problem for Jekyll—for everyone, probably, who has come under Utterson's authority. Utterson's ribald, sadistic sense of humor must be reconciled with the gravity of his claim to spiritual leadership, just as his frank animal smells are blended with the sly but undeniable odor of sanctity. With Hyde there is no problem. That his dingy living room reeks of urine doesn't at all disturb Jekyll, who, as a doctor, can't afford to be squeamish. Hyde is Hyde. But Utterson is always more than Utterson. Or less. And Utterson insists that his admirers accept everything about him. They're not permitted to subtract or add.

It's the same with the words that stream from Utterson's mouth, which never quite closes even when he's not speaking. Long smutty stories. Platitudes and truisms about the good life. And genuine, subtle, almost inhuman wisdom. But Utterson doesn't let you throw out the first two parts and keep the third. You have to keep it all. Is that the secret of harmonious development, of the well-rounded personality, of not being one-sided? If it is, Jekyll will never find the way: he is incapable. And most likely that isn't the secret. Utterson never encourages anyone to imitate him. On the contrary, his sardonic bullying of his disciples suggests that the liberties he grants himself are definitely not for them. Otherwise, why does Utterson lie in bed late, wallowing in his breakfast, while everyone else at the Institute, pupils and staff alike, rises at 6 a.m. and spends most of the day pruning trees, tending the vegetable gardens, milking cows, preparing meals, sewing clothes, mowing lawns, paving driveways, constructing new buildings. "Work," Utterson's basic teaching method, for them; capricious potency, afloat on the sea of liberty, for himself.

Jekyll notices a whip hanging on the wall of the bleak room, presumably a souvenir of Hyde's S-M escapades. Utterson handles his disciples as if he were a wild-animal tamer. But Utterson, who is no stranger to sadism, physical and mental, disapproves of whips. Having observed that each person gives off radiations and emanations (which constitute, according to Utterson, the person's essence), Utterson uses the octave upon octave of emanations that he is capable of emitting—to subdue, subjugate, harass, harness, and finally liberate each of his disciples, near and far, to become a true will. Jekyll would prefer the whip.

In the meantime, Jekyll has sedately abandoned his packing crate for a mauve plastic couch scarred with cigarette burns across the room, while Hyde, who has great difficulty in keeping still and can't remain seated in one place for more than a few minutes, hops off his crate. He is getting more orange juice, pouring more gin: more gin than orange juice this time. While taking note of Hyde's taste and what it reveals about his deterioration—from satanic to eccentric—Jekyll approves of the orange juice, since Hyde has always suffered from a vitamin C deficiency. With a wave of his hand he refuses a second round for himself.

"God damn love," wails Hyde.

"What did you say?" Jekyll asks.

"I said"—Hyde lowers his raucous voice to a growl—"God damn love."

Hyde empties his glass in two gulps. Not only does Hyde seem to have lost most of his flair for moral turpitude, but this vehement drinking indicates that he is going soft. Jekyll is discouraged. "God damn love," he thinks he hears Hyde hiss once more.

Hyde can't seem to keep still, darting about the living room from the bottle on the rattan table to his packing crate and back again, like a morose gorilla. Jekyll leans back on the mauve couch, tired from watching him move so much. He feels drowsy, under water. How long must he go on chasing after Hyde? Are they to go around and around, continuous as a frieze on an urn? He'll never overtake him. Hyde, despite his odd gait, is incredibly light, mobile. You couldn't catch him with a rope, as one could imagine catching Utterson—a bull-like man who moves with ponderous slowness and prefers to be enthroned in a chair or, whenever possible, to lie in bed. Jekyll imagines how he might lasso Utterson and drag him here, to continue the conversation. It's not with Utterson, though, but with this manic lout circling the room that he must try to communicate.

At least the doctor in Jekyll remains undaunted by Hyde's corrosive antics. Jekyll notes that Hyde's constitution looks embattled now. From what can be glimpsed of Hyde's chicken-breasted frame through his wrinkled work shirt, two of whose buttons are missing, he's lost weight, and his cough rivals Camille's.

Making one more effort, Jekyll manages to rouse the eloquent, long-suffering aspirant to psychic unity; and from the couch he aims that part of himself, like a gun, at Hyde. Addressing Hyde, he begins a monologue. Hyde gulps down more gin while Jekyll names the main points on the map of his discontent, expounding on his heartfelt desire to change his life. Utterson comes in for heavy savaging, he and that motley crew of disciples and bastards camping out in Oyster Bay at the Institute for Deprogramming Potential Human Beings.

"But the Work did you a lot of good, right?" Hyde mumbles, still on the run.

How could Jekyll deny that the Work has helped him? That, without the Work, he wouldn't have become as gifted a physician as he is today; that he wouldn't be so calm, controlled, steady, self-observing; that he couldn't so easily inspire trust in and impose his will on colleagues, subordinates, and patients. "Utterson isn't the problem," Jekyll admits. "It's me."

"I don't get it," whines Hyde, abruptly dropping to all fours and crouching in a corner.

"It's . . . wanting to give everything up. I'd like to be . . . Don't laugh! I'd like to be you."

"Wow!" Hyde claps the palm of his hand to his rodent-like forehead. "What a load of middle-class crap! You'd like to be me?" He lurches up, awkward as ever, from the floor. "You'd like to lead my trashy life? Man, you are clean out of your ever-loving skull!"

"But," says Jekyll, "if your life depresses you, why don't you move back to the city?"

"And get busted? Thanks a lot!"

"But things can be arranged, you know that. I'll tell Lanyon."

"That asshole?" Hyde pivots, the bottle in his claw. "He's senile."

"He's not. And you're drunk."

"Just because you keep that shyster alive with these injections of yours, you don't have to defend his health," Hyde rants. "Lanyon couldn't get a D.A. to reduce charges on a baby who landed in the Tombs for stealing a diaper."

"Don't drink so much. I hate to think what your liver looks like."

"Cool it, man!" Hyde snarls, halting his lame progress around the room. "Want to see my tracks?" He fumbles with the left sleeve of his work shirt, tugging it up over his elbow. "Well, I'm clean now, see! And I owe it all to—good—old—booze!" He pats the bottle and then slams it down on the rattan table. Utterson raises his glass of Armagnac, scans the long oval table in the refectory, and proposes a toast. His favorite subject for a toast is a certain kind of idiot. During a high-spirited dinner several years ago, Utterson invented a whole taxonomy of spiritual retardedness; "idiots," as he insisted on calling them, could be classified into ingenious categories and subcategories, the point being to determine into which category each person at the table fell. The game is still being played, with pupils nervously interrogating themselves, and Utterson reserving the right to pronounce the final verdict. Utterson sips the Armagnac and grins.

Jekyll is continuing. "Well, if you won't come back to the city, would you consider moving somewhere else? We could . . ." He hesitates, then plunges. "We could go somewhere together. I mean, I'd go with you."

That does stop Hyde's gyrations, at least momentarily. "What would you want to do that for? Man, you have really flipped your wig!" Jekyll feels, through the strong roots of his hair, his scalp tingling.

"I know it sounds crazy . . ." Jekyll pauses. "But we wouldn't have to stay in one place. We could be on the road most of the year."

"Hey, what is this? A proposition? Don't tell me that after

umpteen years of happy marriage you've discovered you're some kind of fruit. Oh, man, that would be too much!" He falls to the floor, flops over like a dog, then stretches out on his back, convulsed with laughter.

"Cut it out, Eddy!" Jekyll, leaning forward on the couch, is embarrassed. "You know it's not that. It's because . . . I've realized I don't have enough . . . enough imagination. You know what I mean?"

Hyde waves his spindly legs in the air, while pushing both hands into his ribs to stop laughing. "And you think if you hang around with me"—choking and coughing, he sits up—"you'll get more . . . imaginative?"

"Drink some water."

Hyde, shaking his head sullenly, staggers to his feet. "I don't get it." He is wheezing. "You want to toss your career in the garbage can, move out of a rent-controlled apartment, leave your old lady—"

"No," Jekyll interrupts, "I'd like my wife to come with us."

"Far out!" Hyde snorts. "Okay, you want to dump your apartment, drag your wife away from her friends, kiss off Utterson, let down all those poor coons waiting on line at your clinic who think you're Dr. Schweitzer, run out on all those nurses who you never ball . . ." Jekyll nods. "For what?"

"Because I'm not free."

"Free!" Hyde explodes drunkenly. "Grow up, you big baby."

"But it's true. I live a life that's . . . all laid out. Nothing is going to happen to me. I mean, I know what's going to happen to me. I'm thirty-eight, and with my health and family history I'll probably live to be ninety. But I could already write my obituary."

"Big momma's baby!"

"You've already said that."

"Freedom!" Hyde rubs his fist against his eyes. "Man, have you got an old head!"

"Right," Jekyll says. "That's why it's good for me to be with you."

"Well, don't start thinking I can help you! Jeezus, I've got problems of my own." He starts pacing around again. "One more minute and you'll be talking about happiness." He stops in his tracks, gazing fiercely at Jekyll. "Or love." His small eyes are blinking.

"Look, Eddy, I'm really sorry about the way she . . ." Jekyll sees Hyde's swarthy face going livid with distress. "About . . . what's happened to you."

"God damn love," moans Hyde. He wipes his nose with the back of his left hand and pours himself another drink.

But nothing, least of all despair, seems to stop Hyde's incessant, ungainly motility. Jekyll's left foot is falling asleep, and he starts thinking about how late it is. He rises from the couch, stretching his arms above his head.

"Don't split!" Hyde screeches. As Jekyll drops his arms to his sides, Hyde bounds over to where he's standing. "You have to crash here tonight anyway." Thrusting the compact dial of his face close to Jekyll's chest, he whispers, almost gibbering: "You missed the last train."

Jekyll nods. But he doesn't sit down.

"What's wrong now?" Hyde demands belligerently.

"I'd like something to eat."

"How come?" Hyde leers. "I ain't hungry."

Jekyll pushes him aside and heads for the john in the hallway. As he is about to flush the toilet, Hyde starts banging on the door. Jekyll pulls the chain, but nothing happens.

Hyde keeps banging. "Hey!" He kicks the door. "I'll ask my ma to whip up something."

"Does your mother live here with you?" Jekyll says through the door.

"Sure." Hyde kicks the door again. "Since . . . since that broad left."

"But you hate your mother! I remember your telling me that years ago."

"So what!" exclaims Hyde. "She's doing her thing. I'm doing mine. She don't get in my way."

Jekyll opens the door. "I shouldn't be bothering you with my problems."

Hyde is just outside. "No sweat!" Hyde's mouth crumples into a jaunty sneer, meant to be friendly, that shows a mouthful of tar-tared teeth. "I'm glad you popped up, Hank. And I dig your being so out front with me, even if you have gone off your nut."

Jekyll demurs once again, although he has by now given up the hope of persuading Hyde. "Try to put yourself in my position," he adds.

"Are you kidding? Why should I want to do that!" Hyde snarls, while at that very moment Utterson, whatever position he is sitting or lying in, is telling one of his disciples that, if she listens carefully, she will learn how funny the Truth can be.

The next morning, Hyde's ivory-faced mother brings Jekyll an English muffin and a cup of Nescafé in bed. Meanwhile, Utterson is being served his breakfast by the sleepy-eyed Poole. Jekyll wants to ask about Hyde—is he awake? is he hung over?—but decides against it and rolls briskly onto his stomach, pretending to doze off again. Better not ask the old woman any questions and possibly get some in return. Jekyll remembers a rule of military history, best illustrated by Pearl Harbor, according to which it is difficult to hear the true signals because of the surrounding noise—that is, other messages.

After she leaves the attic room, Jekyll gets out of bed, biting into the muffin. Tall sycamores rear above the sloping roof of faded slate outside the window; the gutter is clogged with leaves. Wearing a cashmere dressing gown, Utterson emerges into the corridor and shouts at one of the pupils to go outside and rake the leaves. Then Jekyll puts on his flannel pants and corduroy jacket, goes down the back stairs, through the kitchen (where Mrs. Hyde is immobilized in front of the TV, watching the war), and into the living room. Hyde is kneeling in the corner, fixing a bicycle. It seems strange to think of Hyde with a bike instead of his lethal Harley-Davidson.

"Awake long?"

Hyde looks up and grunts, a different creature from last night: clear-eyed, humanoid, more brutal, more youthful, more frightening. He scratches his bald spot with a screwdriver.

"It's a beautiful day, ain't it?" Jekyll continues.

"Don't patronize me, pal," Hyde says in a menacing tone. "If I want to, I can talk as good as you college boys any day." He turns back to the bike and does something with the pliers.

Jekyll pauses indecisively, then takes a step in Hyde's direction. "What's the Sunday train schedule?"

"Want to leave, huh?"

"I've got to get back by dinnertime."

Hyde slams the pliers on the floor and puts his hands on his razorlike hips. "You mean we're not going to elope and live happily ever after, robbing banks together like Bonnie and Clyde?" Hyde pushes his voice up to a falsetto.

"That's right," Jekyll says. "So what about the trains?"

"There's a local at 3:40 that'll get hubby back home just in time."

Jekyll turns away, in irritation.

"No, wait!" croaks Hyde, standing up and hopping over his tool kit and the bicycle chain. "I've been thinking about our rap last night . . ."

Jekyll turns back.

"Listen, I figured it out. You don't need me. Do it on your own."

"Meaning what?" says Jekyll.

"Do something! Violent." Hyde hisses. "Rob a blind newsie. Molest a child. Mug a fag. Strangle Utterson. Put—" Hyde stops, seeing Jekyll's face blanch, and slaps his stringy thighs. "I got you there, didn't I?" he jeers. "Wow, that horny old geezer really has you by the balls. You should take what he's got that's good for you and run with it. Like me." As if to illustrate what he is saying, Hyde is hopping spastically around the room on one foot.

"Hey, man, didn't you ever commit a crime?"

Jekyll doesn't answer. He is thinking of all the imaginary crimes he has committed, and of all the real crimes he has never imagined. If only he had the force, not the physical but the moral force, just to place his hands on Utterson's heavy veined neck.

"You know," Hyde sneers. "Violence. V-I-O-L—"

"I know how it's spelled," groans Jekyll. He feels a painful contraction around the heart. "*What* violence?"

"Well . . ." Hyde pauses, giving a theatrical (or a gorilla's) imitation of someone thinking. "You're not up to offing Utterson, we got that. Right? So . . . so, how about something easy for a start? Like burning down the Institute. You could always hope that nobody'll get killed."

"You think I'm capable of that?"

"You could try." Hyde has stopped moving, and is picking his nose. "Maybe you could get someone to help you."

"I don't need any help."

"You don't, huh? That's not how you were coming on last night."

Jekyll, who wants to leave, is standing near the hook where his coat is hanging.

"Suppose," Hyde mutters, borne up by a new current of energy, "suppose I tell you someone's already planning to trash the Institute."

"Are you telling me?"

"You don't believe me." Hyde's face flushes.

"I might, if you explain how you know about it."

"I can't reveal my sources." Hyde clears his throat and spits on the floor. "But I'll tell you when. This month, the night of October sixteenth."

Is it envy or terror that Jekyll is feeling? "Are you . . . going to tell Utterson?"

Hyde doesn't answer. He is prancing around his bicycle.

"You've got to!"

"Why?" rages Hyde. "He's telepathic and clairvoyant and all that, ain't he? Let the creep figure it out for himself."

Jekyll doesn't have a reply for this. It seems like a cheap trick. Don't we all inhabit the same space? Jekyll is thinking about crime. He is thinking about Utterson.

A quotation from Utterson: "When the devil has been caged too long, he comes out roaring." Jekyll has the feeling that something is coming to him from the patches of blue in the cloudy sky he sees through the broken windowpane, from the sounds, the smells, the temperature outside—something that he is trying to keep away. Then he abandons himself; a voice whispers over and over: "Free, free, free!"

There is a scene that Jekyll once witnessed, which goes like this: An aged white-haired man is walking along Riverside Drive late one summer evening—he is probably a German-Jewish refugee scholar who teaches at Columbia University—and another man, young, very small, in a black leather jacket, is coming toward him. When they get near each other, the old man nods with stately, unfashionable politeness and stops. It looks as if he is asking directions: he is pointing. He has a complacent, beautiful face. The short youth stands facing him, tapping on a guitar that he carries. He doesn't answer. Then, like the propeller of an old plane, he gradually begins vibrating with anger, stamping his booted muddy feet, brandishing the guitar. The old man takes a step back, looking more disgusted than surprised or fearful. He must have heard that madmen roam the streets, but may have counted on never meeting one. He takes another step back. The short youth clubs him to the sidewalk with his guitar. A flurry of blows fall upon the victim's head and chest and legs. The old man groans, twitches once or twice, and lies still. The short youth goes on prodding and mauling the unresisting body, humming a nasal song.

Watching from a doorway down the street, Jekyll felt that song on his lips, too. "What did it matter?" said the voice. He who had seen so many people die—poor, discarded—and always mustered without stint both compassion and indignation, he who had saved so many lives, patched innumerable bodies and restored them to health, might be pardoned for watching once, just once, without pity, without intervening—not confined to the better part of feelings—as if it were a dream. Who was breaking that old man's bones? If that was Hyde, then he must be stopped.

Jekyll seeks the energy to live out his own acts. Inwardly, he begins composing the new will that he would dictate to Lanyon tomorrow morning. Hyde's aid seems ghostly now. Jekyll realizes that he is alone in a world of monsters, that the struggle between the good magicians and the bad ones is a distraction, if not an illusion. He must go after their chieftain, the master magician, the one beyond good and bad, who has confused and tempted him. Let

Utterson send him all his energy, by whatever conduits are open. This time, he won't give it back.

While Utterson is rolling around in his bed in Oyster Bay, watching Poole scrub the carpet, and Hyde is squatting down by the bike again in Plattsburg, Jekyll, also in Plattsburg, is getting his arms into his coat. Hyde looks up again. "Wait!" he howls. "I've changed my mind."

Jekyll, who is concentrating on certain sensations he may or may not be having in his chest, thinking about the blue light that may or may not be emanating from Utterson at this very moment, feels a stab of alarm. "What?"

"Maybe you were right. That stuff you said last night." There is a strange, repulsive insinuation in Hyde's voice. "About going back to the city."

"What about your mother?" Jekyll is desperate.

"Let her croak," Hyde shouts jubilantly. "I'm coming with you!"

Haunches against his heels, he dances around the bike Cossack-fashion, kicking one scrawny leg and then the other, his left arm high above his head, banging on the fenders with the hammer in his right hand. "I just have to fix this"—Hyde gives the rear fender a terrific smash with the hammer, making a big dent—"then I'll get my other jeans and a sweater from upstairs . . ."

"Don't come!" Jekyll bellows.

"Listen, buddy," Hyde snarls, picking up a huge pair of pliers. He yanks out the front wheel spokes one by one. "I can take a train if I want to. It's a free country."

Jekyll snatches the black cape off the hook and runs at Hyde, throws the cape over him, and seizes the bicycle chain lying on the floor. Hyde is struggling like a hen as Jekyll hits him once, twice, three times—trying, unsuccessfully as it turns out, to kill him—while, at the same moment, Utterson is picking up the phone with the long cord in his bedroom in Oyster Bay to dial the police.

Utterson stands at the blackboard in the Study House. Jekyll sits on the edge of his cot in a dank cell. He's already spent two months in solitary. Jekyll is in solitary, not because his crime, attempted murder, is so serious, but because one week after being put in jail he participated in a prisoners' strike for better food; the strike turned into a riot, and two hostage guards had their throats cut. Jekyll, conceding that it was his duty to make common cause with the mostly black and Puerto Rican prisoners, so much less fortunate than he, finds himself punished more severely than anyone. He is maltreated by the guards and suspected by his fellow prisoners, who elected him their spokesman in the parleys with the negotiator from Albany, of having been too intransigent, thereby making it easier for the Governor to order the National Guard to storm the west wing; during the assault, thirteen prisoners had been shot down, including all the principal leaders of the riot except Jekyll.

It's very cold, the coldest January in years. Jekyll thinks it is still December. Anyway, December or January, no letup in the unremitting freezing spell is predicted. Technically, the prison can claim to be heated; regular deliveries of coal are made, and the coal shoveled into furnaces. But the heat doesn't filter down to Jekyll or to any of the other cells on the floor where prisoners in solitary are lodged. He minds most that his nose is always cold. Also his feet. The prisoners are issued slippers when they arrive at the prison—real leather, Jekyll noted with surprise, though cracked, worn, and a size too big. But they aren't allowed to wear socks. Jekyll, who was once a physical-fitness buff and now weighs one hundred and forty pounds, is extremely weak. If Utterson moves around too much on the platform, Jekyll will topple over.

What Utterson is saying to a class of eager young disciples in the Study House is this: "Remember our lost brothers and sisters." Jekyll, who thinks that today is December 14, remembers that last Sunday was his wife's birthday.

Richard Enfield, his wife's cousin, is visiting Jekyll, who has now been moved from solitary to the east wing, where prisoners are housed in pairs. Jekyll, whose right foot is in a cast because of an accident he had yesterday jumping down from the upper bunk, has permission to receive visitors today in his cell, instead of in the long rectangular visitors' room divided by a floor-to-ceiling grille. "That was a pretty dumb thing you tried to do there," says Enfield, trying to be casual. At first, Jekyll thinks he is referring to the stupid way he wrenched his Achilles tendon and broke a bone in his heel, then realizes Enfield means the attempted murder of Hyde. But he isn't offended. He has already had a loving visit, early this afternoon, from his wife, who brought him a box of chocolates and a roast chicken in aspic. He has had to share the chocolates with his cell mate, a heroin merchant who cut a guard's throat during the riot, but luckily the man turned up his nose at the chicken and Jekyll got to devour it by himself. Jekyll has already put on a little weight (he is up to one hundred and fifty) and the cell is reasonably heated, but Enfield thinks he looks terrible.

Jekyll imagines he is handcuffed and that a chain runs from his wrist to the doorknob of Utterson's bedroom. If he jerked his hands, he could open Utterson's door—being careful not to bang Poole, the sleeping fourteen-year-old acolyte, on the head as the door flies open—and actually see what obscene acts take place in that room in the middle of the night.

"Anything I can bring you?" Enfield asks.

"Sure," says Jekyll. "You can bring me the news of someone's death."

Enfield turns away in pity and disgust, and asks the guard to open the cell door. "Mind how you close the door," Jekyll says. "There's a draft." His cell mate, now exiled to the upper bunk, presses his chocolate-stained mouth into his pillow and grunts unpleasantly. Utterson, taking his afternoon nap, rolls around in his large filthy bed, and shouts for Poole to bring him some fresh coffee. It is time for him to get up and rejoin his pupils in the Study House, to deliver another talk on inner discipline and the proper uses of selfishness. Jekyll watches the door slam shut.

Finally, it is frail old Lanyon who brings Jekyll the news he is waiting for. Hyde has committed suicide: hanged himself in his cellar.

Since it is two weeks later, Jekyll should have been able to receive Lanyon in the visitors' room; but this morning he tripped on his crutches while hobbling from his bunk to the slop pail and cleanly fractured a bone in his left ankle. The prison doctor has just left; the new cast, a pinkish color, is still damp.

"Speaking as your lawyer, I don't know whether this affects your chances for parole or not."

My feet, thinks Jekyll. No, not my feet.

Lanyon is still talking. "Attempted murder is still attempted murder, even if the intended victim dies for whatever reason shortly after."

"Did he leave me a note?" Jekyll demands in a husky voice.

Lanyon hands Jekyll a small envelope that Jekyll tears open. Inside is a sheet of ruled paper from a school notebook, on which is the imprint in lipstick of a large mouth. Lanyon tries to look over Jekyll's shoulder, but Jekyll crumples the paper before the lawyer can see, stuffing it into the top of his right cast.

"What does he say? It could be useful in the file I'm submitting to the parole board."

Jekyll shakes his head. "Did he leave any other messages?" he says coldly.

"For Utterson."

"What did it say?"

"He admits it was he who tried to burn down the Institute on October sixteenth."

"Poor pretentious bastard," says Jekyll, hiding his disappointment.

"Shut up! I'm trying to sleep!" grumbles the murderer in the upper bunk.

During a moment's silence, Jekyll looks down at his handsome, bony hands. "And what did Utterson say to that?"

"You know Utterson." Lanyon laughs, with his discordant, old man's laugh. "He says it would have been fine with him if Hyde had succeeded. He says that everybody is free to do as he or she likes."

"Oh, freedom . . ." Jekyll munches on some vanilla fudge his wife brought him that morning. Leaning back comfortably in his bunk, he settles his legs, encased to mid-calf in plaster, one dry and the other still damp, on the extra pillow he's been given, and smiles. "Don't speak to me about freedom."

DEBRIEFING

... Frail long hair, brown with reddish lights in it, artificial-looking hair, actressy hair, the hair she had at twenty-three when I met her (I was nineteen), hair too youthful to need tinting then, but too old now to have exactly the same color; a weary, dainty body with wide wrists, shy chest, broad-bladed shoulders, pelvic bones like gulls' wings; an absent body one might be reluctant to imagine undressed, which may explain why her clothes are never less than affected and are often regal; one husband in dark phallocratic mustache; unexpectedly successful East Side restaurant owner with dim Mafia patronage, separated from and then divorced in fussy stages; two flaxen-haired children, who look as if they have two other parents, safely evacuated to grassy boarding schools. "For the fresh air," she says.

Autumn in Central Park, several years ago. Lounging under a sycamore, our bicycles paired on their sides—Julia's was hers (she had once bicycled regularly), mine was rented—she admitted to finding less time lately for doing: going to an aikido class, cooking a meal, phoning the children, maintaining love affairs. But for wondering there seemed all the time in the world—hours, whole days.

Wondering?

"About . . ." she said, looking at the ground. "Oh, I might start wondering about the relation of that leaf"—pointing to one—"to that one"—pointing to a neighbor leaf, also yellowing, its frayed tip almost perpendicular to the first one's spine. "Why are they lying there just like that? Why not some other way?"

"I'll play. 'Cause that's how they fell down from the tree."

"But there's a relation, a connection . . ."

Julia, sister, poor moneyed waif, you're crazy. (A crazy question: one that shouldn't be asked.) But I didn't say that. I said: "You shouldn't ask yourself questions you can't answer." No reply. "Even if you could answer a question like that, you wouldn't know you had."

Look, Julia. Listen, Peter Pan. Instead of leaves—that's crazy—take people. Undoubtedly, between two and five this afternoon, eighty-four embittered Viet veterans are standing on line for welfare checks in a windowless downtown office while seventeen women sit in mauve leatherette chairs in a Park Avenue surgeon's lair waiting to be examined for breast cancer. But there's no point in trying to connect these two events.

Or is there?

Julia didn't ask me what I wonder about. Such as:

What Is Wrong

A thick brownish-yellow substance has settled in everyone's lungs—it comes from too much smoking, and from history. A constriction around the chest, nausea that follows each meal.

Julia, naturally lean, has managed lately to lose more weight. She told me last week that only bread and coffee don't make her ill. "Oh, no!" I groaned—we were talking on the phone. That evening I went over to inspect her smelly bare refrigerator. I wanted to throw out the plastic envelope of pale hamburger at the back; she wouldn't let me. "Even chicken isn't cheap any more," she murmured.

She brewed some Nescafé and we sat cross-legged on the living-room tatami; after tales of her current lover, that brute, we passed to debating Lévi-Strauss on the closing off of history. I, pious to the end, defended history. Although she still wears sumptuous caftans and treats her lungs to Balkan Sobranies, the other reason she is not eating is that she's too stingy.

One thickness of pain at a time. Julia may not want to go out "at all," but many people no longer feel like leaving their apartments "often."

This city is neither a jungle nor the moon nor the Grand Hotel. In long shot: a cosmic smudge, a conglomerate of bleeding energies. Close up, it is a fairly legible printed circuit, a transistorized labyrinth of beastly tracks, a data bank for asthmatic voice-prints. Only some of its citizens have the right to be amplified and become audible.

A black woman in her mid-fifties, wearing a brown cloth coat darker than the brown shopping bag she is carrying, gets into a cab, sighing. "143rd and St. Nicholas." Pause. "Okay?" After the word-less, hairy young driver turns on the meter, she settles the shopping bag between her fat knees and starts crying. On the other side of the scarred plastic partition, Esau can hear her.

With more people, there are more voices to tune out.

It is certainly possible that the black woman is Doris, Julia's maid (every Monday morning), who, a decade ago, while down on

St. Nicholas Avenue buying a six-pack and some macaroni salad, lost both of her small children in a fire that partly destroyed their two-room apartment. But if it is Doris, she does not ask herself why they burned up just that much and no more, why the two bodies lay next to each other in front of the TV at exactly that angle. And if it is Doris, it is certainly not Monday, Miz Julia's day, because the brown paper bag holds cast-off clothing from the woman whose seven-room apartment she's just cleaned, and Julia never throws out or gives away any of her clothes.

It's not easy to clothe oneself. Since the Easter bombing in Bloomingdale's third-floor boutique section, shoppers in large department stores are body-searched as they enter. Veined city!

If it is not Doris, Julia's Doris, then perhaps it is Doris II, whose daughter (B.A., Hunter College, 1965), having been bewitched, now lives with a woman the same age as her mother, only fatter, muscularly fat, and rich: Roberta Jorrell, the Queen of the Black Arts; internationally known monologist, poet, set designer, filmmaker, voice coach, originator of the Jorrell System of body awareness, movement, and functional coordination; and initiated voodoo priestess third-class. Doris II, also a maid, has not heard from her daughter for seven years, a captivity of biblical length that the girl has been serving as assistant stage manager of the Roberta Jorrell Total Black Theatre Institute; bookkeeper for Jorrell real-estate holdings in Dakar, Cap-Haïtien, and Philadelphia; decipherer and typist of the two-volume correspondence between R.J. and Bertrand Russell; and on-call body servant to the woman whom no one, not even her husband, dares address as anything other than Miss Jorrell.

After taking Doris, if she is Doris, to 143rd and St. Nicholas, the taxi driver, stopping for a red light on 131st Street, has a knife set against his throat by three brown boys—two are eleven, one is twelve—and surrenders his money. Off-duty sign blazing, he quickly returns to his garage on West Fifty-fifth Street and unwinds in a corner, on the far side of the Coke machine, with a joint.

However, if it is not Doris but Doris II whom he has dropped at 143rd and St. Nicholas, the driver is not robbed but immediately gets a fare to 173rd and Vyse Avenue. He accepts. But he is afraid of getting lost, of never finding his way back. Writhing, uncontrollable city! In the years since the city stopped offering garbage collection to Morrisania and Hunts Point, the dogs that roam the streets have been subtly turning into coyotes.

Julia doesn't bathe enough. Suffering smells.

Several days later, a middle-aged black woman carrying a brown shopping bag climbs out of a subway in Greenwich Village and accosts the first middle-aged white woman who's passing by. "Excuse me, ma'am, but can you tell me the way to the Ladies' House of Detention?" This is Doris III, whose only daughter, age twenty-two, is well into her third ninety-day sentence for being a, etcetera.

We know more than we can use. Look at all this stuff I've got in my head: rockets and Venetian churches, David Bowie and Diderot, nuoc mam and Big Macs, sunglasses and orgasms. How many newspapers and magazines do you read? For me, they're what candy or Quaaludes or scream therapy are for my neighbors. I get my daily ration from the bilious Lincoln Brigade veteran who runs a tobacco shop on 110th Street, not from the blind news agent in the wooden pillbox on Broadway, who's nearer my apartment.

And we don't know nearly enough.

What People Are Trying to Do

All around us, as far as I can see, people are striving to be ordinary. This takes a great deal of effort. Ordinariness, generally considered to be safer, has gotten much rarer than it used to be.

Julia called yesterday to report that, an hour before, she had gone downstairs to take in her laundry. I congratulated her.

People try to be interested in the surface. Men without guns are wearing mascara, glittering, prancing. Everyone's in some kind of moral drag.

People are trying not to mind, not to mind too much. Not to be afraid.

The daughter of Doris II has actually witnessed Roberta Jorrell—stately, unflinching—dip both hands up to the wrists in boiling oil, extract some shreds of cornmeal that she kneaded into a small pancake, and then briefly reimmerse pancake and hands. No pain, no scars. She had herself prepared by twenty hours of nonstop drumming and chanting, curtseying and asyncopated hand clapping; brackish holy water was passed around in a tin cup and sipped; and her limbs were smeared with goat's blood. After the ceremony, Doris II's daughter and four other followers, including Henry, the husband of Roberta Jorrell, escorted her back to the hotel suite in Pétionville. Henry was not allowed to stay on the same floor this trip. Miss Jorrell gave instructions that she would sleep for twenty hours and was not to be awakened for any reason. Doris II's daughter washed out Miss J's bloody robes and stationed herself on a wicker stool outside the bedroom door, waiting.

I try to get Julia to come out and play with me (fifteen years have gone by since we met): see the city. On different days and nights I've offered the roller derby in Brooklyn, a dog show, F.A.O. Schwarz, the Tibetan Museum on Staten Island, a women's march, a new singles' bar, midnight-to-dawn movies at the Elgin, Sunday's La Marqueta on upper Park Avenue, a poetry reading, anything. She invariably refuses. Once, I got her to a performance of *Pelléas et Mélisande* at the old Met, but we had to leave at the intermission; Julia was trembling—with boredom, she claimed. Moments after the curtain rose on the Scene 1 set, a clearing in a dark forest, I knew it was a mistake. "Ne me touchez pas! Ne me touchez pas!" moans the heroine, leaning dangerously into a deep well. Her first words. The well-meaning stranger and would-be rescuer—equally lost—backs off, gazing lasciviously at the heroine's long hair; Julia shudders. Lesson: don't take Mélisande to see *Pelléas et Mélisande*.

After getting out of jail, Doris III's daughter is trying to quit the life. But she can't afford to: everything's gotten so expensive. From chicken, even wings and gizzards, to the Coromandel screen, once owned by a leading couturier of the 1930s, for which Lyle's mother bids $18,000 at a Parke-Bernet auction.

People are economizing. Those who like to eat—a category that includes most people, and excludes Julia—no longer do the week's marketing in an hour at one supermarket, but must give over most of a day, exploring ten stores to assemble a shopping cart's worth of food. They, too, are wandering about the city.

The affluent, having invested in their pocket calculators, are now seeking uses for them.

Unless already in a state of thralldom, like the daughter of Doris II, people are answering ads that magicians and healers place in newspapers. "You don't have to wait for pie in the sky by-and-by when you die. If you want your pie now with ice cream on top, then see and hear Rev. Ike on TV and in person." Rev. Ike's church is not, repeat not, located in Harlem. New churches without buildings are migrating from West to East: people are worshiping the devil. On Fifty-third Street west of the Museum of Modern Art, a blond boy with a shag cut who resembles Lyle tries to interest me in the Process Church of the Final Judgment. "Have you ever heard of the Process?" When I say yes, he goes on as if I'd said no. I'll never get into the 5:30 screening if I stop to talk to him, but I hand over a buck fifty for his magazine; and he keeps up with me, telling me about free breakfast programs the Process runs for poor children, until I spin into the museum's revolving door. Breakfast programs, indeed! I thought they ate little children.

People are videotaping their bedroom feats, tapping their own telephones.

My good deed for November 12: calling Julia after a lapse of three weeks. "Hey, how are you?" "Terrible," she answered, laughing. I laughed back and said, "So am I," which wasn't exactly true. Together we laughed some more; the receiver felt sleek and warm in my hand. "Want to meet?" I asked. "Could you come to my place again? I hate leaving the apartment these days." Dearest Julia, I know that already.

I try not to reproach Julia for throwing away her children.

Lyle, who is nineteen now, called me the other morning from a phone booth at Broadway and Ninety-sixth. I tell him to come up, and he brings me a story he's just completed, the first in years, which I read. It is not as accomplished as the stories that were published when he was eleven, an undergrown baby-voiced pale boy, the Mozart of *Partisan Review*; at eleven Lyle hadn't yet taken all that acid, gone temporarily blind, been a groupie on a cross-country Rolling Stones tour, gotten committed twice by his parents, or attempted three suicides—all before finishing his junior year at Bronx Science. Lyle, with my encouragement, agrees not to burn his story.

Taki 183, Pain 145, Turok 137, Charmin 65, Think 160, Snake 128, Hondo II, Stay High 149, Cobra 151, along with several of their friends, are sending insolent messages to Simone Weil—no Jewish-American Princess she. She tells them there is no end to suffering. You think that, they answer, because you had migraines. So do you, she says tartly. Only you don't know you have them.

She also says that the only thing more hateful than a "we" is an "I"—and they go on blazoning their names on the subway cars.

What Relieves, Soothes, Helps

It's a pleasure to share one's memories. Everything remembered is dear, endearing, touching, precious. At least the past is safe— though we didn't know it at the time. We know it now. Because it's in the past; because we have survived.

Doris, Julia's Doris, has decorated her living room with photographs, toys, and clothes of her two dead children, which, each time you visit her, you have to spend the first half hour examining. Dry-eyed, she shows you everything.

A cold wind comes shuddering over the city, the temperature drops. People are cold. But at least it clears off the pollution. From my roof on Riverside Drive, squinting through the acceptable air, I can see—across New Jersey—a rim of the Ramapo hills.

It helps to say no. One evening, when I drop by Julia's apartment to retrieve a book, her psychiatrist father calls. I'm expected to answer the phone: covering the mouthpiece, I whisper, "Cambridge!" and, across the room, she whispers back, "Say I'm not home!" He knows I'm lying. "I know Julia never goes out," he says indignantly. "She would have," I say, "if she'd known you were going to call." Julia grins—heartbreaking, childish grin—and bites into a pomegranate I've brought her.

What helps is having the same feelings for a lifetime. At a fundraising party on Beekman Place for the New Democratic Coalition's alternate mayoral candidate, I flirt with an elderly Yiddish journalist who doesn't want to talk about quotas and school boycotts in Queens. He tells me about his childhood in a shtetl ten miles from Warsaw ("Of course, you never heard of a shtetl. You're too young. It was a village where the Jews lived"). He had been inseparable from another small boy. "I couldn't live without him. He was more to me than my brothers. But, you know, I didn't like him. I hated him. Whenever we played together, he would make me so mad. Sometimes we would hurt each other with sticks." Then he goes on to tell me how, last month, a shabby old man with stiff pink ears had come into the *Forward* office, had asked for him, had come over to his desk, had stood there, had said, "Walter Abramson, you know who I am?" And how he'd gazed into the old man's eyes, scrutinized his bald skull and shopping-bag body, and suddenly knew. "You're Isaac." And the old man said, "You're right."

"After fifty years, can you imagine? Honestly, I don't know how I recognized him," said the journalist. "It wasn't something in his eyes. But I did."

What happened? "So we fell into each other's arms. And I asked him about his family, and he told me they were all killed by the Nazis. And he asked me about my family, and I told him they were all killed . . . And you know what? After fifteen minutes, everything he said infuriated me. I didn't care any more if his whole family had been killed. I didn't care if he was a poor old man. I hated him." He trembled—with vitality. "I wanted to beat him. With a stick."

Sometimes it helps to change your feelings altogether, like getting your blood pumped out and replaced. To become another person. But without magic. There's no moral equivalent to the operation that makes transsexuals happy.

A sense of humor helps. I haven't explained that Julia is funny, droll, witty—that she can make me laugh. I've made her sound like nothing but a burden.

Sometimes it helps to be paranoid. Conspiracies have the merit of making sense. It's a relief to discover your enemies, even if first you have to invent them. Roberta Jorrell, for instance, has humorlessly instructed Doris II's daughter and others on her payroll exactly how to thwart the enemies of her federally funded South Philadelphia Black Redress Center—white bankers, AMA psychiatrists, Black Panthers, cops, Maoists, and the CIA—with powders, with hexes, and with preternaturally smooth flat stones blessed by a Cuban *santera* in Miami Beach. Julia, however, doesn't think she has any enemies—as, when her current lover again refuses to leave his wife, she still doesn't understand that she isn't loved. But when she goes down on the street, which happens less and less frequently, she finds the cars menacingly unpredictable.

———

Flight is said to help. Dean and Shirley, Lyle's parents, having pulled out of the market last year, have bought into a condominium in Sarasota, Florida, whose City Fathers recently voted, in order to make the city more seductive to tourists, to take out all the parking meters they installed downtown five years ago. Lyle's parents don't know how many weeks a year they can actually spend in the Ringling Brothers' hometown; but there's never been a decade when real-estate values haven't gone up, right? And that crazy Quiz Kid, their son, will always have his room there if he wants it.

It helps to feel guiltless about your sexual options, though it's not clear that many people actually manage this. After eventually finding his way back from Hunts Point into the well-lit grid of more familiar predators, the driver who had taken Doris II to 143rd and St. Nicholas picks up a pale, blond boy with a shag cut who also resembles Lyle and who says, as he gets into the cab, "West Street and the trucks, please."

Lately, my sexual life has become very pure. I don't want it to be like a dirty movie. (Having enjoyed a lot of dirty movies, I don't want it to be like that.)

Let's lie down together, love, and hold each other.

Meanwhile, the real Lyle has again skipped his four o'clock class, Comp. Lit. 203 ("Sade and the Anarchist Tradition"), and is sprawled in front of a TV set in the dormitory lounge. He's been watching more and more television lately, with a preference for serials like *The Secret Storm* and *As the World Turns*. He has also started showing up at student parties, instead of rebuffing his roommate's kindly, clumsy invitations. A good rule: any party is depressing, if you think about it. But you don't have to think about it.

I'm happy when I dance.

Touch me.

What Is Upsetting

To read *Last Letters from Stalingrad*, and grieve for those lost, all-too-human voices among the most devilish of enemies. No one is a devil if fully heard.

To find everyone crazy—example: both Lyle and his parents. And to find the crazy particularly audible.

To be afraid.

To know that Lyle will be introduced to Roberta Jorrell next week at an elegant SoHo loft party given in her honor after her speech at New York University; be recruited by her; drop out of college; and not be heard from again for at least seven years.

To feel how desperate everyone is. Doris, Julia's Doris, is being evicted from her apartment. She not only has no money to pay a higher rent; she wants to go on living in the place where her children perished.

To learn that the government—using information that the law now requires be recorded on tape and stored indefinitely by banks, the telephone company, airlines, credit-card companies—can know more about me (my more sociable activities, anyway) than I do myself. If necessary, I could list most of the plane trips I've taken; and my old checkbook stubs are in a drawer—somewhere. But I don't remember whom I telephoned exactly four months ago at 11 a.m., and never will. I don't think it was Julia.

To find in myself the desire to stop listening to people's distress.

To be unsure of how to exercise the powers I do possess.

Julia had once fallen under the spell of an ex-ESP researcher, then a specialist in the North American Indian occult, who claimed to know how to help her. Most people who meet Julia, stunned by her vulnerability, take a crack at helping her; the pleasure of her beauty, which is the only gift Julia has ever been able to make to other people, helps too. The sorceress in question, Martha Wooten, was white, Westchester-born, crisp, a superb tennis player—rather like a gym teacher; I thought, condescendingly, she might be good for Julia, until as part of a program for freeing Julia from her demons, she had her bay at the full moon on all fours. Then I swooped back into Julia's underfurnished life, performed my old rites of counterexorcism—reason! self-preservation! pessimism of the intellect, optimism of the will!—and Martha Wooten vanished, metamorphosed, rather, into one of the Wicked Witches of the West, setting up in Big Sur as Lady Lambda, head of the only Lucifer cult that practices deep breathing and bioenergetics analysis.

Was I right to de-bewitch her?

To be unable to change one's life. Doris III's daughter is back in jail.

To live in bad air. To have an airless life. To feel there's no ground: that there is nothing but air.

Our Prospects

Aleatoric. Repetitious. On a Monday, after taking Doris, Julia's Doris, home from cleaning Julia's apartment, the taxi driver stops to pick up three fourteen-year-old Puerto Ricans on 111th and Second Avenue. If they don't rob him, they will get in the cab, ask to be taken to the juice bar in the alley by the Fifty-ninth Street Bridge, and give him a big tip.

Not good. A hand-lettered sign pasted at eye level on the bare brick wall of a housing project on the corner of Ninetieth and Amsterdam reads, plaintively: Stop Killing.

Wounded city!

Although none of the rules for becoming more alive is valid, it is healthy to keep on formulating them.

Here's a solid conservative rule, deposited by Goethe with Eckermann: "Every healthy effort is directed from the inner to the outer world." Put that in your hashish pipe and smoke it.

But let's say, or suppose, we're not up to being healthy. Then there's only one way left to get to the world. We could be glad of the world, if we were flying to it for refuge.

Actually, this world isn't just one world—now. As this city is actually layers of cities. Behind the many thicknesses of pain, try to connect with the single will for pleasure that moves even in the violence of streets and beds, of jails and opera houses.

In the words of Rev. Ike, "You Can Be Happy Now." By an extraordinary coincidence, there is one day when Doris, Doris II, and Doris III—who don't know each other—may all be found under the

same roof: in Rev. Ike's United Church and Science of Living Institute, attending a 3 p.m. Sunday Healing and Blessing Meeting. As for
their prospects of being happy: none of the three Dorises is convinced.

Julia . . . anybody! Hey, how are you? Terrible, yes. But you laughed.

Some of us will falter, but some of us will be brave. A middle-aged
black woman in a brown coat carrying a brown suitcase leaves a
bank and gets into a cab. "I'm going to the Port of Authority,
please." Doris II is taking the bus to Philadelphia. After seven
years, she's going to confront Roberta Jorrell and try to get her
daughter back.

Some of us will get more craven. Meanwhile, most of us will never
know what's happening.

Let's dig through the past. Let's admire whatever, whenever we
can. But people now have such grudging sympathy for the past.

If I come out to dinner in my space suit, will you wear yours? We'll
look like Dale and Flash Gordon, maybe, but who cares. What everybody thinks now: one can form an alliance only with the future.

The prospects are for more of the same. As always. But I refuse.

Suppose, just suppose, leaden soul, you would try to lead an exemplary life. To be kind, honorable, helpful, just. On whose authority?
    And you'll never know, that way, what you most long to know.
Wisdom requires a life that is singular in another way, that's per-
verse. To know more, you must conjure up all the lives there are,
and then leave out whatever fails to please you. Wisdom is a ruth-
less business.

But what about those I love? Although I don't believe my friends can't get on without me, surviving isn't so easy; and I probably can't survive without them.

If we don't help each other, forlorn demented bricklayers who've forgotten the location of the building we were putting up . . .

"Taxi!" I hail a cab during the Wednesday afternoon rush hour and ask the driver to get to Julia's address as fast as he can. Something in her voice on the phone lately . . . But she seems all right when I come in. She'd even been out the day before to take a batik (made last year) to be framed; it will be ready in a week. And when I ask to borrow a back issue of a feminist magazine that I spy, under a pile of old newspapers, on the floor, she mentions three times that I must return it soon. I promise to come by next Monday. Reassured by the evidence of those petty forms that Julia's hold on life often takes, I'm ready to leave. But then she asks me to stay on, just a few minutes more, which means that it's changing; she wants to talk sadness. On cue, like an old vaudevillian, I go into my routines of secular ethical charm. They seem to work. She promises to try.

What I'm Doing

I leave the city often. But I always come back.

I made Lyle give me his story—his only copy, of course—knowing that, despite his promise, if I returned it to him, he'd burn it, as he's burned everything he's written since he was fifteen. I've given it to a magazine editor I know.

I exhort, I interfere. I'm impatient. For God's sake, it isn't *that* hard to live. One of the pieces of advice I give is: Don't suffer future pain.

And whether or not the other person heeds my advice, at least I've learned something from what was said. I give fairly good advice to myself.

That late Wednesday afternoon I told Julia how stupid it would be if she committed suicide. She agreed. I thought I was convincing. Two days later she left her apartment again and killed herself, showing me that she didn't mind doing something stupid.

I would. Even when I announce to friends that I'm going to do something stupid, I don't really think it is.

I want to save my soul, that timid wind.

Some nights, I dream of dragging Julia back by her long hair, just as she's about to jump into the river. Or I dream she's already in the river: I am standing on my roof, facing New Jersey; I look down and see her floating by, and I leap from the roof, half falling, half swooping like a bird, and seize her by the hair and pull her out.

Julia, darling Julia, you weren't supposed to lean any farther into the well—daring anyone with good intentions to come closer, to save you, to be kind. You were at least supposed to die in a warm bed—mute; surrounded by the guilty, clumsy people who adored you, leaving them frustrated and resentful of you to the end.

I'm not thinking of what the lordly polluted Hudson did to your body before you were found.

Julia, plastic face in the waxy casket, how could you be as old as you were? You're still the twenty-three-year-old who started an absurdly pedantic conversation with me on the steps of Widener Library—so thin; so prettily affected; so electric; so absent; so much younger than I, who was four years younger than you; so tired already; so exasperating; so moving. I want to hit you.

How I groaned under the burden of our friendship. But your death is heavier.

Why you went under while others, equally absent from their lives, survive is a mystery to me.

Say we are all asleep. Do we want to wake up?

Is it fair if I wake up and you, most of you, don't? Fair! you sneer. What's fair got to do with it? It's every soul for itself. But I didn't want to wake up without you.

You're the tears in things, I'm not. You weep for me, I'll weep for you. Help me, I don't want to weep for myself. I'm not giving up.

Sisyphus, I. I cling to my rock, you don't have to chain me. Stand back! I roll it up—up, up. And . . . down we go. I knew that would happen. See, I'm on my feet again. See, I'm starting to roll it up again. Don't try to talk me out of it. Nothing, nothing could tear me away from this rock.

THE WAY WE LIVE NOW

At first he was just losing weight, he felt only a little ill, Max said to Ellen, and he didn't call for an appointment with his doctor, according to Greg, because he was managing to keep on working at more or less the same rhythm, but he did stop smoking, Tanya pointed out, which suggests he was frightened, but also that he wanted, even more than he knew, to be healthy, or healthier, or maybe just to gain back a few pounds, said Orson, for he told her, Tanya went on, that he expected to be climbing the walls (isn't that what people say?) and found, to his surprise, that he didn't miss cigarettes at all and reveled in the sensation of his lungs being ache-free for the first time in years. But did he have a good doctor, Stephen wanted to know, since it would have been crazy not to go for a checkup after the pressure was off and he was back from the conference in Helsinki, even if by then he was feeling better. And he said, to Frank, that he would go, even though he was indeed frightened, as he admitted to Jan, but who wouldn't be frightened now, though, odd as that might seem, he hadn't been worrying until recently, he avowed to Quentin, it was only in the last six months that he had the metallic taste of panic in his mouth, because becoming seriously ill was something that happened to other people, a normal delusion, he observed to Paolo, if one was thirty-eight and had never had a serious ill-ness; he wasn't, as Jan confirmed, a hypochondriac. Of course, it was hard not to worry, everyone was worried, but it wouldn't do to panic, because, as Max pointed out to Quentin, there wasn't any-thing one could do except wait and hope, wait and start being careful, be careful, and hope. And even if one did prove to be ill, one shouldn't give up, they had new treatments that promised an arrest of the disease's inexorable course, research was progressing. It seemed that everyone was in touch with everyone else several times a week, checking in, I've never spent so many hours at a time on the phone, Stephen said to Kate, and when I'm exhausted after the two or three calls made to me, giving me the latest, instead of switching off the phone to give myself a respite I tap out the num-ber of another friend or acquaintance, to pass on the news. I'm not sure I can afford to think so much about it, Ellen said, and I suspect my own motives, there's something morbid I'm getting used to, get-ting excited by, this must be like what people felt in London during the Blitz. As far as I know, I'm not at risk, but you never know, said Aileen. This thing is totally unprecedented, said Frank. But don't you think he ought to see a doctor, Stephen insisted. Listen, said Orson, you can't force people to take care of themselves, and what makes you think the worst, he could be just run down, people still do get ordinary illnesses, awful ones, why are you assuming it has to be *that*. But all I want to be sure, said Stephen, is that he under-stands the options, because most people don't, that's why they won't see a doctor or have the test, they think there's nothing one can do. But is there anything one can do, he said to Tanya (according to Greg), I mean what do I gain if I go to the doctor; if I'm really ill, he's reported to have said, I'll find out soon enough.

And when he was in the hospital, his spirits seemed to lighten, according to Donny. He seemed more cheerful than he had been in the last months, Ursula said, and the bad news seemed to come almost as a relief, according to Ira, as a truly unexpected blow, according to Quentin, but you'd hardly expect him to have said the same thing to all his friends, because his relation to Ira was so different from his relation to Quentin (this according to Quentin, who was proud of their friendship), and perhaps he thought Quentin wouldn't be undone by seeing him weep, but Ira insisted that couldn't be the reason he behaved so differently with each, and that maybe he was feeling less shocked, mobilizing his strength to fight for his life, at the moment he saw Ira but overcome by feelings of hopelessness when Quentin arrived with flowers, because anyway the flowers threw him into a bad mood, as Quentin told Kate, since the hospital room was choked with flowers, you couldn't have crammed another flower into that room, but surely you're exaggerating, Kate said, smiling, everybody likes flowers. Well, who wouldn't exaggerate at a time like this, Quentin said sharply. Don't you think *this* is an exaggeration. Of course I do, said Kate gently, I was only teasing, I mean I didn't mean to tease. I know that, Quentin said, with tears in his eyes, and Kate hugged him and said well, when I go this evening I guess I won't bring flowers, what does he want, and Quentin said, according to Max, what he likes best is chocolate. Is there anything else, asked Kate, I mean like chocolate but not chocolate. Licorice, said Quentin, blowing his nose. And besides that. Aren't *you* exaggerating now, Quentin said, smiling. Right, said Kate, so if I want to bring him a whole raft of stuff, besides chocolate and licorice, what else. Jelly beans, Quentin said.

He didn't want to be alone, according to Paolo, and lots of people came in the first week, and the Jamaican nurse said there were other patients on the floor who would be glad to have the surplus flowers, and people weren't afraid to visit, it wasn't like the old days, as Kate pointed out to Aileen, they're not even segregated in the hospital any more, as Hilda observed, there's nothing on the door of his room warning visitors of the possibility of contagion, as there was a few years ago; in fact, he's in a double room and, as he told Orson, the old guy on the far side of the curtain (who's clearly on the way out, said Stephen) doesn't even have the disease, so, as Kate went on, you really should go and see him, he'd be happy to see you, he likes having people visit, you aren't not going because you're afraid, are you. Of course not, Aileen said, but I don't know what to say, I think I'll feel awkward, which he's bound to notice, and that will make him feel worse, so I won't be doing him any good, will I. But he won't notice anything, Kate said, patting Aileen's hand, it's not like that, it's not the way you imagine, he's not judging people or wondering about their motives, he's just happy to see his friends. But I never was really a friend of his, Aileen said, you're a friend, he's always liked you, you told me he talks about Nora with you, I know he likes me, he's even attracted to me, but he respects you. But, according to Wesley, the reason Aileen was so stingy with her visits was that she could never have him to herself, there were always others there already and by the time they left still others had arrived, she'd been in love with him for years, and I can understand, said Donny, that Aileen should feel bitter that if there could have been a woman friend he did more than occasionally bed, a woman he really loved, and my God, Victor said, who had known him in those years, he was crazy about Nora, what a heartrending couple they were, two surly angels, then it couldn't have been she.

And when some of the friends, the ones who came every day, waylaid the doctor in the corridor, Stephen was the one who asked the most informed questions, who'd been keeping up not just with the stories that appeared several times a week in the *Times* (which Greg confessed to have stopped reading, unable to stand it any more) but with articles in the medical journals published here and

in England and France, and who knew socially one of the principal doctors in Paris who was doing some much-publicized research
on the disease, but his doctor said little more than that the pneu-
monia was not life-threatening, the fever was subsiding, of course
he was still weak but he was responding well to the antibiotics,
that he'd have to complete his stay in the hospital, which entailed
a minimum of twenty-one days on the I.V., before she could start
him on the new drug, for she was optimistic about the possibility
of getting him into the protocol; and when Victor said that if he
had so much trouble eating (he'd say to everyone, when they coaxed
him to eat some of the hospital meals, that food didn't taste right,
that he had a funny metallic taste in his mouth) it couldn't be good
that friends were bringing him all that chocolate, the doctor just
smiled and said that in these cases the patient's morale was also an
important factor, and if chocolate made him feel better she saw no
harm in it, which worried Stephen, as Stephen said later to Donny,
because they wanted to believe in the promises and taboos of today's
high-tech medicine but here this reassuringly curt and silver-haired
specialist in the disease, someone quoted frequently in the papers,
was talking like some oldfangled country G.P. who tells the family
that tea with honey or chicken soup may do as much for the patient
as penicillin, which might mean, as Max said, that they were just
going through the motions of treating him, that they were not sure
about what to do, or rather, as Xavier interjected, that they didn't
know what the hell they were doing, that the truth, the real truth,
as Hilda said, upping the ante, was that they didn't, the doctors,
really have any hope.

Oh, no, said Lewis, I can't stand it, wait a minute, I can't believe it,
are you sure, I mean are they sure, have they done all the tests, it's
getting so when the phone rings I'm scared to answer because I
think it will be someone telling me someone else is ill; but did

Lewis really not know until yesterday, Robert said testily, I find that hard to believe, everybody is talking about it, it seems impossible that someone wouldn't have called Lewis; and perhaps Lewis did know, was for some reason pretending not to know already, because, Jan recalled, didn't Lewis say something months ago to Greg, and not only to Greg, about his not looking well, losing weight, and being worried about him and wishing he'd see a doctor, so it couldn't come as a total surprise. Well, everybody is worried about everybody now, said Betsy, that seems to be the way we live, the way we live now. And, after all, they were once very close, doesn't Lewis still have the keys to his apartment, you know the way you let someone keep the keys after you've broken up, only a little because you hope the person might just saunter in, drunk or high, late some evening, but mainly because it's wise to have a few sets of keys strewn around town, if you live alone, at the top of a former commercial building that, pretentious as it is, will never acquire a doorman or even a resident superintendent, someone whom you can call on for the keys late one night if you find you've lost yours or have locked yourself out. Who else has keys, Tanya inquired, I was thinking somebody might drop by tomorrow before coming to the hospital and bring some treasures, because the other day, Ira said, he was complaining about how dreary the hospital room was, and how it was like being locked up in a motel room, which got everybody started telling funny stories about motel rooms they'd known, and at Ursula's story, about the Luxury Budget Inn in Schenectady, there was an uproar of laughter around his bed, while he watched them in silence, eyes bright with fever, all the while, as Victor recalled, gobbling that damned chocolate. But, according to Jan, whom Lewis's keys enabled to tour the swank of his bachelor lair with an eye to bringing over some art consolation to brighten up the hospital room, the Byzantine icon wasn't on the wall over his bed, and that was a puzzle until Orson remembered that he'd recounted without seeming upset (this disputed by Greg) that the boy he'd recently gotten rid of had stolen it, along with four of the *maki-e* lacquer boxes, as if these were objects as easy to sell on the street as a TV or a stereo. But he's always been very generous, Kate said quietly, and though he loves beautiful things isn't really attached to them, to things, as Orson said, which is unusual in a collector, as Frank commented, and when Kate shuddered and tears sprang to her eyes and Orson inquired anxiously if he, Orson, had said something wrong, she pointed out that they'd begun talking about him in a retrospective mode, summing up what he was like, what made them fond of him, as if he were finished, completed, already a part of the past.

Perhaps he was getting tired of having so many visitors, said Robert, who was, as Ellen couldn't help mentioning, someone who had come only twice and was probably looking for a reason not to be in regular attendance, but there could be no doubt, according to Ursula, that his spirits had dipped, not that there was any discouraging news from the doctors, and he seemed now to prefer being alone a few hours of the day; and he told Donny that he'd begun keeping a diary for the first time in his life, because he wanted to record the course of his mental reactions to this astonishing turn of events, to do something parallel to what the doctors were doing, who came every morning and conferred at his bedside about his body, and that perhaps it wasn't so important what he wrote in it, which amounted, as he said wryly to Quentin, to little more than the usual banalities about terror and amazement that this was happening to him, to him also, plus the usual remorseful assessments of his past life, his pardonable superficialities, capped by resolves to live better, more deeply, more in touch with his work and his friends, and not to care so passionately about what people thought of him, interspersed with admonitions to himself that in this situation his will to live counted more than anything else and that if he really wanted to live, and trusted life, and liked himself well enough (down, ol' debbil Thanatos!), he *would* live, he would be an exception; but perhaps all this, as Quentin ruminated, talking on the phone to Kate, wasn't the point, the point was that by the very keeping of the diary he was accumulating something to reread one day, slyly staking out his claim to a future time, in which the diary would be an object, a relic, in which he might not actually reread it, because he would want to have put this ordeal behind him, but the diary would be there in the drawer of his stupendous Majorelle desk, and he could already, he did actually say to Quentin one late sunny afternoon, propped up in the hospital bed, with the stain of chocolate framing one corner of a heartbreaking smile, see himself in the penthouse, the October sun streaming through those clear windows instead of this streaked one, and the diary, the pathetic diary, safe inside the drawer.

It doesn't matter about the treatment's side effects, Stephen said (when talking to Max), I don't know why you're so worried about that, every strong treatment has some dangerous side effects, it's inevitable, you mean otherwise the treatment wouldn't be effective, Hilda interjected, and anyway, Stephen went on doggedly, just because there *are* side effects it doesn't mean he has to get them, or all of them, each one, or even some of them. That's just a list of all the possible things that could go wrong, because the doctors have to cover themselves, so they make up a worst-case scenario, but isn't what's happening to him, and to so many other people, Tanya interrupted, a worst-case scenario, a catastrophe no one could have imagined, it's too cruel, and isn't everything a side effect, quipped Ira, even *we* are all side effects, but we're not bad side effects, Frank said, he likes having his friends around, and we're helping each other, too; because his illness sticks us all in the same glue, mused

Xavier, and, whatever the jealousies and grievances from the past that have made us wary and cranky with each other, when something like this happens (the sky is falling, the sky is falling!) you understand what's really important. I agree, Chicken Little, he is reported to have said. But don't you think, Quentin observed to Max, that being as close to him as we are, making time to drop by the hospital every day, is a way of our trying to define ourselves more firmly and irrevocably as the well, those who aren't ill, who aren't going to fall ill, as if what's happened to him couldn't happen to us, when in fact the chances are that before long one of us will end up where he is, which is probably what he felt when he was one of the cohort visiting Zack in the spring (you never knew Zack, did you?), and, according to Clarice, Zack's widow, he didn't come very often, he said he hated hospitals, and didn't feel he was doing Zack any good, that Zack would see on his face how uncomfortable he was. Oh, he was one of those, Aileen said. A coward. Like me.

And after he was sent home from the hospital, and Quentin had volunteered to move in and was cooking meals and taking telephone messages and keeping the mother in Mississippi informed, well, mainly keeping her from flying to New York and heaping her grief on her son and confusing the household routine with her oppressive ministrations, he was able to work an hour or two in his study, on days he didn't insist on going out, for a meal or a movie, which tired him. He seemed optimistic, Kate thought, his appetite was good, and what he said, Orson reported, was that he agreed when Stephen advised him that the main thing was to keep in shape, he was a fighter, right, he wouldn't be who he was if he weren't, and was he ready for the big fight, Stephen asked rhetorically (as Max told it to Donny), and he said you bet, and Stephen added it could be a lot worse, you could have gotten the disease two years ago, but now so many scientists are working on it, the American team and the French team, everyone bucking for that Nobel Prize a few years down the road, that all you have to do is stay healthy for another year or two and then there will be good treatment, real treatment. Yes, he said, Stephen said, my timing is good. And Betsy, who had been climbing on and rolling off macrobiotic diets for a decade, came up with a Japanese specialist she wanted him to see but thank God, Donny reported, he'd had the sense to refuse, but he did agree to see Victor's visualization therapist, although what could one possibly visualize, said Hilda, when the point of visualizing disease was to see it as an entity with contours, borders, here rather than there, something limited, something you were the host of, in the sense that you could disinvite the disease, while this was so total; or would be, Max said. But the main thing, said Greg, was to see that he didn't go the macrobiotic route, which might be harmless for plump Betsy but could only be devastating for him, lean as he'd always been, with all the cigarettes and other appetite-suppressing chemicals he'd been welcoming into his body for years; and now was hardly the time, as Stephen pointed out, to be worried about cleaning up his act, and eliminating the chemical additives and other pollutants that we're all blithely or not so blithely feasting on, blithely since we're healthy, healthy as we can be; so far, Ira said. Meat and potatoes is what I'd be happy to see him eating, Ursula said wistfully. And spaghetti and clam sauce, Greg added. And thick cholesterol-rich omelettes with smoked mozzarella, suggested Yvonne, who had flown from London for the weekend to see him. Chocolate cake, said Frank. Maybe not chocolate cake, Ursula said, he's already eating so much chocolate.

And when, not right away but still only three weeks later, he was accepted into the protocol for the new drug, which took considerable behind-the-scenes lobbying with the doctors, he talked less about being ill, according to Donny, which seemed like a good sign, Kate felt, a sign that he was not feeling like a victim, feeling not that he *had* a disease but, rather, was living *with* a disease (that was the right cliché, wasn't it?), a more hospitable arrangement, said Jan, a kind of cohabitation which implied that it was something temporary, that it could be terminated, but terminated how, said Hilda, and when you say hospitable, Jan, I hear hospital. And it was encouraging, Stephen insisted, that from the start, at least from the time he was finally persuaded to make the telephone call to his doctor, he was willing to say the name of the disease, pronounce it often and easily, as if it were just another word, like boy or gallery or cigarette or money or deal, as in no big deal, Paolo interjected, because, as Stephen continued, to utter the name is a sign of health, a sign that one has accepted being who one is, mortal, vulnerable, not exempt, not an exception after all, it's a sign that one is willing, truly willing, to fight for one's life. And we must say the name, too, and often, Tanya added, we mustn't lag behind him in honesty, or let him feel that, the effort of honesty having been made, it's something done with and he can go on to other things. One is so much better prepared to help him, Wesley replied. In a way he's fortunate, said Yvonne, who had taken care of a problem at the New York store and was flying back to London this evening, sure, fortunate, said Wesley, no one is shunning him, Yvonne went on, no one's afraid to hug him or kiss him lightly on the mouth, in London we are, as usual, a few years behind you, people I know, people who would seem to be not even remotely at risk, are just terrified, but I'm impressed by how cool and rational you all are; you find us cool, asked Quentin. But I have to say, he's reported to have said, I'm terrified, I find it very hard to read (and you know how he loves to read, said Greg; yes, reading is his television, said Paolo) or to think, but I don't feel hysterical. I feel quite hysterical, Lewis said to Yvonne. But you're able to *do* something for him, that's wonderful, how I wish I could stay longer, Yvonne answered, it's rather beautiful, I can't help thinking, this utopia of friendship you've assembled around him (this pathetic utopia, said Kate), so that the disease, Yvonne concluded, is not, any more, out there. Yes, don't you think we're more at home here, with him, with the disease, said Tanya, because the imagined disease is so much worse than the reality of him, whom we all love, each in our fashion, having it. I know for me his getting it has quite demystified the disease, said Jan, I don't feel afraid, spooked, as I did before he became ill, when it was only news about remote acquaintances, whom I never saw again after they became ill. But you know you're not going to come down with the disease, Quentin said, to which Ellen replied, on her behalf, that's not the point, and possibly untrue, my gynecologist says that everyone is at risk, everyone who has a sexual life, because sexuality is a chain that links each of us to many others, unknown others, and now the great chain of being has become a chain of death as well. It's not the same for you, Quentin insisted, it's not the same for you as it is for me or Lewis or Frank or Paolo or Max, I'm more and more frightened, and I have every reason to be. I don't think about whether I'm at risk or not, said Hilda, I know that I was afraid to know someone with the disease, afraid of what I'd see, what I'd feel, and after the first day I came to the hospital I felt so relieved. I'll never feel that way, that fear, again; he doesn't seem different from me. He's not, Quentin said.

According to Lewis, he talked more often about those who visited more often, which is natural, said Betsy, I think he's even keeping a tally. And among those who came or checked in by phone every day, the inner circle as it were, those who were getting more points, there was still a further competition, which was what was getting on Betsy's nerves, she confessed to Jan; there's always that vulgar jockeying for position around the bedside of the gravely ill, and though we all feel suffused with virtue at our loyalty to him (speak for yourself, said Jan), to the extent that we're carving time out of every day, or almost every day, though some of us are dropping out, as Xavier pointed out, aren't we getting at least as much out of this as he is. Are we, said Jan. We're rivals for a sign from him of special pleasure over a visit, each stretching for the brass ring of his favor, wanting to feel the most wanted, the true nearest and dearest, which is inevitable with someone who doesn't have a spouse and children or an official in-house lover, hierarchies that no one would dare contest, Betsy went on, so we are the family he's founded, without meaning to, without official titles and ranks (we, we, snarled Quentin); and is it so clear, though some of us, Lewis and Quentin and Tanya and Paolo, among others, are ex-lovers and all of us more or less than friends, which one of us he prefers, Victor said (now it's us, raged Quentin), because sometimes I think he looks forward more to seeing Aileen, who has visited only three times, twice at the hospital and once since he's been home, than he does you or me; but, according to Tanya, after being very disappointed that Aileen hadn't come, now he was angry, while, according to Xavier, he was not really hurt but touchingly passive, accepting Aileen's absence as something he somehow deserved. But he's happy to have people around, said Lewis; he says when he doesn't have company he gets very sleepy, he sleeps (according to Quentin), and then perks up when someone arrives, it's important that he not feel ever alone. But, said Victor, there's one person he hasn't heard from, whom he'd probably like to hear from more than most of us; but she didn't just vanish, even right after she broke away from him, and he knows exactly where she lives now, said Kate, he told me he put in a call to her last Christmas Eve, and she said it's nice to hear from you and Merry Christmas, and he was shattered, according to Orson, and furious and disdainful, according to Ellen (what do you expect of her, said Wesley, she was burned out), but Kate wondered if maybe he hadn't phoned Nora in the middle of a sleepless night, what's the time difference, and Quentin said no, I don't think so, I think he wouldn't want her to know.

And when he was feeling even better and had regained the pounds he'd shed right away in the hospital, though the refrigerator started to fill up with organic wheat germ and grapefruit and skimmed milk (he's worried about his cholesterol count, Stephen lamented), and told Quentin he could manage by himself now, and did, he started asking everyone who visited how he looked, and everyone said he looked great, so much better than a few weeks ago, which didn't jibe with what anyone had told him at that time; but then it was getting harder and harder to know how he looked, to answer such a question honestly when among themselves they wanted to be honest, both for honesty's sake and (as Donny thought) to prepare for the worst, because he'd been looking like *this* for so long, at least it seemed so long, that it was as if he'd always been like this, how did he look before, but it was only a few months, and those words, pale and wan-looking and fragile, hadn't they always applied? And one Thursday Ellen, meeting Lewis at the door of the building, said, as they rode up together in the elevator, how is he *really*? But you see how he is, Lewis said tartly, he's fine, he's perfectly healthy, and Ellen understood that of course Lewis didn't think he was perfectly healthy but that he wasn't worse, and that was true, but wasn't it, well, almost heartless to talk like that. Seems inoffensive to me, Quentin said, but I know what you mean, I remember once talking to Frank, somebody, after all, who has volunteered to do five hours a week of office work at the Crisis Center (I know, said Ellen), and Frank was going on about this guy, diagnosed almost a year ago, and so much further along, who'd been complaining to Frank on the phone about the indifference of some doctor, and had gotten quite abusive about the doctor, and

Frank was saying there was no reason to be so upset, the implication being that *he*, Frank, wouldn't behave so irrationally, and I said, barely able to control my scorn, but Frank, Frank, he has every reason to be upset, he's dying, and Frank said, said according to Quentin, oh, I don't like to think about it that way.

And it was while he was still home, recuperating, getting his weekly treatment, still not able to do much work, he complained, but, according to Quentin, up and about most of the time and turning up at the office several days a week, that bad news came about two remote acquaintances, one in Houston and one in Paris, news that was intercepted by Quentin on the ground that it could only depress him, but Stephen contended that it was wrong to lie to him, it was so important for him to live in the truth; that had been one of his first victories, that he was candid, that he was even willing to crack jokes about the disease, but Ellen said it wasn't good to give him this end-of-the-world feeling, too many people were getting ill, it was becoming such a common destiny that maybe some of the will to fight for his life would be drained out of him if it seemed to be as natural as, well, death. Oh, Hilda said, who didn't know personally either the one in Houston or the one in Paris, but knew *of* the one in Paris, a pianist who specialized in twentieth-century Czech and Polish music, I have his records, he's such a valuable person, and, when Kate glared at her, continued defensively, I know every life is equally sacred, but that *is* a thought, another thought, I mean, all these valuable people who aren't going to have their normal fourscore as it is now, these people aren't going to be replaced, and it's such a loss to the culture. But this isn't going to go on forever, Wesley said, it can't, they're bound to come up with something (they, they, muttered Stephen), but did you ever think, Greg said, that if some people don't die, I mean even if they can keep them alive (they, they, muttered Kate), they continue to be carriers, and that means, if you have a conscience, that you can never make love, make love fully, as you'd been wont—wantonly, Ira said—to do. But it's better than dying, said Frank. And in all his talk about the future, when he allowed himself to be hopeful, according to Quentin, he never mentioned the prospect that even if he didn't die, if he were so fortunate as to be among the first generation of the disease's survivors, never mentioned, Kate confirmed, that whatever happened it was over, the way he had lived until now, but, according to Ira, he did think about it, the end of bravado, the end of folly, the end of trusting life, the end of taking life for granted, and of treating life as something that, samurai-like, he thought himself ready to throw away lightly, impudently; and Kate recalled, sighing, a brief exchange she'd insisted on having as long as two years ago, huddling on a banquette covered with steel-gray industrial carpet on an upper level of The Prophet and toking up for their next foray onto the dance floor: she'd said hesitantly, for it felt foolish asking a prince of debauchery to, well, take it easy, and she wasn't keen on playing big sister, a role, as Hilda confirmed, he inspired in many women, are you being careful, honey, you know what I mean. And he replied, Kate went on, no, I'm not, listen, I can't, I just can't, sex is too important to me, always has been (he started talking like that, according to Victor, after Nora left him), and if I get it, well, I get it. But he wouldn't talk like that now, would he, said Greg; he must feel awfully foolish now, said Betsy, like someone who went on smoking, saying I can't give up cigarettes, but when the bad X-ray is taken even the most besotted nicotine addict can stop on a dime. But sex isn't like cigarettes, is it, said Frank, and, besides, what good does it do to remember that he was reckless, said Lewis angrily, the appalling thing is that you just have to be unlucky once, and wouldn't he feel even worse if he'd stopped three years ago and had come down with it anyway, since one of the most terrifying features of the

disease is that you don't know when you contracted it, it could have
been ten years ago, because surely this disease has existed for years
and years, long before it was recognized; that is, named. Who
knows how long (I think a lot about that, said Max) and who knows
(I know what you're going to say, Stephen interrupted) how many
are going to get it.

I'm feeling fine, he's reported to have said whenever someone
asked him how he was, which was almost always the first question
anyone asked. Or: I'm feeling better, how are you? But he said
other things, too. I'm playing leapfrog with myself, he is reported
to have said, according to Victor. And: There must be a way to get
something positive out of this situation, he's reported to have said
to Kate. How American of him, said Paolo. Well, said Betsy, you
know the old American adage: When you've got a lemon, make
lemonade. The one thing I'm sure I couldn't take, Jan said he said
to her, is becoming disfigured, but Stephen hastened to point out
the disease doesn't take that form very often any more, its profile is
mutating, and, in conversation with Ellen, wheeled up words like
blood-brain barrier, I never thought there was a barrier *there*, said
Jan. But he mustn't know about Max, Ellen said, that would really
depress him, please don't tell him, he'll have to know, Quentin said
grimly, and he'll be furious not to have been told. But there's time
for that, when they take Max off the respirator, said Ellen; but isn't
it incredible, Frank said, Max was fine, not feeling ill at all, and
then to wake up with a fever of a hundred and five, unable to
breathe, but that's the way it often starts, with absolutely no warning, Stephen said, the disease has so many forms. And when, after
another week had gone by, he asked Quentin where Max was, he
didn't question Quentin's account of a spree in the Bahamas, but
then the number of people who visited regularly was thinning out,
partly because the old feuds that had been put aside through the

first hospitalization and the return home had resurfaced, and the flickering enmity between Lewis and Frank exploded, even though Kate did her best to mediate between them, and also because he himself had done something to loosen the bonds of love that united the friends around him, by seeming to take them all for granted, as if it were perfectly normal for so many people to carve out so much time and attention for him, visit him every few days, talk about him incessantly on the phone with each other; but, according to Paolo, it wasn't that he was less grateful, it was just something he was getting used to, the visits. It had become, with time, a more ordinary kind of situation, a kind of ongoing party, first at the hospital and now since he was home, barely on his feet again, it being clear, said Robert, that I'm on the B list; but Kate said, that's absurd, there's no list; and Victor said, but there is, only it's not he, it's Quentin who's drawing it up. He wants to see us, we're helping him, we have to do it the way he wants, he fell down yesterday on the way to the bathroom, he mustn't be told about Max (but he already knew, according to Donny), it's getting worse.

When I was home, he is reported to have said, I was afraid to sleep, as I was dropping off each night it felt like just that, as if I were falling down a black hole, to sleep felt like giving in to death, I slept every night with the light on; but here, in the hospital, I'm less afraid. And to Quentin he said, one morning, the fear rips through me, it tears me open; and, to Ira, it presses me together, squeezes me toward myself. Fear gives everything its hue, its high. I feel so, I don't know how to say it, exalted, he said to Quentin. Calamity is an amazing high, too. Sometimes I feel *so* well, so powerful, it's as if I could jump out of my skin. Am I going crazy, or what? Is it all this attention and coddling I'm getting from everybody, like a child's dream of being loved? Is it the drugs? I know it sounds crazy but sometimes I think this is a *fantastic* experience, he said shyly; but there was also the bad taste in the mouth, the pressure in the head and at the back of the neck, the red, bleeding gums, the painful, if pink-lobed, breathing, and his ivory pallor, color of white chocolate. Among those who wept when told over the phone that he was back in the hospital were Kate and Stephen (who'd been called by Quentin), and Ellen, Victor, Aileen, and Lewis (who were called by Kate), and Xavier and Ursula (who were called by Stephen). Among those who didn't weep were Hilda, who said that she'd just learned that her seventy-five-year-old aunt was dying of the disease, which she'd contracted from a transfusion given during her successful double bypass of five years ago, and Frank and Donny and Betsy, but this didn't mean, according to Tanya, that they weren't moved and appalled, and Quentin thought they might not be coming soon to the hospital but would send presents; the room, he was in a private room this time, was filling up with flowers, and plants, and books, and tapes. The high tide of barely suppressed acrimony of the last weeks at home subsided into the routines of hospital visiting, though more than a few resented Quentin's having charge of the visiting book (but it was Quentin who had the idea, Lewis pointed out); now, to insure a steady stream of visitors, preferably no more than two at a time (this, the rule in all hospitals, wasn't enforced here, at least on his floor; whether out of kindness or inefficiency, no one could decide), Quentin had to be called first, to get one's time slot, there was no more casual dropping by. And his mother could no longer be prevented from taking a plane and installing herself in a hotel near the hospital; but he seemed to mind her daily presence less than expected, Quentin said; said Ellen, it's we who mind, do you suppose she'll stay long. It was easier to be generous with each other visiting him here in the hospital, as Donny pointed out, than at home, where one minded never being alone with him; coming here, in our twos and twos, there's no doubt about what our role is, how we should be, collective, funny, distracting, undemanding, light, it's important to be light, for in all this dread there is gaiety, too, as the poet said, said Kate. (His eyes, his glittering eyes, said Lewis.) His eyes looked dull, extinguished, Wesley said to Xavier, but Betsy said his face, not just his eyes, looked soulful, warm; whatever is there, said Kate, I've never been so aware of his eyes; and Stephen said, I'm afraid of what my eyes show, the way I watch him, with too much intensity, or a phony kind of casualness, said Victor. And, unlike at home, he was clean-shaven each morning, at whatever hour they visited him; his curly hair was always combed; but he complained that the nurses had changed since he was here the last time, and that he didn't like the change, he wanted everyone to be the same. The room was furnished now with some of his personal effects (odd word for one's things, said Ellen), and Tanya brought drawings and a letter from her nine-year-old dyslexic son, who was writing now, since she'd purchased a computer; and Donny brought champagne and some helium balloons, which were anchored to the foot of his bed; tell me about something that's going on, he said, waking up from a nap to find Donny and Kate at the side of his bed, beaming at him; tell me a story, he said wistfully, said Donny, who couldn't think of anything to say; *you're* the story, Kate said. And Xavier brought an eighteenth-century Guatemalan wooden statue of St. Sebastian with upcast eyes and open mouth, and when Tanya said what's that, a tribute to eros past, Xavier said where I come from Sebastian is venerated as a protector against pestilence. Pestilence symbolized by arrows? Symbolized by arrows. All people remember is the body of a beautiful youth bound to a tree, pierced by arrows (of which he always seems oblivious, Tanya interjected), people forget that the story continues, Xavier continued, that when the Christian women came to bury the martyr they found him still alive and nursed him back to health. And he said, according to Stephen, I didn't know St. Sebastian didn't die. It's undeniable, isn't it, said Kate on the phone to Stephen, the fascination of the dying. It makes me ashamed. We're learning how to die, said Hilda; I'm not ready to learn, said Aileen; and Lewis, who was coming straight from the other hospital, the hospital where Max was still being kept in the I.C.U., met Tanya getting out of the elevator on the tenth floor, and as they walked together down the shiny corridor past the open doors, averting their eyes from the other patients sunk in their beds, with tubes in their noses, irradiated by the bluish light from the television sets, the thing I can't bear to think about, Tanya said to Lewis, is someone dying with the TV on.

He has that strange, unnerving detachment now, said Ellen, that's what upsets me, even though it makes it easier to be with him. Sometimes he was querulous. I can't stand them coming in here taking my blood every morning, what are they doing with all that blood, he is reported to have said; but where was his anger, Jan wondered. Mostly he was lovely to be with, always saying how are *you*, how are you feeling. He's so sweet now, said Aileen. He's so nice, said Tanya. (Nice, nice, groaned Paolo.) At first he was very ill, but he was rallying, according to Stephen's best information, there was no fear of his not recovering this time, and the doctor spoke of his being discharged from the hospital in another ten days if all went well, and the mother was persuaded to fly back to Mississippi, and Quentin was readying the penthouse for his return. And he was still writing his diary, not showing it to anyone, though Tanya, first to arrive one late-winter morning, and finding him dozing, peeked, and was horrified, according to Greg, not by anything she read but by a progressive change in his handwriting: in the recent pages, it was becoming spidery, less legible, and some lines of script wandered and tilted about the page. I was thinking, Ursula said to Quentin, that the difference between a story and a painting or photograph is that in a story you can write, He's still alive. But in a painting or a photo you can't show "still." You can just show him being alive. He's still alive, Stephen said.